imagine murder

A JOHN LENNON MYSTERY

imagine murder

A JOHN LENNON MYSTERY

DEAN THOMPSON

with *Thom Moon & Victoria Hallerman*

TUCKER

DS

PRESS

To Barry Greenberg, who never stopped trying

-FOREWORD-

In the fall and winter of 1971, John Lennon and Yoko Ono made New York City their permanent home. Living first in a series of suites at the St. Regis Hotel, the couple eventually sublet an apartment on Bank Street in Greenwich Village. Around that same time, they invested in a somewhat shabby two-story loft building in a warehouse district that was coming to be known as Soho.

At this location, on Broome Street near the corner of West Broadway, they incorporated a new business entity, calling it simply Joko Films. Allen Klein, the manager John had originally promoted to take over his and the other Beatles' business affairs—after the untimely death of Brian Epstein—established his headquarters in Midtown Manhattan, near the New York offices of Apple Records.

To staff Joko Films, the Lennons hired a small group of young people, many, coincidentally, from Cincinnati, including Dean Thompson, the author of this book, originally hired to sell the film *Imagine*, to television. Dean also functioned as an unofficial office manager.

With the exception of obvious celebrities, most of the characters and many of the situations in this book are fictional. The structures, both of Joko Films and of the Lennons' household on Bank Street, are accurate or true to form. Many conversations included in the text actually occurred, their contexts altered to suit the narrative.

-PROLOGUE-

Fade to Black

8:40 P.M, Thursday, June 15, 1972

Stephanie Bradley was staring out of the second-floor window, watching the wind blow trash westward, right down the middle of Broome Street: discarded coffee cups, food wrappers, sections of all three New York dailies, and more than the occasional feather from the poultry slaughterhouse still in business one block east. All of it made the small street feel that much more derelict as night approached.

Three hours earlier, Maria and David had left to go uptown. She imagined one of those familiar black limousines that were such a part of the Joko scene still sitting in front of 496 Broome. If it were, would she have quickly shut the flattop and sprinted down the stairs to join her colleagues? But the cars were long gone.

The overhead lights were off, as they were whenever she and others were screening or editing film footage. The preview screens were hard enough to see clearly without the added glare. For the same reason, the black window shades stretched down from the ceiling and covered the other five large windows facing Broome, almost touching their sills. Slowly she pulled down the shade of the window from which she'd been observing the street. She pushed away the rest of the muffin she'd been chewing on while watching night fall.

The first muffin had gone down quite well during breakfast; but now, not quite halfway through the second, she was feeling logy and feared an upset stomach coming on. Good thing she'd skipped the anchovies at lunch. She walked back toward the flattop and suddenly felt that she might be sick. She went to the corner of Edit One and into the half bathroom. After flicking on the light, she paused for a second to check herself in the mirror; her tummy seemed to settle. So as not to be tempted to take any risks with food for the rest of the day, she deposited the rest of muffin number two into the toilet, where it was soon flushed away.

Back on her stool, she checked her watch again. It was still not quite nine o'clock. What had her husband said? Would he call from his business trip tonight—or check with her in the morning? No matter, he had the line-four number here at the studio. If he wanted to call, he could reach her easily enough.

She sat facing the edit device, resolved to put in another hour at least. The flattop made a low, clattering racket all its own as she sped forward and back, looking at the same scene for the tenth or seemingly hundredth time that day. Maybe I should put back in the helicopter shot of the rowboat approaching the small island in the water folly, *she thought, fingering a lengthy strip of film that dangled around her neck.*

She was in the habit of keeping two or three strips of cut footage there, instead of hanging them within arm's reach of her stool. "Inserts," she called these—some only a few inches in length and others several feet long, but never more than a few seconds on-screen. "These are my wannabes: they may really want to be in the film," she'd explained once to Bill when he asked about the 16mm necklaces that were a constant part of her daily attire.

"I'm just not sure, but I want them right at hand, so I can look at them, hold them up to the light, and then, if I want, cut in all or part of the scene really quick. You know, the footage that really wants to be there I keep close to me, so I won't forget it."

She was reaching for one of these segments, impulsively pulling it from the back of her neck in order to check one more time, beginning the process of cutting it into the B roll on the platter system. Damn, *she thought,* another small cut! *There were always, or so it seemed, two or three tiny paper cuts right below her hairline and above where any collar might protect her. Her husband complained they never seemed to go away— never seemed to heal. "I know" she explained, waxing poetic to try to make him understand the visceral import they held for her, "but these little cuts are more or less physical proof to me at any time that I'm really able to do what I want to do, that I'm able to work with film and, with it, help mold an entire piece into a story where pictures and angles lead the audience literally through a scene and into a situation. It's why I love editing film. It's like theater except I'm able to almost pick up each member of the audience and move them around without them leaving their own theater seat or couch. It's the true magic of the Magic Lantern."*

Her husband, Jeffrey, had heard this explanation in various forms, but he seldom paid attention. His young wife, he was sure, could do far better for her own career, and for their household, getting a better job, doing something for one of the networks, even joining the union or returning to NYU, changing majors from film into something more practical—and finishing her degree. She listened with a bit more attention than he offered, but it only hardened her resolve.

After hours especially, Steph enjoyed the whir and spin, sometimes of all six reels simultaneously, under her control. Back and forth, pausing, then fast-forwarding through a segment. Then, through careful manipulation, slowing the entire process in search of just that right place to make a cut, add a scene or clip a track. However, tonight the movement of the reels, the constant spooling and unspooling—along with the continuous flickering of the screens—were not helping the once-mild nausea that seemed to be building. She felt dizzy, more than a bit clammy, and for just a second, she feared she might topple from her stool.

Just take a break, *she said to herself.* You have nowhere to go, no deadlines tonight. Maybe go over and lie on the couch for ten, fifteen minutes and let this pass.

The couch was covered with—what was it, plastic? Naugahyde? It was both cool and inviting, yet rough and unyielding against her right cheek as she first lay, then curled into a fetal position.

She slipped into and out of a dreamlike state. The dizziness was less, but the nausea was getting worse. As a result, she didn't notice footfalls on the wooden stairs up to the second-floor workspace. Then the entire space began to spin, counterclockwise, she thought. The room must be rewinding. She blacked out for just a few seconds.

When she returned to consciousness, she realized she was now unable to move, bathed in her own sweat. Shadows made by the streetlights below danced on the ceiling above her. For a moment, she imagined she was still watching footage spooling out. Some of the pieces she worked on, after all, were quite surreal. This imagery might have fit right in. Then again, there was no sound, no audio track, no hum and clatter of the edit bay itself.

She sensed without panic that her life might be leaving her. There was no pain, no tunnel of light, no distant path. Could death really be this undramatic? Then again, there will be plenty of drama when they find me; a lot of people will be upset: John, his manager, all those lawyers, and Yoko, Maria, David, even Jeffrey.

Why hadn't she gone with David and Maria—where was it again? To a studio, a concert? A club? Maybe in another city. If only it had been convenient to leave work behind for just one evening. If only. Then again, how inconvenient was it going to be to be found on the couch in Edit One? No time to shut down the K-E-M, properly store the reels, and spool up the audio track. Her eyes drifted toward the massive flattop floating across the room. No glow from the screen. Had someone else turned it off? Had she? Or had it gone to sleep all by itself?

Her thoughts blurred and then seemed to seize up. In her editor's mind, she was seeing herself both from a distance and through failing eyes. Long shot to establish, quick cut to reveal the empty doorway, change POV to my position, quick cut to empty stool, and yes, a twelve-frame cross dissolve to the shadows on the ceiling. *At once she was aware of not breathing. The flickering light on the ceiling, which had become a large screen, dimmed and went out. It was well after dark on a Thursday night, and now the room was deadly quiet.*

The blow, when it came, was not felt at all; it was inconsequential.

—CHAPTER 1—
"MORNING, JOKO FILMS"

10:00 A.M., MONDAY, JUNE 12, 1972

"Hey, like, yo, I mean is this *the* Joko Films?"

"Yeah," I replied, "I'm sure this is the only one."

"Great," said the unsure voice.

And then the man at the other end of the line hesitated, uncertain, "I mean I don't suppose John is around?"

"Uh, no."

"Okay, then I guess I'd better tell you."

"Tell me what?" I inquired flatly. I was pretty sure I knew what kind of news he had was so important. And I had nothing better to do this morning, so I settled in.

"Hey, I know it may sound crazy, but the world–I mean the entire fucking world—is going to end on July 19. I know this for a fact, man."

I leaned forward and glanced at the torn calendar taped to the wall next to my desk. Flipping the page to July, I lowered my voice to its most confidential tone, "Sorry, man. All of the nineteenth is taken."

"Taken? Whaddaya mean?"

"It's taken. Two Rastafarians booked it already, called last week. The entire world will be consumed by fire on Wednesday, July 19, midafternoon as I recall. The only way to avoid this conflagration is apparently for us to get the Beatles back together to sing 'Give Peace a Chance' at the Albert Hall on the morning of the nineteenth."

""Hey man, that's bullshit! I mean, what the fuck? The Albert Hall? All I'm askin' to save the world is maybe an album dedication for me, or a donation to The Anarcho-Pacifist Children of Henry David

6

Thoreau."

"Well," I said, polite as any good office manager, "I do have Monday of that week open, but the rest of mid-July is packed with apocalyptic predictions. Now if you were to have a feeling about something on the week of the twenty-fourth, we could talk?"

"Fuckin' Rastafarians!" the voice muttered, but he seemed willing to compromise. "I'll check my charts, like maybe I am off by a week or so."

"Smart of you to check," I assured him. "Don't want to do half-ass work when it comes to the end of the world. Get back to me when you're sure."

"Yeah man, you're right. Thanks."

Alone at last, only the dial tone for company, I replaced the receiver. The first "business" call of the day was over, and given that Joko Films's office number was unlisted, there might not be another for a couple of hours. How the number got out to that crowd, I don't know. They talk among themselves?

My job was still relatively new. I had originally been hired with the vague idea that I would help make and sell a film to television, but the film was still in the works, and none of our roles were all that clearly defined. I didn't even have a supervisor or boss to report to on a regular basis. The hours were flexible, the modest salary seemed to arrive as promised, and the working environment was overwhelmingly wonderful.

Maria Anastasia, Joko's "secretary," had an even looser schedule than mine and apparently a less fully formed work ethic. This morning she still hadn't wandered in.

To my surprise, Bill Frost appeared, unusually early, gripping a Led Zeppelin coffee mug.

"Another one?" he quipped, pointing to the calendar.

I let the June page fall back into place on my "End of the World" calendar, its title scrawled above "Superior Lumber."

"Told 'em the nineteenth's booked; he'll get back to me."

Bill took a slurp from his cup. His morning "coffee" was, more often than not, either a White Russian from home or some brandy from a stash he had tucked away in one of the edit rooms. If there was someone who could get away with that, it was Bill, a golden boy at Joko Films, standing here before me in his self-styled uniform: Frye boots, leather pants, and an electric-blue shirt beneath a leather-buttoned vest made from some kind of Afghan carpet. Two or three chains and one string of glass beads seemed to be holding his neck in place, topped by what some would call an aristocratic head, with close-cropped curls that ran long in the back. His profile—if not his countenance—could, in a smoky club, be mistaken for Dylan's.

"Did we have any calls last week?" he wondered.

"Believe it or not, we've been able to work in two more apocalyptic predictions: one from a defrocked priest in Altoona, the other called in by someone alleging to represent the Future Farmers of America."

A *Village Voice* article that spring had pointed out that many fringe groups—which I suspected were only one or two players deep—were predicting the end of all things at various points throughout the summer. The article claimed that the Aztec calendar had found some or another day in July or August particularly auspicious, something about the "ruins of rationality." The Aztecs, or the *Voice*, had inspired more than a few "prophets" to declare the imminent end of the planet. The means by which it would end was left for them to predict.

A number of these groups reached out to our office to tell us the when and the how of the apocalypse, but even more importantly, to suggest some means of saving the planet or at least part of it. These all required that our famous boss and/or some of his friends would perform a particular feat, always involving the individual on the phone.

Speaking of the boss, John took a great deal of pleasure in hearing about these predictions of Earth's demise. There was a group from Salt Lake City calling itself the Radical Wing of the Brigham Young Brigade, and then there was The Loyal Order of Perpetual Peyote—he relished this one—which claimed to operate from a commune near Flagstaff. Roughly a half dozen chapters, real or otherwise, of the Students for a Democratic Society seemed almost more interested in the end of the world than the end of the war. Someone representing the New Age War Council of the Seminole Nation reminded me, while he was at it, that his tribe had never unilaterally signed a peace treaty with the U.S.

A right-wing organization calling itself Students for a Stronger America had its finger in the apocalypse pie too. I tracked them all carefully on our calendar. Although if they were off by a few days, would it have mattered?

"What is it today: fire, ice, or massive flood?" Bill asked.

"Didn't specify," I said.

"And the Reds?"

"Swept the Expos over the weekend," I responded, "and before you ask, yes, they're still in first."

He nodded agreeably and took his cup of whatever back toward the first-floor kitchen area and up the stairs to one of the two edit rooms on the second floor.

We'd both grown up in Cincinnati, and though I was the real Reds fan, he felt it necessary to bond daily over our mutually agreed splinter sect of hometown baseball. For me especially, the Reds had become a kind of ersatz religion since I'd relocated to New York three years earlier.

Though I now considered myself a New Yorker, I wondered if I would ever lose the sense—or was it the reality?—of having grown up as a true Midwesterner.

What was I really doing at Joko Films when I wasn't tracking the apocalypse or following baseball? I was a general manager of sorts, head of sales, a jack-of-all-trades for this little-known, rock-star-led production company hidden at 496 Broome Street in Soho, an area slowly taking on a new identity. This area, regardless of alleged eastern, western, and southern boundaries, was indeed south of Houston Street, which everyone agreed marked its northern border. At one time, the area was a suburb for New York's first downtown. However, the quaint Federal-style wooden homes had been replaced nearly a century ago with mostly two- and three-story brick and cast-iron structures that housed all forms of light manufacturing, retailing, and office space. One of those worksites was 496 Broome.

The outside of the two-story building where we worked bore faded letters painted on the window, "Marwood Press." Whoever or whatever Marwood Press had been, it had ceased to exist sometime in the midsixties. Our boss, John Lennon, had acquired the empty building for a little more than $40,000 the year before. He and Yoko lived in an apartment on Bank Street, but the *Sgt. Pepper* uniforms in our basement and the nine-foot guitar leaning against the left side wall of the high-ceilinged space bore witness to its owner. One corner of the wide-open space near the guitar served as storage for dozens of clothing boxes that arrived almost daily from shops around New York, the West Coast, and overseas. Joko Films also served as a receiving and shipping drop for the Lennons.

The door to Broome Street swung open, and Stephanie Bradley, our assistant film editor, closed it behind her. After fiddling with the unreliable inner front door—"Darn thing never closes the first time!" she said to no one in particular—she continued across the open space that served as both our reception area and office space for Maria and me.

"Coffee?" she asked.

This, like Bill's inquiry about baseball, was more or less a morning ritual.

"I try never to touch the stuff, remember?" I said.

This brought Steph up to a full stop; she smacked her forehead.

"Why can't I remember that? I often get a second cup wondering why I don't ever see him with morning coffee. Maybe it will sink in and I'll remember it's because you don't drink morning coffee."

"Or coffee anytime," I added. "But thanks."

The antithesis of Bill in many ways, Stephanie—sometimes Stephie to us—was nearly a foot shorter, at five foot three and remarkably unconventional for the unconventional times. She wore well-ironed blouses with Peter Pan collars tucked into starched khakis or blue jeans with a crease. Counterculture she was not, but in her own way, she was very weird. Her most unusual attribute was that she was married.

She seemed a little out of place in a rock star's film company, reminding me of any number of characters from 1960s sitcoms, like Laura Petrie, Mary Tyler Moore's character on *The Dick Van Dyke Show*. I imagined she used Ivory Soap, as both she and the product were, hypothetically, almost totally pure.

"So, is there anything I can get you that you might want first thing in the morning? Some orange juice? A bagel? Cocoa?" she asked.

"Actually," I responded, "I used to keep a box of Nestlé's Quik back in the kitchen when I first arrived, but Bill wiped it out during an attack of the munchies one weekend in April. Said he ate it right out of the box with a spoon, liked it because he didn't have to chew too much."

"Yikes, that's weird! Then again, I mean, really, I don't know what everyone sees in drugs. I mean I tried marijuana a couple times back in college. Didn't do a thing for me."

"Try inhaling?" I asked.

"Well, no, not really. I mean I never smoked cigarettes, so it just made me cough. I don't think I could have inhaled."

"Makes quite a difference," I said. "Kind of like rinsing your mouth out with bourbon and then spitting it out: won't have much impact."

"I don't like bourbon either," Stephie remarked. Then she glanced at the tiny Bulova on her left wrist.

"Golly! I gotta get upstairs, set up the reels in Edit One before Sam arrives. You know he hates waiting first thing in the morning. Says it interrupts his creative flow. See you later."

I leaned over the back of my chair.

"Well, we sure as hell wouldn't want to interrupt any kind of magic coming from Sam Heintzelman now, would we?"

Stephie paused briefly, turning not quite halfway around, "You're too hard on Sam. Once you get to know him, really get to work with him, you realize what insight, what genius he really has. You need to give him more of a chance, David."

Then she was gone. Unlike Bill, you could barely hear her footfall on the backstairs. Stephie was the only film editor at Joko, though she had been introduced to me as an assistant when I came on board back in March.

"Okay," you might say, "no full-time editors and only one assistant editor in a film company with two edit rooms?" My thought exactly when I first began working at Broome Street. Two rooms, replete with all things state-of-the-art, including splicing blocks, rewinders, strip bins, and the one central component, a six-spool flatbed film editing machine for both A and B reels and audio.

"I've never seen a Steenbeck quite like that," I'd commented to Bill during my introductory tour of the facilities. "Newer model?"

"That's cause it's not a Steenbeck. Both machines are K-E-M's, German made and distributed here by the French."

"Seems awkward," I said. "What about maintenance, or parts?"

"There's some old Ukrainian guy from Long Island City who can fix 'em when he's sober, but anyhow, that's why we have two edit suites."

"In case we get really busy?" I speculated.

"No," he said, "because the damn machines break down all the time. We constantly have to cannibalize the machine in Room 2 to keep editing in Room 1."

"So why don't we get rid of both of them and go with Steenbeck?"

"Stop, too logical. She figured out through numerology that it was far better to have equipment come to us from Europe by way of Argentina, then to the West Coast, San Francisco, I think, and on to New York."

"Better than sending a truck to the Steenbeck showroom at Forty-fourth and Eighth?" I asked.

"Didn't work out for her numberswise," Bill said.

"She" was Yoko Ono, feared yet, despite her reputation with the press, sometimes also admired by most of the employees.

"Always remember, man," Bill continued, "everything with Yoko, at least most things, is done that way. Numerology rules."

I was reviewing that conversation while sorting through some pieces of mail, when the obstinate front door was suddenly attacked from the outside. I thought I might have heard a key in the lock, the deadbolt click and then refuse to turn while at the same time, the doorknob rattled violently and was twisted to no effect. Eventually there was the sound of relentless pounding, followed by a not-so-muffled voice hollering, "Open! Open you suv un a bitch. Anybody in there? C'mon! Somebody open up—it's me."

With that, the stubborn door exploded inward, revealing Sam Heintzelman himself, our Great Director.

Six four or six five, with shaggy brown hair and a Pecos Bill-style mustache, Sam usually came clothed in his own self-styled uniform: denim work shirt, jeans jacket, wide leather belt, and boots; but his role was changing, and with it, his garb. As he evolved from sharing production duties with Bill to making directorial and editing decisions for and with John and Yoko, his clothing began to reflect his elevated sense of his own stature. Today, he was wearing something like denim jodhpurs, billowing out at the hips, then tapering narrow to the calf, tucked into heavily polished riding boots that had likely never seen a stable. He had begun to carry what looked like an old British officer's swagger stick—or was it just a beat-up riding crop?—for effect. I made a mental note to suggest we do Secret Santa if I stayed at this gig through December, if for no other reason than to satisfy my longing for someone to give him a burgundy beret to top it all off.

"Goddamn door!" Sam's opening salvo had been shot in my direction. "How many times you gotta sit there and listen to people complain about the fuckin' goddamn door without doin' something about it? You need to get it fixed!"

This particular morning, Sam's wife, Christine, glided in behind the great director himself. Chris was tall as well, nearly five feet ten in flats, and in her early thirties. Unlike Sam, she had a round, soft, approachable look, her skin a muted milky white, hair a striking mahogany-black color, cut short to frame a heart-shaped face. She generally wore either long flowing dresses or a short dashiki over jeans. She wasn't hiding anything. Though she had borne a set of twins, her figure had not suffered. For a generally shy woman, she could be surprisingly sarcastic, a combination I found both interesting and appealing.

"Morning, David," she said, trailing Sam across the space. "We had to drop the boys off at Little Red early, some sort of rehearsal they were in, and I—well we—felt we should look in on the school, you know, to show support."

"Support my ass," said Sam. "Goddamn private school, freakin' expensive, probably just lookin' for more money. Next thing you know, they'll be holdin' graduation ceremonies for fifth graders. Next year, for sure, we look again at public school, you hear?"

"Of course, dear," Chris said in a somewhat mocking fashion. "The boys could use the experience mingling with drug dealers, to get a better sense of our society. . . . Sam, aren't you going to say good morning to David?"

Without looking over his shoulder, Sam grunted something unintelligible as he passed my desk, hardly pausing to drop off a series of folded invoices that materialized from his front pockets. It was a fluid movement.

"Here's some lab bills and my expense report for the last two weeks; approve 'em and get 'em up to the office for payment, and then you can do, well, whatever you guys do down here, okay?"

"Why, David, aren't you positively thrilled that the father of my children has given you a menial task to complete, as well as his permission to do absolutely nothing productive after you've completed the task, which is probably his responsibility in the first place? Then again, I'm pretty sure he actually is the father of my children."

The quip caused Sam to glare over his right shoulder for just a second, never decreasing his stride toward the back of the building. Under his breath, he muttered, "Never changes; same shit, different outhouse."

Chris paused at the corner of my desk, and I feared, not for the first time, to expound one or more grievances.

"I, for one, David, am glad you're here." She laid a casual hand on my left shoulder. "I mean, before there was no sense of order in this place. I swear Sam didn't get reimbursed for his out-of-pockets for months at a time."

Then Sam stuck his head back in from the hallway and interrupted.

"Dah-veed," he said, pronouncing my name as he imagined the French would.

"Sam-u-el," I fired back, knowing he hated the full version of his name.

"Staff all assembled?" he asked, glancing toward Maria's empty desk.

Did five people constitute a group large enough to be considered a staff?

"Bill and Stephie are upstairs, I'm here, with a pile of nonsense to wade through, and you're standing in front of me in jodhpurs, looking roughly like an oversized Spitfire pilot. Yeah, we're mostly all here."

"You know," he grumbled, "you need to do something about Maria's habitual lateness. I mean if you want to pretend to be some kind of manager, then act like it. Take control!"

"You, on the other hand," joked Chris, "could just pretend to be a studio mogul or the second coming of John Ford."

"Someday you're going to really tick me off," Sam hissed, and without further comment, he continued toward the stairs.

Sam, Chris, Bill, and I were the Ohio contingent. Bill and I had attended the University of Cincinnati around the same time. Both of us were in radio/TV. Chris was from Cleveland; she and Sam had met upstate.

I'd gotten this gig after running into Bill near Times Square the previous winter. Finding out Sam was part of the team had been the only bummer. Christine was a bonus; she took away the sting of working with her husband.

Still standing by my desk, Christine emitted one long sigh.

"Oh well, we all do what we do. And sometimes for reasons we've forgotten. For the record, Robbie and Ted really are his sons, though it sometimes pisses him off to recall that I was having an affair with a man at his father's art school till shortly before we were married."

"Thanks," I said, "for all that information!" I didn't know what else to say.

She beamed back, her blue eyes lit with some crazy hot notion.

"Gotta keep him guessing. Guessing, if not interested. Right?"

"I . . . I suppose so," I stuttered, uncertain why she was sharing her marital discord with me.

Another weird married couple. Maybe the only married people in the entire New York film business who happened to work for Joko. Marriage was, in New York's creative worlds, completely out of style.

A peal of high-pitched, girlish laughter drifted down from the second floor. It was undoubtedly Stephie, to my knowledge the only person who both understood and appreciated Sam's humor.

"That happen a lot?" inquired Chris, staring at the ceiling.

"A bit, I suppose," was my lame answer.

With that, Chris shrugged and then reached into the oversized straw bag she perpetually carried.

"David, before I forget, I brought muffins. Baked them last night. I threw in some blueberries I had left over from making jam. Thought you and the rest of, well, the staff, might like them. Next week, I hope to have some extra strawberry jam. I use my mom's recipe, and it's all the boys and I can do to deal with it. Sam says he hates jams and jellies; I think especially mine."

Jam. Okay. Easier to chat about than Sam's paternity. With that, Chris said goodbye. I was sorry to see her go.

Less than an hour later, the staff was finally complete. Maria Anastasia, who arrived just in time to beat out the mail delivery, was a striking, twenty-one-year-old Italian American. She was confident, with the stance and assertiveness of a native New Yorker, delivered with more than a touch of the city's outer-borough accent. At nearly five nine, she wore her dark hair in long, wavy tresses that ended below her shoulders. She was slim, with eyes so dark brown they actually seemed black and a smooth, deep-tanned complexion. Not traditionally beautiful, she was striking.

"Like sorry I'm late. I was stuck on a fuckin' bus for over an hour. I mean, it was ridiculous."

I was tempted to point out that it probably would have taken less than an hour for her to walk from the apartment in Chelsea she still shared with her parents downtown to Joko, but her all-purpose retort, "Whatevah!" was inevitable, so I said nothing.

And so the day unreeled: expense reports to review and approve, the occasional real business phone call, and two or three more "end of the world" warnings.

So, ya know," said Maria, as I was putting additional information into the EOW calendar, "you'd think it would be a helluva lot easier for somma deez wack jobs to put on a sandwich board and walk around town like those one-panel cartoons.

"Maybe," I said. "But then they wouldn't get the satisfaction of telling their friends they'd notified J&Y about their predictions."

"Whatevah," was all Maria had to say on the topic.

I was deep into reviewing a nine-page invoice from DuArts covering lab costs of a recently shot beach scene for *Imagine*, the film we were working on upstairs, when Maria interrupted me again. Obviously bored, she'd answered the phone.

"It's a loyah. One of John's. Wants to talk to you," she said, coming out for a moment from behind her moss-green IBM Selectric. "Line one."

An officious young man in the legal profession got right to business.

"That flaky idea of yours, giving the film company to the Democrats to help with the election? The people at the DNC want to talk about it. Can you be in DC on Friday morning?" he asked.

I hadn't suggested giving away the company. Just working out a deal.

The Nixon administration was threatening John with deportation on various charges, so his involvement in any campaign to put a Democrat in the White House next January would be frowned upon in the extreme. "No concerts, no public appearances, definitely no major financial contributions, and no public endorsement of any Democratic presidential candidate will be tolerated," one senior attorney had warned the previous month.

But John and Yoko desperately wanted to be involved, to see that Nixon never got a second term. How to do it? I'd proposed giving the Dems unlimited access to our facilities and our accounts with film labs and equipment companies, where we could bury the costs involved; that would be as good as a cash contribution but wouldn't call attention to itself. Maybe we could even get involved in some of the production.

"Okay, kid, why don't you come by my office first thing tomorrow morning? We're two floors beneath Klein's, same building, the entire floor. Just ask for me, and if I'm tied up I'll leave an envelope at the front desk—DNC address, itinerary—all that stuff."

With that, he gave me his name, the name of the firm, and his direct telephone number, just to be safe. He continued, "Just see you're there on time, look somewhat presentable, and don't curse a lot. Do you have anything you can wear outside of jeans?"

Before I could respond, he rang off.

—CHAPTER 2—
YES, BUT YOU MISSED A WHOLE BUNCH

12:10 P.M., TUESDAY, JUNE 13, 1972

For the first time I could remember, Maria was in before me. In fact, probably everybody was. I had started the day in Midtown at the attorney's office as requested. There'd been no self-important lawyer or envelope waiting for me when I arrived. I cooled my heels till nearly eleven when a harried, balding man in his midthirties bustled into reception, gave me a preemptive handshake, and passed me the promised information.

"Sorry, kid. Got backed up. You haven't been here long, have you?"

Without waiting for an answer, he hurried back into the inner sanctum, pausing only briefly before rounding a corner.

"Boots?" he spat out, observing my Frye cavalry footwear. "Don't any of you ever wear shoes and socks?" He didn't wait for an answer.

"You took your own sweet time," observed Maria as I fiddled with the front door latch.

"Told you yesterday. Had to start the day at some lawyer's office uptown." I waved the envelope at her and headed for my desk. "Any messages? Did that order of film stock arrive from Kodak? Did I miss anything good?"

"No, of course no messages—and yes, you missed a whole bunch."

"Such as?"

"Well, let's see. Stephie's upstairs, that's normal, but Bill was on time—big surprise. Then Chris showed up with Sam again—second morning in a row. Both of them were in, even before Stephie. Then there were these two characters who said they were sent over here to see you about work or something."

"Two characters? Where from? Who sent them?"

"Dunno from where. But Farah called from Bank Street when I first came in—might I point out, I was here real early, like 9:45 — anyhow she said J&Y wanted you to meet with these guys."

"Are they still here?"

"Nah. You missed 'em by a good hour. Now I remember: they're from England. Well, one of them sounded English; the other, an American I'm pretty sure I met before. Danny or something. Worked in the movies here or somewhere. Somehow got hooked up with John and Yoko a couple years back. Pretty much ran their mansion outside of London or something like that. Anyway, they said they'd stop back tomorrow or the next day. And oh yeah, Sam ducked them big time. When I buzzed upstairs to the edit room, he told me to tell 'em he wasn't in and wouldn't be in —and that story was good for either of them any time they came looking."

"Pretty all inclusive," I remarked. "Did either of them leave a résumé? A phone number? Some way to get in touch?"

"Nope—don't think so. In fact, they spent most of their time back in the kitchen talking with Chris, who covered for Sam. She did unload a batch of cookies on them but told me there were also two muffins in a bag on top of the fridge just for you, next to some stuff she left for Stephie. She's becoming a genuine grocery delivery service."

More than a bit peckish, I headed for the kitchen in search of the baked goods. As promised, the muffins were on top of the fridge in a bag, fresh as could be and, I soon found, more than tasty. I was just getting comfortable on the stool, considering a second muffin, when I noticed another paper bag on the counter next to me. I saw it contained a couple of squat jars of something as well as a paper napkin wrapped around yet a third muffin. On the floor between the stools was a piece of Joko stationery with a note scrawled, "For Stephie. No one else—just her." I put the bag and note together on the counter, assuming the two had been meant for each other. Then I gave in to the second muffin, rationalizing I'd probably skip lunch.

Less than ten minutes later, I was back at my desk preparing to do some actual work when Maria called from across the room.

"Whoa, quite a week for you," she announced. "A second call. Guy says he's a friend, says his name is Paul Buck, or Brick—something like that. He's on line three."

"Hello . . . Paul? You in town?"

Paul Bloch was an acquaintance of mine from my first job who had until recently been running a small management agency on the West Coast, trying to sign second- and third-tier rock bands for what he and his two partners earnestly claimed would be "honest, forthright, and sincere management." The only real accomplishment of the management team was to get the drummer of a San Francisco-based psychedelic band to wear one of its branded T-shirts on a photo shoot that wound up on the back of an album. As a result of their honest and forthright approach to the recording industry, Paul and his people had gone out of business more than a year ago.

"Sort of in town," he answered. "In and out. Look, David, is what I hear pure? Are you running a film company for John Lennon? Is that where I'm reaching you?"

"Well, nobody really runs this company. It more or less drifts along, but, yes, I do work here. It's actually not a bad gig. How did you find me?"

"Don't remember. Might have gotten the number from Sutherland over at *Billboard*. Anyway, I have a super big favor to ask of you, man."

"And that would be?" I said.

"Look, I've got this short-term gig booking talent for this year's Muscular Dystrophy Telethon, you know—the Jerry Lewis thing that runs every Labor Day weekend."

"You mean," I interjected, "telethons actually have talent bookers? I thought celebrities wandered into the studio and onto the set pretty much at random, you know, Jerry's friends and all that."

Paul laughed in spite of himself. "Hey, that's maybe the way they portray it. But every section of every hour of the entire show—I mean it's on the air for like twenty-one-and-a-half hours every year—is booked solid. It raises millions for those kids. And, well, I'm not the only talent booker, and each of us has to produce. They brought me on for really just two reasons."

"Because you're smart and good-looking?" I suggested.

"Two additional reasons," he responded. "I have long hair, and they think I can book some younger acts, some rock celebrities. I mean, the Jerry Lewis audience is aging. The telethon's ratings demographics keep skewing older every year."

"And if only the good-looking yet shaggy-haired Paul Bloch could land John Lennon to appear on this year's telethon, that would mean all the difference to Jerry and his kids, not to mention ratings and demographics," I said.

"Well, exactly," Paul responded. "I mean, do you think there'd be any chance? Like, do you really talk to John? Do you know him? Would you ask him? I mean, I really need this gig. I got a couple shots of work for the fall, even a possibility at NBC, but this summer is looking bleak if I can't keep this job. What do you think?"

No surprise. All of us who had anything to do with John were automatically targets for anyone digging for a favor from one of the world's most recognized mortals.

"You know, unbelievably, you might be in luck. I've heard, I can't quite remember when, that John is actually a fan of Jerry Lewis, thinks he's genuinely funny. Now that I think about it, that may be one of the things that keeps John Lennon from being an almost perfect human being."

"Terrific! I mean, like, you have access to John? I mean, you talk with him and everything?"

I was tempted to brag that I saw John nearly every day, but instead I responded, "And pretty much everything. I don't know when I can bring it up, but I promise I will try to ask, you know, see if there's any interest at all."

I began turning the pages of the Superior Lumber calendar ahead through July and August, noting the first weekend in September. "So the telethon is on, let's see, Sunday the third, runs into Monday the fourth?"

"Right on," Paul said enthusiastically. "And you know, it's broadcast from here in the city, the ballroom complex at the Americana Hotel uptown, convenient for John and whatever band he can put together. I hear he is really putting together a band, right?"

"More or less," I answered. "So, you would want John to perform, hopefully, with his band, and of course Yoko?"

"Definitely. And Yoko, I mean, why not? They've got to be the most famous couple on Earth right now. I mean, we could build an entire segment around interview time with Jerry, maybe some other guests; it would be terrific! Look, David, don't fuck with me. You think this could really happen?"

"Don't mention it to anybody, and definitely don't count on it. Believe me, if I didn't know that he was actually aware of Jerry Lewis and thought he was funny, I wouldn't ask. I mean, you don't understand how many requests, how much stuff comes through here all the time. At least you're not telling me the world is going to end if he doesn't deliver."

"What?"

"Never mind."

"Like, I'm sure it must be overwhelming! Look, anything you can do—anything. Just let me know as soon as you can. Okay?"

Paul then rattled off phone numbers for his brand-new temporary office, his sublet apartment in Chelsea, and the house he shared back in Malibu. "Both the apartment and the place in California have answering services. Call anytime—I mean anytime. And thanks, man, really."

"Did that guy Paul Brick really work for Gary Lewis? You know, Gary Lewis and the Playboys"? Maria wondered aloud. "I mean, I think they're really cool! I even, can you believe it, actually bought one of their albums. Cash. I paid out of pocket!"

Really? I thought. You work in John Lennon's company and you're swooning over Gary Lewis? I couldn't figure Maria, but she probably had the most extensive record collection this side of WNEW-FM, relying on freebies and DJ copies, which flowed freely from office to office on a regular basis. One British-issue *Sgt. Pepper* could easily be traded for the entire month's release catalog from Epic or Columbia, an exchange rate of roughly fifteen or twenty to one.

"No, not Gary Lewis, Jerry Lewis. You remember, comedy team of Martin and Lewis in the fifties? I think Gary Lewis might be his son, actually."

"Whatevah," Maria said. "Don't remember Jerry Lewis much, but I know Dean Martin. His singing sucks. Must be all the drinking."

I happened to be staring at a poster Maria had tacked above her desk. It had been there since before I arrived at Joko. It was two images side by side: on the right, arrayed in a flamboyant red waistcoat cut away to reveal a gold-buttoned white silk vest and tight white men's breeches and a pair of shiny riding boots, strode the very image of the mascot for Johnnie Walker Scotch, his top hat tilted rakishly on his patrician head. The image in the opposite cell was of a bearded grinning and somewhat disheveled youth sitting on an orange crate in a barren room, his left hand cupping a joint. The legend over both images read "Johnny paper? or Johnnie Walker?" The world that produced Dean Martin and Jerry Lewis had taken a significant turn.

—CHAPTER 3—
THE VISIT

11:35 A.M., WEDNESDAY, JUNE 14, 1972

"You're kidding? I mean, you're not being serious?" An incredulous Maria Anastasia cradled the phone shoulder to cheek as she rose from her desk. "You mean they're awake already and out? Okay, Yeah, like I'm really surprised. We'll keep an eye out for 'em. Yeah, soon as they get here I'll call. Bye."

"And that was?" I asked after she had hung up.

"Do you like listen to all my calls?" she shot back. "There is absolutely no privacy here. No decorum."

"Decorum? Good word."

"Call it what you want, but there's still no privacy."

It was the start of another day at Joko, a Wednesday. Back when I worked a normal job, Monday through Friday—some overtime with an occasional responsibility on a Saturday—Wednesday was "hump day," halfway to the weekend, so I always looked forward to Wednesday. But the world of J&Y seemed to be a seven-day-a-week merry-go-round. Wednesday was now remarkable only for the new edition of the *Village Voice*. This particular morning, true to form, my weekly copy of the *Voice* had already migrated from my desk to Maria's.

"Well, pardon me," I replied. "After all, I'm pretty sure you listen to all my phone calls."

"It's my job," she declared. "I'm supposed to know what's going on around here all the time. Like does anybody keep track of stuff around here? Besides, if I don't have an idea of what goes on, you know, if I'm not able to talk about stuff intelligently with John and Yoko, be able to answer Farah's questions when she calls, like maybe someone from the apartment or Klein's office would be sent down here. Look, consider me an important—what's that word?—luzon? Someone who keeps in touch with everybody for all our benefit, dig?"

"Luzon? Isn't that in the Philippines? I think you mean liaison, you know, a go-between."

"Whatevah," Maria said flatly. "Anyway, that was Farah, and she called to give us a heads-up that J&Y are actually walking down here from the apartment on their own—in broad daylight—alone."

"No fuckin' way! By themselves?" I'd heard the day before that Yoko was planning to come down to screen the latest rough with Sam and Stephie, but nobody had given us a time. "Are you sure? By themselves?"

"Says Farah. She has her finger on Yoko's pulse better than anybody."

The indefatigable Farah Freedwoman was one of the only constants at "the apartment," a snug little three-room duplex on Bank Street that John and Yoko called home. It was, oddly enough, a sublet.

"Believe it or not, I've got me a landlord," John had mentioned back in early April. "He's a drummer, that Joe Butler who beats for the Lovin' Spoonful, Sebastian's group. They're on the road pretty much nonstop . . . better them than me . . . so we've got an open-ended arrangement. Groovy place, and Joe's a great guy. Then again, we're seldom late with the rent," he'd concluded with a wry smile.

Whether John was an owner, renter, whatever, there was no doubt in anyone's mind that the place was ruled by Farah. The twenty-two-year-old force of nature—born Francine Miriam Friedman—had been happily on her way to becoming one of Long Island's newest generation of Jewish-American heiresses. Then, the fall of her senior year at Sarah Lawrence, she suddenly informed her parents she would not return to finish school. Originally what had been a summer internship at the office of John's manager—Allen Klein— had left her open to recruitment by Yoko at the Bank Street digs.

Staffed by an ongoing parade of houseboys, clueless assistants, and part-time clericals, the apartment was the center of John and Yoko's world. Nobody really knew where most of the staff came from. Like Freedwoman, Maria had started either at Allen Klein's ABKCO office or the nearby Apple Records offices uptown. There she was noticed and adopted by John or Yoko, or both. Other employees appeared from nowhere, staying a short while, then either fading away or simply disappearing without warning, but there was always Farah. I wondered whether her parents were more upset at her (formal?

informal?) name change or the fact that she'd failed to report for her final year of English lit on the Bronxville campus.

I suspected Yoko's factotum got her strident and superior style of management from a no-nonsense mother who probably ruled the family manse in Cedarhurst with a steady hand. It didn't hurt that the Divine Ms. Freedwoman had the full faith and credit of Yoko Ono, or that Yoko had also studied at and left Sarah Lawrence in the early 1950s. Alumni solidarity?

Not ten minutes after Maria got the warning call—a period during which the entire five-person staff scurried about tidying up—there was a faint, polite knock on the interior front door. Maria had been standing near it, anticipating the arrival while fretting that something might happen to them "out there, on the loose, in the streets."

She opened the door, and there, backlit by the late-morning sun from Broome Street, stood the couple. Yoko, just past five feet tall, was clad entirely in black." She wore a high-collar, black silk blouse with billowing sleeves tucked into modest palazzo pants, the effect completed by a pair of half boots with hardly any heel. Yoko never seemed at all concerned about height; she played nine or ten feet tall at all times.

Next to her, on her left, stood John Winston Lennon. From any distance, from any angle, and regardless of lighting or atmospheric intrusion, there was no doubt to even the most casual observer that he was, indeed, who he was. Like Yoko, he wore a black beret, tilted on his head and favoring his left side. It complemented Yoko's, which was canted towards the right. John wore jeans, long and somewhat bell-bottomed, more or less obscuring his footwear. This particular morning, he wore a collarless denim shirt under a frayed, well-worn army fatigue jacket. It was rumored that the garment had been sent by a grateful admirer whose disabling war wound, his "ticket out of 'Nam," had been, he felt, a direct result of his belief in peace and love overcoming hate and war. This revelation he attributed to John's music.

"Well . . . are we fuckin' surprised?" John said as he walked into his film company. Maria searched for words, not a common occurrence in her life, and then took a giant stride backward.

In the most unpretentious manner imaginable, the couple were like royalty. Not standard rock 'n' roll variety -- Kris and Rita, Mick and Carly--but actual larger-than-life significant figures. In fact, royalty might not be the best way to describe J&Y; they were like deity.

Now remembering to respond to John, I choked out, "Yes, more than a bit surprised, more than a little worried. More than a bit concerned that . . ."

Standing near my desk, John turned his attention directly to me.

"I, we . . . don't know what the big deal is. Why all of you seem to be so concerned. Farah actually sent a limo cruisin' up and down the high street lookin' for us to see if we needed a ride, or even rescuin', from whatever all of you fear is on the streets that might rise up and gobble us down. Caught up to us two three blocks back and followed us all the way down here. We are adult people, more than capable of walkin' about on our own, ya know?"

Yoko said, "And I think, John and I think, you know, that it's really important that we get out into the streets, that we, you know, fit in, become part of this city. I don't think so much that we are noticed as much as you people fear, you know. I don't think we stand out very differently at all."

Okay, I thought, *nothing different about a midsized Englishman and a diminutive Japanese woman wearing matching berets, he in a now-famous fatigue jacket, wearing the wire frames whose style was beginning to bear his name, walking around hand in hand in Manhattan. What was there to notice?* The only important thing was that this time, they had made it all the way down Seventh Avenue—if the Village had a "high street," I guess that was it—then into Soho without incident. Maybe we did worry about them too much.

With no more ceremony or discussion, J&Y passed Maria's and my desks, heading for the back room. John stopped for a moment, glanced at the calendar on the wall, and said simply, "David, where the fuck is Altoona?"

Before I could answer, he and Yoko turned down the hallway, then up the staircase to Edits 1 and 2. When they had disappeared, I picked up the receiver, punched in the intercom, and before Bill could say anything, I uttered our internal alert phrase, "Give Ireland back to the Irish."

"Thanks, man," he said. "We're racked up and ready to screen."

"So, David," Maria said, easing coyly, or so she thought, into a discussion, "why do you guys use that song lyric about giving Ireland back? Why do you say that to each other when like Yoko is just getting into the building? It's a code, right?"

"Something like that," I said. "If you answer that incoming call, I'll explain it to you."

Maria pulled an exaggerated furrowed-brow face, stuck out her tongue and picked up the phone on her desk.

In less than thirty seconds she called out, "It's yours, another freak predicting the end of the world."

I sighed and punched in line one, "Apocalyptic Notation Department, this is Mr. Johnson, can I help you?"

"Uh, like I wanna talk to somebody to warn you guys about a killer earthquake gonna hit the East Coast in a week. Did I get the right place?"

Unfortunately, he had. Before I could get much deeper into the call, the walls, the ceiling, and even the floor began to vibrate. Wow, was one of these loonies actually on target?

Of course not: John and Yoko were on-site. When they were screening, the audio monitors were always cranked up. I didn't have to go upstairs to know how the room looked: John and Yoko hunched over the K-E-M editor, Stephie perched on a stool operating the controls, Bill to her left waiting to change a reel or audio spool at a moment's notice. Behind the group, Sam no doubt paced slowly back and forth, slapping his riding crop against first one leg, then the other. He made comments, mostly reinforcing whatever John or Yoko said, while inside I knew his emotions were churning. I was learning what it was like to watch somebody watch your work, not knowing what they are thinking.

From where I sat downstairs, the repetitive back-and-forth of certain segments was not quite irritating, but more or less mesmerizing. For example, the solo piano intro to John's "Imagine," or at least the first few seconds of it, was run to and fro at least fifty times that afternoon. After an entire day seated beneath Edit One, absorbing chunks of the music track, the first thing I'd do on arriving home might be to pull out my own copy of Imagine and place the needle on the entire cut of the song to make up for hearing only a snippet hour after hour. The only way to get the repetitive bars of "Jealous Guy" or "How Can You Sleep" or whatever out of my head was to finally hear the entire song.

And then, just as suddenly as they arrived, John and Yoko left. It was not quite four o'clock, and the limo that had been idling outside Broome Street for nearly five hours stood open and ready to whisk them away.

"I think we'll go directly uptown to Record Plant, have them bring in a meal, till the band's all set up," John commented as he strode past my desk. "Why don't you and Maria come up later on, if you wish. Maria is so good at studio, knows when not to interfere, knows when we need something. She's a treasure. And David, you're not half bad your own self."

I grinned shyly, nodding toward John, "Well, thanks."

"You know when to be quiet. That's likewise important," John said, smiling back.

An evening, any evening, at Record Plant was magic. Whether they were laying down tracks or using the space as one of the city's most expensive rehearsal halls, "The Plant," as all of us very cool insiders referred to it, was a genuine slice of what we imagined would be rock 'n' roll history rolled out in real time. Dozens of musicians—name acts and famous sidemen, backup singers with multiple albums in their own names—and scads of producers and engineers whose work we'd all grown up with were as common in the hallways, lounges, control rooms, and studios of Record Plant as the ever-present haze of pot and cigarette smoke. I never got tired of going there, and I vowed almost every night I hung out, or more likely early morning heading home, that I would not forget what I'd seen or heard in the previous four, five, or ten hours. However, I often found it hard to remember the following afternoon. I figured I might regret that someday.

The front door, so difficult for most of us to shut effectively on the first try, slipped obediently into its frame as John and Yoko left.

"Weren't you going to mention something about that Jerry Lewis guy who called yesterday?" Maria said. "He is Gary's father; I checked with my friend May, uptown. Still doesn't mean that Dean Martin can sing."

"I'll get around to mentioning it in due time."

And I would try very hard to see if John Lennon would want to appear on this year's Jerry Lewis telethon, but I wasn't about to make the request at the risk of appearing to be just another person in his life seeking a favor on behalf of a friend. I didn't want to ask for more of him, for more of his life, than was fair. So many of us looked to him as not only a music icon with ideals and standards to be admired, but as someone who was much more than any kind of rock 'n' roller. We needed him to be John Lennon on so many levels at all times. It was pressure that I was not going to attempt to increase, even if he did think Jerry Lewis was funny.

—CHAPTER 4—
SOCK AND DANNY
10:50 A.M. THURSDAY, JUNE 15, 1972

"Whaddaya think it means? All this stuff? This scribblin'? Couldn't be appointments, could it, Dan?"

The speaker was a scruffy man, somewhere between twenty-five and forty, who had taken up comfortable residence in my desk chair. Easing in through the tricky inner door at Joko, I managed to take in his bewildering presence. However, it was the second visitor who demanded even greater attention. That would be a rather fit fellow doing what might be called a jig on my desktop while at the same time hooting and grunting like an ape. It was late for me to be getting to work, but the session at Record Plant and the subsequent group "breakfast" at Home, J&Y's favorite late-night hangout, had lasted till nearly four. Now it was nearly noon as I made my tentative entrance. Unbelievably, Maria had beaten my time again. She turned and, from behind her newly installed marmalade-color IBM Selectric that must've appeared overnight, nodded toward my desk.

"Sorry, David. Those two have been here since I walked in, maybe an hour ago. Same two guys who were here the other day. Said they wanted to talk to you, and didn't want to hang out back in the kitchen again. The one on your desk making the monkey sounds says the smell of burnt coffee gives him a headache."

It seemed as if no one at Joko knew how to make coffee. We were a film production company, so it seemed almost irreligious not to have a pot on the burner at all times. Truth be known, only Stephie drank the stuff, and she brought it in. Bill drank anything alcoholic; Sam affected a love for tea. Maria actually drank water—from bottles she bought somewhere near her parents' home in Chelsea. She actually bought individual-size bottles of water, a new idea, chucking them in the fridge with a large and obvious "Don't Touch" sticker, then threw them out when she was done and went out and purchased more.

Also unbelievable was the state of my desk as I approached it. The burly male in my chair continued to page through the makeshift "End of the World" calendar tacked to the exposed brick while his companion actually stood on top of my blotter; he was hopping up and down like a gorilla or chimpanzee, arms thrust out and bent at the elbows, seeming to scratch himself in an aggressive fashion while hooting and snuffling to no one or nothing in particular.

"Guy messin' with your calendar is a fella named Socrates; he has a last name, but I didn't catch it," Maria chimed in, seeing my bewilderment.

"Socrates is quite enough to begin with," I muttered, standing stock-still in the middle of the room, trying to absorb the spectacle.

"Man on your desk, like him I know. Name is Richter, Dan Richter. He used to be kind of a Farah Freedwoman at John's country house in Tittenhurst, the place in England where a lot of *Imagine* was shot. I think the other guy is like his assistant, or whatever."

"And could you, since you say you know the guy on my desk, explain what he's doing?"

"Oh, that. He was in a movie a while back, the space baby thing. What was it called? 'The Ultimate Trip?' or '2001 Trips?'"

2001: A Space Odyssey? Did he work on the movie or simply catch some sort of jungle fever in the opening scene?"

"Word is he worked with the director, Stanley something, can't think of his name."

How was it Maria could tell you the tour bus driver for almost any band currently on the *Billboard* Hot 100 yet fail to know the name of one of this century's great film directors?

"Guy says he trained all the apes to act like apes, or maybe it was men in costume."

At this point, Richter's companion, bored finally by paging through the calendar, began to make cawing sounds, roughly like what you'd hear from a large jungle bird. Some people did call Joko a zoo; now maybe we'd morphed into one.

Richter began to beat his chest, huffing even more aggressively, kicking the hell out of a stack of Eastman film invoices and trampling my blotter into near submission.

"Hi, guys," I began. "Was either of you looking for me?"

The one named Socrates blessedly stopped trying to imitate a mynah bird and turned slowly in my chair to face me. Richter, however, continued working on the blotter.

"You David?" Socrates said in a thick British accent, which I thought had more than a hint of the North Country in it, while pointing a thick finger my way.

"Yep, I'm David alright, not Tarzan, and I understand neither of you is Jane, though apparently your friend has seen all of the films, 'cuz he's doing a pretty good imitation of Cheetah."

"The fuck you talkin' about? I'm Sock and that's Danny. And you sez you're David, so where does that leave Tarzan or this guy named Cheater?"

"Sorry, bad joke," I said. Then, pointing toward Richter, whose desktop energy level seemed to be diminishing, I asked, "Does he eventually run down? Do you have to unplug him, or is there an off switch?"

"Nope. It's the openin' monolith discovery dance from 2001. Danny choreographed it, dontcha know. Taught all the other dancers moves, them perfect gestures. Once he starts, he's got to go through the entire thing in real time."

"Well, as I recall, the film ran about two and a half hours, so I imagine, no matter what, he'll be done before lunch."

And then, as if on cue, and with one final blow to his chest and a mighty apelike holler in the direction of the nonfunctioning sprinkler head on the ceiling, Dan Richter leaped from my desk, landing nimbly on the floor, and turned himself into a rather ordinary, if not athletic, male human in his early thirties.

"Hey, I'm Dan Richter, you've probably heard of me, or at least seen my work. John and Yoko sent us over to meet with you—you are David Johnson?—to see if we could be of use here at the studio while we're in town. Socrates and I have more or less run out of things to do at John's UK place, so we thought we'd pop over and see if a hand needed lending with the operation here in America. Just tryin' to be helpful, you know, to be of use."

Not your usual job applicant, but truth was this was how people were hired at Joko; they wandered in. That said, I was at a complete loss as to what to do with either of these characters. Richter, clad in jeans, sandals, and some sort of dress shirt, two buttons opened at the neck and sleeves rolled to his elbows, was the very picture of eager anticipation, grinning broadly, eyes sparkling with more than awareness and more or less leaning into, but not across, the two or three feet that separated us. His companion, however, was the antithesis of interest. He had begun to paw through the top drawer of my desk, ripping open two or three packets of that thick, orangey goop that comes in every bag of Chinese carryout, you know, the stuff you never seem to want to put on any food even if you run out of soy sauce and mustard. He deftly ripped open the end of each packet, thrust the majority of each into his mouth, then smoothly sucked out the remainder and, closing his eyes, groaned with satisfaction.

"Loves his Oriental," Richter stated. "Can't get enough, no matter where we are. If you think he's happy now, you should watch him with a good curry!"

"I can't wait. But Dan, or is it Danny?"

"Please, call me Dan," he said.

"Well Dan, nobody told me, or us, you guys were coming over, and I'm at a bit of a loss as to what to do with you, either one of you. I mean, we're . . . "

"We're both well schooled, well skilled in the film arts, David. As I'm sure you know, I had my time with Stan Kubrick, and have worked on several other films with J&Y." Here he paused, to make certain I was aware that he was aware of how one used the Lennons' initials during common, in-crowd slang. "I'm sure you've seen them, the movies. And, well, those wonderful people thought that Ball and I couldn't help but be of use here at your New York studios."

"His other name is Ball?" I asked. "First or last?"

"Sock, stand up here," commanded Richter, "and meet David Johnson. David, meet Socrates Ball."

Ball somehow levered himself out of my chair and thrust a sticky, orange-covered paw in my general direction for a manly handshake— or was it to wipe some of the Chinese goop onto my jacket? I wasn't sure which.

"Charmed, I'm sure," I said, turning back toward Richter. "You know, Sam Heintzelman is really the guy you should talk to. I mean, you know we have no true studio here, just a couple of edit rooms, one of which is usually working upstairs. Why don't I ring up and see if Sam has a moment to . . . "

"Sorry, won't work," Maria said from across the room. "The Great Director isn't in yet; nobody's seen him. Chris says he didn't come home last night, so I think you're stuck."

As suddenly as she had piped up, Maria found a great deal of work to do in the bottom file drawer of her desk.

It was then that a true angel of mercy appeared in the hallway to my left.

"Oh, really terrific! You're here!" Steph Bradley said as she entered the front room. "Didn't you remember? You promised to have either breakfast or lunch with me today. You know, go over the edit notes from yesterday's screening and put together a lab budget for the next working rough? I'd have Bill join us, but he's in conference in the back."

"In conference" was code for Bill's—or anyone else's—need to sleep something off or recover from a lack of sleep after a studio night.

"Of course, I was just going to mention Dan here, and Socrates . . . "

"Sock, call me Sock," said the hairy image who had retaken my chair. He was now reduced to toying with those small salt and pepper packets that find their way to the back of desk drawers nationwide. "Don't much like Socrates; it was me mum's idea. Me dad didn't like it either, but then he quit us before I turned one, so mum thought he'd given up his vote. Don't much like me dad, his memory. I'd chuck him about if he went and popped up afront of me. Finish him proper, if not a thorough beatin'. Anyway, call me Sock."

"Quite a bit of anger you have there," I observed. Turning to Stephie, I continued, "Looks like it's going to have to be lunch, and I know how important this is. So just give me a few minutes to wrap things up here and I'll buzz you upstairs."

"Neat!" Stephie said. "We can go around the corner to that new place, the Spring Street something or other. Just let me know."

Of course, there'd been no discussion of a breakfast or lunch, and we seldom if ever worked a budget for any phase of any project at Joko Films. I assumed that Steph had simply overheard some of my byplay with the uninvited Richter and Ball and had decided to come to my rescue.

"Well okay, I guess Sock and I will be off, though we do need to spend time soon with you and Mr. Heintzelman. We're busy tomorrow. Let's get together next week—say a late lunch or maybe even drinks and dinner."

"Wow! That would be terrific! But again, Sam is really the guy you have to talk to."

"Well, but Fran, you know, the pushy one over at John's flat, says you pretty much run the place. Would be you who figured out what to do with us," Sock Ball interjected.

Good old Fran, always the joker. "Let's see what we can work out Monday or Tuesday next week."

Now, surprisingly, Ball turned, looked at the calendar and left a smear of orange substance on several squares at the beginning of next week, seeming to mark a spot for several appointments in the near future.

"Says here Monday's all taken up with some kind of massive explosion startin' in some place called Utah, a brigade led by a guy name of Brigham Young. What's this? A special effects scene for a major piece with Lennon? We could help there. I've been a key grip on three or four films, one of which wasn't even a porno, and Danny, well, fuck, he can do almost anything. Where is Utah? Across the river in Jersey?"

"Close," I said. "That brigade thing, it's kind of a joke. In fact, the entire calendar is full of things people call in, claiming to predict the end of the world. I keep my real calendar, well, sort of, in the top right-hand drawer."

Here Richter jumped in. I think he was beginning to see the three-card monte byplay that would lead them round in circles until no one sat with either of these two for whatever reason in the next few days. "We'll ring you up on Monday," he said. "I think Sock got your calendar confused with friends of his, boys from the Angry Brigade, you know, in the UK. Kind of like the SDS over here, or the Weather Underground."

"Not no more. Don't like 'em," said Ball, who now was showing he could actually walk upright, in addition to destroying fast food detritus, as he moved toward the front door. "Don't like 'em no more. Too lefty, too pinko. Me mum says all of us English-speakin' peoples got to turn more to the right. Mum used to be Labor, but she's voted Tory the last two times. You know, accordin' to Mum, we all need a war every now n' again just to clear shit up."

"Clear shit up? That sounds important."

"'Tis important. Y'know, like that bloke Darwin used to say, important to thin the herd. Survival of the fittest, like wif the use of heritage power, separates weak from strong."

"Heritage power?" I said. "What is that?"

"Don't mind Sock," said Richter, "he just runs on a bit . . ."

Then, before he had to break out a leash or possibly a whip and chair, Richter began to herd his sidekick through the front room and toward the door leading to Broome Street.

"Again, don't mind Sock," he said. "He's full to his eyelids with opinions. Often doesn't think things through. We'll look you up— and Mr. Heintzelman—Monday, Tuesday, and I'm sure we'll work something out."

With that, Richter and Ball were gone, if far from forgotten, as the mess that was my desk plainly showed.

"That was weird. Definitely weird," Maria commented, suddenly losing interest in the empty Pendaflex files in her drawer. "Damn good thing Sam didn't come in."

"Why's that? I could have passed them on to him; told them how important he is. He would have spent the better part of today and tomorrow reinforcing that."

"Not that," Maria said. "Thank God, he didn't hear them calling him 'Mr. Heintzelman.' Once he heard that, he'd want all of us to do that."

There was a light tap on my right shoulder from behind. "Lunchy lunchy?" Steph Bradley inquired.

I turned and gave her a genuinely broad smile and said, "Most definitely, and it's on me."

–CHAPTER 5–
LUNCH ON SPRING STREET
12:15 P.M., THURSDAY, JUNE 15, 1972

"I think I read about this place in Gael Greene's column," I told Steph as we cozied up at a corner table in the recently opened Spring Street Bar; we had just put in our orders with a lackadaisical waitress.

"This is really a pretty keen, okay place!" Steph replied enthusiastically.

For Soho, an area populated mostly by light manufacturing and warehouse buildings, with hardly any spots for lunch or drinks, let alone dinner, the bar was a giant step forward. Bill had told me that a month or so before I came to work at Joko, it was nearly impossible to get so much as a sandwich within walking distance after one thirty or two in the afternoon. "Like everybody's supposed to have eaten by one. I mean, who does that? I'm not really awake and getting hungry for anything until two or three." he'd complained. For the sake of all of us, the Spring Street Bar was the first glimmer of a truly evolving work setting, as the neighborhood's hours and offerings began to be more in tune with the rest of the city.

"Who's Gael Greene? Wait a minute, that's probably a dumb question; she's a restaurant reviewer, right?" Steph queried, hesitantly.

"Just me trying to be in the know. Yes, Gael Greene does restaurant reviews, the *Voice*? Or no. I think it's *New York*— maybe." I affected nonchalance.

"You know, I like you," Steph replied, grinning broadly. "I mean, not like that, you know, boy and girl like. I mean, oh jeez, I'm married, mostly, and, well, you know what I mean, don't you?"

"Sure. I think you mean you like me, you appreciate the overwhelming sense of professionalism and responsibility I bring to the company in spite of the fact that on a daily basis, I'm really not quite sure what I'm doing half the time. I'm learning tons about this business, particularly about film. I didn't study it much in school. And I'm downright tickled to be in the middle of anything as cool as the world of John and Yoko."

"Thanks, that bailed me out nicely." Steph took a huge pull on a straw she slid deftly into a large glass of iced tea, which our waitress had recently deigned to deliver, sliding it slowly across the table.

"Fine," I said. "So, I've got to thank you again for getting me out of there before those two guys commandeered my entire afternoon. How much did you hear from the kitchen before you blessedly barged in?"

"Enough to know there is nothing they could possibly do here that wouldn't put them underfoot and in the way all the time," Steph noted. "And then there's the more athletic guy . . . "

"You mean Dan?"

"Yeah, that one. I mean I have heard of him, and he does go way back with John—and Yoko too. And you know as well as I do how much the I-know-John-and-Yoko-real-good-better-than-you goes. You know what I mean."

"Boy, do I! I have to admit it is so very refreshing to know that Maria, even though she's probably the youngest at Joko, has seniority—time of service—on all of us. Yet she never uses it, like others. Hope I never fall into that trap."

"So, you tell people where you work—and for whom?" Stephie inquired.

"For whom? No. At first I thought I might, but then there's the issue of believability. I mean I called up my old college roommate one morning about a month after I started. I wanted to tell him where I was, what I was doing."

"Why did you wait a month?" Steph asked.

"Well, he's in the army, and it took me a while to get his new home number. I had to track down his mom."

"She gave you a phone number for him in Vietnam?"

"No. Thankfully, he was drafted but posted to Hawaii, which he's currently keeping safe from the hordes of godless communism. I think we'll get him back in one piece, maybe even with a decent tan. Anyway, I think he believed me pretty much from the beginning, although he was a bit bent out of shape 'cause I woke him up."

"Was it a weekend? Did you call from home before you left?" Steph inquired.

"No, midmorning, I used Apple Records long distance privileges from the office. What I forgot was the time zone difference between New York and Honolulu. I woke him and his roommates up, I fear. Later, much later, he called back and did ask, quite seriously, if I was for real. Even Thom had to ask a second time, you know, make sure. That taught me a lesson."

"Which was?"

"To be careful how I use this, well, new-found power. If my old roommate had to double-check for believability, what would a casual acquaintance think? You know, the 'Oh yeah, you work for John Lennon!' and, the person's thinking, 'Right. And I'm going on the road with the Dead, just the domestic part of the tour.'"

"Been there. Done that. Yeah, I tend to keep my mouth shut, no need to advertise. All of this will be in my memoirs someday," Steph said.

Our food came. She had the house salad with double dressing—Gael Greene would hardly approve—while I had the cheeseburger platter with extra pickles, fries, and, just to prove I really was born and raised in Ohio, a side order of mayonnaise for both.

"Mayo on the burger?" Steph quipped. "Okay, that's weird, probably Midwestern. All of you heartlanders are simply strange. But you dip french fries in it as well. What's with that?"

"First, I like it," I responded. "It also proves I'm very cosmopolitan, with European overtones. I read in an old Agatha Christie that Hercule Poirot, and most Belgians, prefer their fries with a side of mayo, or better still, aioli." I took a bite of the burger, rare, with Swiss instead of cheddar. Chewing thoughtfully, I inquired, "So, again, is this just a rescue mission, or did you really want to talk about something?"

Steph paused, a forkful of salad midway between bowl and mouth, and slowly blushed. She stayed that way for an uncomfortable period of time, perhaps only five seconds, but nonetheless the pause felt odd to me.

"Oh well, maybe there was something else."

After that nonstatement, she poked around the nearly full bowl for another hefty forkful, guaranteeing it would be impossible for her to comment further for more than a moment or two. Then, chewing slowly, she took some time to compose her thoughts.

"So," I said snappily, "I would be a less than inquisitive man if I didn't go back and pick up on just one thing you said a few minutes ago."

Her blush was beginning to recede; she looked better with a bit of color, I reflected. Another forkful of iceberg in waiting, she nodded vigorously, encouraging me to continue. Anything, I thought, so that I could talk and she did not have to.

"You said, 'mostly.' That you were married 'mostly.' I'm an unmarried person, so enlighten me. What did you mean by that?"

The blush came back, even deeper this time. I took another bite of burger, favored four or five more fries with mayonnaise, wondering if they call them french fries in Belgium, assuredly not chips, as in England. I was waiting her out; she'd exhaust her salad eventually. After more than a full minute of silence and another small forkful, Steph cleared her throat and patted her mouth with one of the tiny cocktail napkins provided by the lackluster waitress.

"I don't think I can finish this. Maybe I should stop ordering extra dressing. I always do that, but today, for some reason, my stomach feels off."

Then she sat up straight and looked me square in the eye. "Well, okay. 'Mostly' really means that, well, I mean I should say that I am married, really. Haven't you met Jeffrey yet? I mean, he's a dreamboat. Every girl I knew, not just in the film program but my sorority . . . "

"They have sororities at NYU?" I asked.

She nodded. "And Jeffrey, well, he got his BA at Columbia but decided he wanted his MBA from a different school, and, anyway, New York University is considered to be more or less the ninth Ivy, right?"

"Sure, along with Boston College, Colgate, Michigan, large parts of Northwestern, and Cal Berkeley."

Steph giggled. "Good point. To be truthful, Jeffrey, and especially his father, wanted him to go on at Columbia, and his grades were okay, but there was an incident—no big deal, really—and, well, as it turned out, happily for me, Jeffrey enrolled in NYU for his business degree. So we met and, well, I was the lucky girl."

She smiled brightly, and took another pull on her straw, and I watched carefully as her face returned to its normal shade of porcelain.

"Did you marry right out of college?" I asked.

"No, actually, it was over Christmas break my senior year. By then, Jeffrey had been out of school a few months and actually landed the job at JWT."

"J. Walter Thompson, the ad agency?"

"Uh-huh. He's kind of graduated from their junior account training program. I mean, it's a coveted way to start in the business.

Jeffrey was so fortunate to land a spot there, even if his dad pulled a few strings. But when you meet Jeffrey, and I hope you do, I'm sure you'll like him. Don't mention the part about his father; he's really sensitive about that. He wants to, you know, believe that he's doing things on his own."

"Was it a big wedding? I mean, I guess, that scheduling something like that during the holidays would be quite difficult. It would take a lot of planning, you know, guests, a church."

Her face reddened yet again. Now she took on a stern countenance. "Don't you know what a Christmas wedding means, especially during a woman's last year in college?"

"I'm, well, not pretending. What significance does it have?"

And then I remembered a very sad, hastily arranged wedding at a small suburban chapel attended by me and my then girlfriend, Liz, and maybe a half dozen others on a rainy Saturday in December in my own senior year. A good friend of Liz's, I think a suite mate in one of the high-rise dorms, was marrying a guy, some kind of salesman, midtwenties—doing it before she began to show. She gave birth just after the couple moved out of town to somewhere in Indiana early the following spring. Never did return to school, never graduated as far as I knew.

It was my turn to blush. Then, before I could begin to cover my tracks, Stephanie spoke up.

"I was still in the first trimester, but my parents, well, they thought it would be best if—how did my mother put it?—it would be best if I looked, you know, more the part of an innocent bride than one who'd already been spoiled."

Steph held my eyes a moment; then her eyes dropped, as if something of great interest required studying in her half-empty salad bowl. Then, just as suddenly, she leveled her eyes back on mine, "And well, before you ask, I, I mean we, lost the baby in February. It's one of the reasons I dropped out of NYU. Ironic, isn't it? Almost funny, in a sad way."

"Steph, I'm sorry, really. That was stupid of me," I said quickly. "I was prying. None of my business how you're married, if you're married, or why and when you married." Then, trying to kid her out of her awkward position, I added, "Well, gee whiz, after all, I like you, a lot too."

That worked more or less. She looked back up at me. "Married. It's a term, you know. It's a situation that I always thought I would find myself in. Always looked forward to it. But now, it just feels, well, strange. Strange to be married."

"Fewer and fewer people seem to be doing it," I put in, trying to assist.

"Do you know, I went to a party at Sam and Christine's, early January, less than a week after New Year's. It was at their apartment. There were lots of people—hardly anyone I knew except for Bill and Maria. And of course Maria left early with two girlfriends to go hear a new band at some club in Brooklyn. Bill arrived mostly comatose and then finished the job in less than an hour. Jeffrey, well, Jeffrey always seems to find someone to talk to, and he was off in one corner with a couple of other business-type guys discussing stuff that was totally out of the moment. They were comparing mileage, gas mileage—can you imagine? Then Jeffrey decided he would bring up the subject of tax shelters. It was boring; I ran away to the other side of the living room."

"Sounds like a lot of fun; sorry I wasn't part of the group back then," I said with more than a bit of sarcasm.

"Yeah, you could have rescued me. Anyway, some guy comes up to me, really good-looking. Maybe a bit older than me. Really cute. I knew I was about to get hit on. You know, I was looking forward to it, good for my self-confidence."

"And did he?" I said.

"Oh yes, for sure. Graphically. Went into great detail about how he would remove certain . . . well, you know. I didn't handle it well."

"Really? I find that hard to believe."

Steph threw the wadded up small napkin in my general direction. "Yeah, well, it's amazing how he stopped being cute quick. Anyway, I gave him what I thought would be the ultimate defense, you know, the end to all pickup lines. I looked him straight in the eye, thanked him, and told him I was married."

"I guess that would do it," I said.

"You know what he said next? He looked at me, smiled, laughed quietly, and said, 'Married? Why?'"

"And you said?"

"Nothing. What answer can you give to that? It made me think. How many people I've met, especially in our business, are really married? How many of my girlfriends from school are married? How many have stayed married if they were? What's wrong with the world? What's wrong with being married?"

Assuming most of Steph's last speech was rhetorical, I kept my mouth shut for a moment. "Not to be a plagiarist," I said, "but the times they are a-changin'. People are too. I'm not quite sure I'll ever get married. Don't see the point."

We were both silent for a minute or so. And then, sensing an opportunity to change the subject, Stephanie sighed and said, "There are some things I want to talk through with you. I mean, you spend a lot more time with them, J&Y, especially off-site. I never get up to Record Plant. Jeffrey either wants me home around the time he gets home or there are agency events, dinners, parties, things like that that spouses—they actually call us 'spice'—are encouraged to attend. I wonder sometimes if that's hurting my career here. And then there's Yoko."

"What about her?" I asked.

"She scares me. Does she scare you?"

"A little bit," I lied. "No, let me be straight, quite a bit. And not so much scare as intimidate. I think most people feel that way around her. But the real mystery to me is whether she's completely unaware of that fact or if she is totally aware of it and uses it. I can't really tell."

"Well, anyway," Steph went on, "she scares the living heck out of me. She'll make changes, more or less demand them. After all, it's her—their—film. But she won't talk directly to me. She'll look right at Bill, tell him, or more often direct the change toward Sam, even though she knows I'm the one who will make the edits, put the next rough together, mark it up, and—after Sam reviews—get it to the lab. She knows I do this, and I think she knows I do it really well, but she seldom—I mean hardly ever—tells me directly. It's unnerving."

I nodded. I'd also had a couple of encounters with Yoko. "Then again, you do have a protector in Sam.

"Yeah, I do." And she added quickly, "I should be grateful. But it's all so, well, confusing."

Again, silence. Then the waitress broke the spell.

"The check," she stated flatly, dangling the crinkled piece of green paper between us. "Are we gonna split it? Or fight for it?"

"Seriously?" I said. "In honor of today, the Seventeenth Annual Inappropriate Waitress Interruption Day, I was thinking of stiffing you and climbing out a window in the men's room."

"From what I've observed, no men's room; they're both unisex, and trust me and your nose, neither has a window."

She dropped the check where my plate had been. I grabbed it. "Dessert?" I asked Stephie.

"Thanks, no. Actually, I'm not feeling too well."

Making good on my promise, I paid, and we left.

—CHAPTER 6—
THE ANGRY BRIGADE
8:10 P.M., THURSDAY JUNE 15, 1972

We were in the hallway just outside Studio A at Record Plant, where John and his recently discovered, somehow still-evolving band, Elephant's Memory, were laying down additional tracks. "We're not even really workin' together, just datin'," he'd said about the band more than a month back. Here in the hallway, John was just killing time. A rare chance to just hang with the man. Not sure why, but I asked about the Angry Brigade.

"Where'd you dig that one up—and fuckin' why? More than a bit arcane, dontcha think?" John asked me. For some reason, Dan Richter's comment about the Brigade had stuck in my head, so I'd figured I'd inquire of an actual Englishman what he knew about the group.

"Somethin' about Grosvenor Square, a bombing or a plot some three, four years back. Strictly nonsense," John continued, recalling the Brigade in the late sixties. "Your SDS over here seem a lot more violent, a lot more intent upon tryin' to end violence usin' violence, which of course is completely stupid. The SDS are a lot more active, I think a bit more destructive, than the Angry Brigade ever was."

"Was?" I asked. "You don't think they're around anymore?"

"Don't really know; could care less. Whatever they were up to, whatever they tried—a few bombs?—nothing consequential, a lot less, what would it be, sound and fury, less of that than your average neighborhood Guy Fawkes bonfire. In fact, whoever the head guy was, I heard he got arrested and sent away somewhere for a good stretch of time, and he said he realized after all was over that he might have been the only 'angry' bloke in the Brigade. All the folks around him who were supposed to help stir up all the trouble—bomb places, change things—were more like the 'extremely cross' brigade after all. In other words, far from fuckin' really angry. Makes you think about anger, you know, as a concept."

"Concept? I've never thought of anger as conceptual," I said.

"Now you're soundin' like Yoko. I mean I've often thought about the forms anger can take, not to mention what brings it on. I mean, I hear that sometimes, just sometimes, I can be what is called 'an angry drunk.'"

"Well, I'm sure . . . "

"Don't bother, I do read my own press now and again, despite myself. However, I don't recall bein' angry or peevish. Didn't think I had anything botherin' me when I started. But more than one person has said my anger in a situation like that can be intimidatin'."

"Hope I never have to see that."

"Likely not. One thing Yoko has helped with—has insisted upon—is my cuttin' down alcohol." Here John paused and did that looking-up-past-me-toward-the-ceiling thing that seemed to indicate he was collecting his thoughts. He continued, "I mean, anger takes many forms, is expressed by people in different ways. Ways that might surprise."

"That makes sense," I agreed. Not surprisingly, the topic brought Sam Heintzelman to mind. I paused, to think how angry or bitter Sam might actually be, which could account for his rather dark moods or sudden outbursts.

"So," John said, "I'm findin' that sometimes you can't even know someone's angry when they are. And the very fact they might be holdin' it in could mean their anger is much, much greater than someone who simply smashes a bottle or finds a way to strike a wall."

John settled his eyes on mine, grinned slightly, and said, "I think we're wanderin' off topic. The Angry Brigade. You're askin'—why?"

"Well, we were visited by Dan Richter and his sidekick."

"Ah! The relatively famous Socrates Ball. Like the name, but don't think much of anything about his character. Only brought him on over there 'cause Dan vouched for him, and Yoko and I thought Dan could use the help; after all, Tittenhurst is a sprawlin' property. Sorry if he's underfoot. I'm hopin' he and Danny will get bored and head back to England."

"Do you miss it, England, I mean?"

"Gotta tell ya, New York, we love it. It's a real pleasure to live in our small, two-room flat 'stead of that massive, ramblin' house. Yoko and I, we're livin' like students, with little more than we really need. It's a pleasure."

"I couldn't agree more," I said. "By the way, as long as you're schooling me on modern Brit trivia, have you ever heard of heritage power?"

"Heritage power? Now that's a new one; if the Angry Brigade were supposed to be the risin' up of the people, you know, the middle and lower classes, then maybe this heritage power you mention is a movement that springs full out of the House o' Lords. Funny actually to even think of somethin' risin' up from the upper class; it's a bit redundant. Could it have something to do with primogeniture?"

"Don't know."

"And is that another bit of nothin' you picked up from the rather frothy Socrates Ball?"

"Yeah, but if you don't know what it means, it's lost on me; probably not important."

With that, an engineer stuck his head into the hallway. "We're back up. Sorry for the delay."

Apparently, some wire or other had come loose, causing the session to break at eight, less than an hour after it had begun. John moved, almost dutifully, toward the studio along with a half dozen or so others who'd gathered in the hallway or adjacent lounge. Some had straggled into the living-room-like environment for which Record Plant had become famous.

In addition to the technical and acoustic requirements of a recording studio, comfortable living spaces had made The Plant in New York—and LA—instantly successful. Gone were the bright white walls, hardwood or concrete flooring, and overhead fluorescents of the past, replaced by large leather couches, throw pillows, beanbag chairs, muted lighting, and soft color schemes, which became the model for recording studios everywhere.

"John, you know, really likes it here; he's comfortable, and the feel, the overall feeling, you know, is very conducive to creativity and expression," Yoko had commented during one of my first visits, back in early April.

Most of us at the film company had, more or less, an open-ended invite to drop by and hang out at sessions. However, it was made clear from the very beginning that like well-behaved children, we were to be seen, not heard. It was only during this unscheduled break that I felt I could approach John and query him about the British protest group Ball had mentioned.

I didn't like Socrates Ball. There was an aura of malevolence about him that made him an altogether uncomfortable piece of work. I again gave a silent prayer of thanks to Stephie for bailing me out, insisting we go to lunch.

I'd asked her if she'd like to come along to Record Plant and hang out for a while at the end of the day. "I mean, I don't think I've ever seen you up there. Gotta tell ya, it's an amazing experience, a great scene."

"Nah, that's not me, but thanks for asking, David, really," Stephie had said. "I know, I know, every night there I could be experiencing so much. But Yoko left a lot of changes in the third and fourth reels of *Imagine*, and I have Sam's notes too, so I think I'll work late here and get a jump on things for tomorrow. Sam will probably show up and want to review the most recent rough."

"You sure?" I asked. "I mean you said at lunch you weren't feeling well and . . ."

"Nah," Stephie said, jumping in, "it comes and goes. I'll be okay."

With Sam still among the missing, and Bill gone midafternoon, Maria and I had called a car for our trip to West Forty-fourth. It was around 5:30. To close the interior door at Joko, it was necessary to give it a firm pull, which I did before locking it. Then I looped the large, case-hardened steel Master padlock through the hardware on the security gate. From the outside, it appeared to be locked. This would make it more convenient for Steph later that evening. Not for the first time, I stood and looked back at the nondescript two-story building before stepping into the limo. All the windows were either dark or shaded, and to anyone on the street, it looked for all the world like Marwood Press—gold letters stenciled on glass —was closed for business on an early evening in late spring. I stared a bit longer, then yielded to Maria from within the car.

"C'mon!" she urged. "We can grab a sandwich on the way; you know how John hates when there's too much food floating around the studio. Get in here!"

—CHAPTER 7—
SEEMS TO BE CALLED THE WATERGATE

9:00 A.M., FRIDAY, JUNE 16, 1972

It had been an unusually early morning. I was sitting in the back of a stuffy Washington cab on the way to my appointment at the Democratic National Committee headquarters. My mind began to wander to Stephie and the stilted connection over lunch at Spring Street. There was so much more I wanted to ask her.

Where had she grown up? And how? I wondered if she liked her parents—and if they actually loved her. Was she an only child? Had she ever been happy? Did she remember her first kiss? (Silly thought—who doesn't?). Any steady boyfriends before Jeffrey? Was her marriage at all happy?

Somehow. I resented him. *Okay, David*, I thought, *she's a married person. Even in this year, 1972, in Downtown NYC, that meant something. And while there had been no overtures, no opening whatsoever, yesterday's lunch had been pleasantly flirtatious—hadn't it? If anything, her marriage had made the flirtation safe, even a bit forbidden. Delicious, as a matter of fact.*

"Here we are, chief, 2600 Virginia Northwest, and this destination today is yours for only $7.60 not including the rather generous gratuity which I'm sure you're contemplating."

"The price is reasonable," I responded, "but where's the meter? How do you know what to charge?"

The driver turned ninety degrees to his right to look at me directly, then tapped his head with his left hand.

"All retained here, my friend. My brain is like a well-oiled machine. I compute all fares in my noggin, without reference to the taxi commission's most recent zone fare chart, which I believe was last altered during the second—maybe the third—Roosevelt administration. We're on a zone system in the District. Big loser is me, the driver. When traffic's tough and we sit bumper to bumper, the fare's the same, no matter what."

I peered up at an office building, the home of the DNC, and my ten o'clock appointment. The structure looked like a massive window air-conditioner having fallen from one of God's bedrooms and lodged on its side.

"Seems to be called Watergate," I said, getting out my money clip and peeling off a ten for the driver. "Why is that?"

"Development's only six, maybe seven years old. Before that, the whole area was called the Water Gate. The National Symphony and a couple of pickup orchestras gave concerts here summers going back to the 1930's; before that it was simply the end of the C&O Canal, which had an actual water gate—part of the canal's lock, about a hundred yards upriver." He pointed to the right of the eleven-story structure.

"You are a genuine fount of information," I said.

"Now you don't want change, do you?" he asked, slipping the folded ten into his shirt pocket and handing me a blank receipt.

"How could I?" I replied.

I left his two-tone cream-over-black cab, sliding out into the June morning. Washington was usually hot and sticky from late May to October, that time when the Redskins are often mathematically eliminated, but this particular day was actually springlike, the morning air carrying a crisp optimism. As I approached the building lobby, the structure stopped resembling an air-conditioner and morphed somehow into a carelessly assembled stack of Melmac plates on the bottom shelf of a cupboard. So ugly!

There was no real lobby security, just a pair of rent-a-guards, broad shouldered, with buzz cuts and blue blazers over khaki trousers. I asked what floor the Democratic National Committee was on, gave my name, and signed in. They pointed me to the elevators.

The DNC reception area featured a low granite-topped desk, where a not-quite-middle-aged woman wearing wire rims assessed me gravely as I approached. With even the hint of a mustache, she could have passed for a descendant of Teddy Roosevelt. *Well, it is Washington*, I thought.

"May I help you?" she inquired, lacking the outward appeal—or warmth—of a bag of frozen peas.

"Mr. O'Brien, Larry O'Brien. My name is . . . "

"Ah, yes, Mr. Johnson, from New York City. You are expected, though Mr. O'Brien is running quite late this morning. Please, take a seat, and I'll let you know as his day progresses."

As his day progresses? I slid dejectedly into one of the ocher Italian-design couches lined up on either wall of reception. They faced several coffee tables replete with stacks of thick, full-color brochures featuring a smiling Lyndon Johnson and Hubert Humphrey glad-handing constituents at some long-ago fairground. I found it interesting there was no old literature for Humphrey-Muskie, the losing ticket in 1968. The table nearest where I sat offered two issues of *Reader's Digest*, one from January and the other from May 1971; several copies of *Field & Stream*; and a tattered *Sports Illustrated* less than three weeks old, for which I was grateful. After paging through it, I busied myself with the morning's *Washington Post*, picked up at the airport.

Less than a half hour later, around 10:15, I rose to see how "Mr. O'Brien's day" was progressing. Then again at 10:35. No news, but somehow time passed more pleasantly than I might have imagined, spurred on by a check of the National League standings—the Reds still solidly in first place in the Western Division. There was even a brief mention of their manager, Sparky Anderson, in the *Post*, Shirley Povich's column: a rundown of possible candidates for Manager of the Year.

Then, there was the redhead. She'd strode purposefully from an elevator less than five minutes after I'd resigned myself to my seat. Instead of formally checking in at reception, she had nodded knowingly to the woman behind the desk and seated herself on the opposite couch. She was tall, probably six feet in her boots, and she had waist-length hair punctuated by luminous green eyes that were impossible to ignore.

Thumbing through reading matter we probably weren't reading, we smiled at each other without feeling the need to communicate further, two apparently lost souls abandoned in a waiting room. Was she staring? I wasn't dressed like most visitors to an upscale Washington office. It was a uniform alright, just not a DC uniform: dress denims, jacket, jeans, work shirt, newer pair of Frye boots, thick leather belt. If she'd had X-ray vision, she might have wondered at the dozen or so record albums and other Apple Corps-branded items, autographed and initialed for O'Brien or whoever might want them, favors from John that I was carrying in my large saddlebag.

My reverie was finally interrupted by a burst of activity at the reception desk. A short, well-dressed man wearing a double-breasted brown Edwardian suit with a ruffled navy-blue dress shirt conferred with the receptionist. He then smiled, nodded to the redhead, urging her not to get up, and came my way. Standing, I towered over him. Before I could say a word, he began.

"Hi, I'm Peter! Peter Trapote. I work here at the Democratic National Committee." He spoke with a burst of pride that seemed to urge me to hug him, then pose with him for a picture he could send to his hometown paper, wherever that might be.

"Good for you," I said. "You work for Mr. O'Brien?"

"No," he said, "I don't work directly for him. I work mostly in the broadcast area, spot distribution, duplication, and some production."

Having used my best response already, I nodded an "attaboy" toward him, then tried to squeeze in a question. "You do know that I'm here representing . . . "

"Of course, of course. We all know why you're here and who you work for."

He was standing nearly on tiptoe, all five foot six of him, beaming a bright, toothy smile my way, eyes glistening beneath granny glasses. *Style* must be catching on everywhere, I thought. The boss had 'em in all colors.

"Well, I'm flattered," I said, "but I've been here for over . . . " I noticed Peter was glancing behind me, hoping perhaps I was shielding someone on the couch between myself and the wall.

He said, "But you are alone. I guess they aren't with you, are they?"

I was accustomed to this. Almost every night in New York I had a choice of two or three places to go: parties, dinners, concerts large and small, a screening or viewing of a rough cut of an upcoming film that was seeking support, all invitations meant for John and Yoko. Invites mailed, slipped under doors, or hand delivered by messenger, accompanied by large floral displays, exotic or common foodstuffs, newly released books and records, or, in one recent memorable delivery, a dozen silk shirts, six each for the boss and his wife, in matching colors.

So, I would show up at the Bitter End, the VIP entrance of Madison Square Garden, the stage door of the Academy of Music, a fifth-floor walk-up loft on the West Side, or the Rizzoli screening room to listen, to view, to experience, and mostly to apologize. John and Yoko couldn't make it, but they'd insisted that I—sometimes with a guest but more often alone—come to assure the group's manager, the singer-songwriter, or the aspiring filmmaker that he, John, and yes, Yoko, very much wanted to be there and wanted me to tell them later all about the wonderful evening they had missed.

From the saddlebag, I'd pull out a couple of record albums, signed and dated, which in most cases were received gratefully. All would be well. I often wondered what became of these albums—with John's signature scrawl on the back, the day's date, sometimes even the time of the signing. Were some framed? Set aside and never opened? Well hidden in a wall safe or secret compartment in a bedroom armoire?

So here I was, showing up at yet another meeting to disappoint all around me, the flimsy substitute for a real live ex-Beatle—and Yoko.

"I'm sure," I said, "that I confirmed on Wednesday that I'd meet alone with Mr. O'Brien about the prospects of our working on behalf of Senator McGovern. It was understood that our efforts would be behind the scenes, providing film support, commercial production, whatever we could do. J&Y would of course not be able to personally . . ."

Wrinkling his nose, and dusting the left cuff of his Edwardian suit, Trapote said, sotto voce, "Janey—who's Janey?"

"No," I said, "J and Y," spacing out the initials around the conjunction to make it clearer.

"Yes," Trapote responded, "of course, J and Y for John and Yoko. so very far out."

I added, as a lame excuse, "They were recording until three or four this morning."

"A brand-new album?" he gushed. "Do you have tracks with you?"

"No. I work in the film company. Many of us go by Record Plant after work and hang out and listen to what's happening. But believe me, John and Phil don't let anybody touch those tapes, ever!"

"Is Phil John's manager?" he asked.

Did this clown ever read a copy of *Billboard* or . . .

"Phil, Phil Spector. He's producing the album with John."

Then my sight line drifted north of Peter. The redhead had stood up and approached wordlessly, simply smiling, nodding, and staring. This, too, was not uncommon. As Steph and I had discussed, where we worked and for whom we worked were, for most people, a kind of magical fairy dust.

On this particular morning, the guy in the weird, ruffled blue shirt and now apparently the redhead both knew for whom I worked. They had that transfixed look in their eyes.

"Okay," I said, "I'm sorry they're not here. However, they are greatly concerned with this election. John and Yoko want to do everything possible to see that Nixon does not get a second term—I mean everything we can do.”

This “everything” excluded the most obvious contribution that could be made. It had already been discussed that a series of large outdoor concerts might be held to raise not only money, but more importantly voter awareness of the apparent Democratic nominee, mild-mannered George McGovern, the junior senator from South Dakota. However, by late May, through channels far above my pay grade, word had come down that should the Lennons attempt to raise money or hold concerts of this type for the Democratic cause, the Nixon administration would double and redouble efforts, already well underway, to deport John—and possibly Yoko too.

Now close-up, the redhead was even more stunning. In her boots, she towered over the diminutive Trapote and was able to look me directly in the eye.

“She has a super voice,” Trapote said, abruptly, introducing a new topic. Yet somehow I was not at all surprised.

“Does she now?” I said, “And I just bet you happen to have . . . ”

“Yes, yes, back in my office, er, my workspace, a tape of her and the group’s most recent session. It’s, I mean, she’s terrific! And guess what?”

“Let me take a shot,” I mused. “No, don’t tell me. Let me guess: you are her manager.”

“Almost. I’m her assistant manager!”

I wondered briefly if Brian Epstein, the Beatles' famous first manager and the one individual credited with helping to craft the group from scratch, had ever had an assistant manager? Doubtful.

“So, if you just come over here,” he said, gently grabbing my elbow, “I’ll be able to play you . . . ”

“Gosh,” I said, “I’d really like that, but I’m here to talk with Mr. O’Brien about the McGovern campaign.”

“Oh, that,” the newly minted assistant manager said. “Well, that’s nice.” At this point, Trapote lowered his voice nearly to a whisper. “It’s a Friday, and I don’t think Larry’s in today. In fact, hardly anybody’s here.”

“But . . . ”

“I know, I know, someone should have called you and rescheduled. Truthfully, people are already beginning to reposition themselves for, you know, well, whatever will happen after November.”

“You mean you guys have already given up? Hell, he’s not even officially nominated yet!” I said.

"We'll put up a good fight, but let's face it, CREEP, you know, the Committee to Re-elect the President, is overwhelmingly funded. Nixon is not exactly unpopular, and this whole opening-up-China thing, well, you've gotta admit, it's pretty spectacular."

It was actually the first time I'd heard the president's campaign organization—pronounced "creep"—referred to by its acronym. How strange it was that anybody would brand themselves in such a way.

"In fact," Trapote continued, "why don't we listen to Katie's tape? I'll order in some sandwiches, and you can tell us what you think."

How often had this already happened, in my first few months working at Joko? It was a strange dynamic, empowering and belittling at the same time. Nobody cared that my primary responsibility was to the film company, just that I had access to John, who—if he would only listen to the reel of tape, pressing, or some sort of audiocassette that would be thrust upon me—would for sure agree the next big thing was right there before us all. Ordinarily, I'd roll with it, but it was a long trip under false premises, and I was pissed.

Also, I wondered if the redhead could even talk, let alone sing. She hadn't uttered a sound. As if on cue she said, "Peter, this is nuts. You mean this gentleman came all the way down here from New York, you've intercepted him in reception, had me come in to meet him, and all along you knew that no one in the office would have the time for him?"

Already, I liked her a little.

"Look, Peter," I said, "why don't you ship me a copy of the tape?"

His face collapsed. For a moment I feared he would cry.

Checking my watch, I said, "Okay, look, I've got about a half an hour. I can get a cab out front, still make it back to National in time for the one o'clock shuttle. I'll give you that."

The grin reappeared. "Super," he said, "just super!" He then turned and began to bustle around the reception desk and toward the hallowed spaces that must have housed the Democratic Party brain trust. "Oh," he said over his shoulder, "this is Katie. Katie, meet Dave. But let's hurry!"

"Johnson," I inserted. "David Johnson. Good to meet you."

She placed her cool, soft right hand briefly in mine while both of us maintained our pace behind Trapote. "Of course. And I'm Katie Steigerwald, but believe me, everybody just calls me Katie."

"I don't blame them," I said.

Trapote's office, or workspace, looked like it had once been a supply closet: long, narrow, poorly lit, and completely unventilated.

One whole wall was lined with a dozen or more tape decks, most of which were cranking away making copies of commercials, interviews, or whatever, barely audible on a large central speaker with the sound level quite low.

"Forget this shit," he said, and one after another, he snapped off all the decks that were running. He then opened a drawer and took out a seven-inch plastic reel, three quarters full of tape, and slapped it onto an Ampex 601 tape deck at the far end of the space. "Close your eyes," he said, "you're about to hear an angel."

"*Good grief!*" I thought. "*Who writes this guy's stuff?*"

Katie rolled her eyes, then blushed and took one step back. Then she turned and bolted from the room.

"She can't stand to watch people listen to the demos; she gets very nervous."

She needn't have been nervous. The bass was loud and trying desperately to keep up with the lead guitar, and both were at constant odds with the drummer. There was a flute player, unusual for rock, who was far more than adequate, in fact, rather good. But the vocals were indeed stunning.

"She is quite good," I said, "I mean very good!"

"Really?" he gushed. "You mean you really like her?"

Before I could answer him, he too was out the door. I heard him shout her name once, twice, then his voice faded. He returned less than a minute later. "She's gone. She does that. I told you she was nervous and shy. You want a copy of the tape?"

I never voluntarily asked for a copy of the tape—or the manuscript, sheet music, full-length novel, album design, whatever. Often, the copies turned out to be original, the only by-product of a disappointed, never-to-be-discovered artist.

"Okay, so she's gone, and so too should I be," I said. As always, I was having second thoughts about accepting the tape. However, the Edwardian suit had come prepared.

"Here's a copy I already ran off for you this morning," he said. "A brand-new box and everything."

New box for an old tape, perhaps? I wondered if the other track of the tape might contain sample commercials loudly proclaiming the McGovern campaign slogan, "Come Home, America." As it turned out, it did not.

In the cab back to National, I stuffed the tape into my saddlebag next to the several undistributed albums. While scouting new talent wasn't in my job description, I really did think she was great. I had every intention of having John take a listen.

Wait. First, I'd play it for Stephie. She was a trained editor; not only had a good eye, but a great ear for music too. That's what I'd do, let Steph Bradley hear Katie's soaring soprano and tell me what she thought.

I barely made the shuttle. The plane was only about two-thirds full, so my saddlebag and I were able to dominate a window and middle seat. The onboard ticketing process completed, I pushed my seat back as far as it would go, stretched out my booted feet, and tried to clear my head. Overall, what a wasted day. No Larry O'Brien. No meetings with marketing types. And the result: no offer to make Joko Films an important cog in the elect George McGovern effort.

As I winged my way home, back in DC, it happened that five nondescript men were checking into two hotel rooms at the Howard Johnson's across the street from the building I had just left. They were about to have a far worse time in the Watergate than I had.

—CHAPTER 8—
WHAT HAVE YOU DONE
WITH HER?

3:15 P.M., FRIDAY, JUNE 16, 1972

"David Johnson . . . Mr. David Johnson . . . come to the nearest white courtesy phone . . . arriving Washington, DC, passenger David Johnson . . ."

Though saddled for a lifetime with one of the world's most common surnames, I was pretty sure I was the only arriving passenger in LaGuardia's old Marine Air Terminal named David Johnson. I began to search for a white courtesy phone, irritated that because of the call, I'd be last in a long taxi line.

"This is David Johnson," I said smartly, picking up the receiver.

The operator, routinely courteous, responded, "Yes, thank you, Mr. Johnson. One moment for your party."

There was a bit of a clunk, then a buzz. "Please, go ahead," she urged someone on the other end, who needed no coaxing.

"Where are you?" an anxious Farah asked.

"Well, you paged me. Where else would I be? At LaGuardia."

"No," she said, expressing exasperation, "I mean where are you heading?"

"Well, I'm at an airport. I thought Paris for dinner, then off to Rome, just for the weekend. I hear it's . . ."

"You know? You're just not funny. And the pathetic thing is, you think you are!" Farah insisted. "Get to the fucking office!"

"Which office?" I asked.

"*The* office, your office, idiot! You know—that hovel on Broome

Street where you guys sometimes work."

What was so important on a Friday afternoon that I should put in just an hour or so at Joko? J&Y weren't recording that night, so I could just go home and catch the Reds and Mets on the Sears Silvertone in glorious black-and-white. But Farah's tone was intense.

"Is something wrong?" I asked.

"You might say that," Farah responded testily. "Sam didn't show for work today. Bill is there, but he's stoned, and Maria keeps calling up, crying, asking when you're coming in. And I'm here trying to run things and making damned sure Yoko and John stay away from that building."

"You mean Broome Street? What the hell is going on?"

"Just get your ass there," was the terse reply.

"I'll get back in the cab line and be there within the hour. However . . ."

Having gotten the desired result and passed on instructions, Farah did what she usually did: she hung up abruptly.

The cab dropped me in front of 496 Broome. The security gate, usually left open when anyone was working within the building, was pulled across, yet padlocked from the inside.

I maneuvered my hand through the gate, got my key into the padlock, popped it open, and fumbled for my key to the front door, but I needn't have bothered. The door was flung open in front of me. A tear-stained, disheveled Maria Anastasia stood shuddering just inside.

She grabbed my left arm. "Get in here, please!" She slammed the door behind me. It bounced back open, and after a second shove, she threw the bolt, then stood in front of me, fighting back more tears. "Well, what are we going to do?" she said.

"About what? And we can start by turning on the light. Fuck, it's dark in here," I said.

"I don't want anyone to know we're in here," she said. "I don't want to call attention to the place."

"Sure, sure," I said. "No one is ever supposed to think there's a film company in here, let alone one owned by John Lennon."

"No," she exclaimed. "It's something else." Then with her right hand extended, she pointed to the ceiling. "It's 'cause of what's upstairs."

"So . . . what's upstairs?"

Without answering the question, Maria led the way, both of us stumbling through the outer office. I banged my ankle on my own chair, left well away from my desk. Then we felt our way down the connecting hallway and through the kitchen, where Maria stubbed her toe on a stool left near the counter.

"Can we at least turn a light on back here?" I asked.

She found the switch, and the room brightened.

The rather sudden flash of overhead lighting and a few sconces did not, however, disturb a recumbent Bill Frost, splayed out on a large leather beanbag chair at the far side of the sitting area. He was snoring gently and seemed to be smiling in his sleep.

"How long has he been there?" I asked.

"Ever since I got here. Hell, I don't know. Look, David, I mean, like, let's just go upstairs and get this over with."

"Get what over with?" I insisted. "Just tell me what the . . . "

Maria grabbed my right arm with both of hers and began trying to drag me to the back stairs, which we found without further incident.

I went up first to the loft area that housed the two edit suites. Somewhere in one of the rooms a small radio was tuned to WNEW-FM. Pink Floyd, "Obscured by Clouds."

The only way into Edit One was through the second edit area; I noticed the door between the two was half-open.

"You go in. I'll stay here," Maria said.

"Why?" I asked again. I could hear nothing—no machine noise, no soundtrack, nothing. I assumed with Sam still not here, Steph must have knocked off early.

"Look, just go in there," she insisted. She seldom sounded authoritative. "Please," she added, sounding more like Maria. "Please, go on. I mean, like, it's terrible, just awful."

Maybe we'd been burglarized? I approached the door and opened it fully.

Steph lay face down on the floor, right in front of the couch, which was six or seven feet from the flattop. I could see from across the room that her head was canted at an unusual, if not impossible, angle to her body, and a small amount of blood had pooled underneath. I noticed a small, rust-like smear on the couch itself.

"I think she's, like, maybe . . . well, no longer with us," Maria said from the other room. "I mean she's here but gone."

"What you mean is she's dead, right?" I said.

"Yeah, like definitely."

"And you know this how?"

"Okay, my mother's brother, my Uncle Vito, runs a funeral parlor in Bay Ridge, and, well, like, I yoosta help out, and, well, believe me, David, I know dead people. Stephanie is definitely . . . "

"Got it!" I said. I couldn't take one more step forward. I realized my heart rate had skyrocketed. Right there on the floor in Edit One was what had been the woman I'd had lunch with just yesterday, the woman I had kidded with, learned more about, and yes, flirted with. Why did I suddenly feel guilty? This was a loss unlike any I'd ever encountered. I really didn't know her very well. Now for sure I wished I could know her better.

All I could say was "Did you call anyone? J&Y? The police?"

"Uh, well, I didn't," Maria said, having now moved tentatively into the edit room. "I mean no one's called J&Y. I called Farah. I mean, like, I didn't know what else to do."

"Of course you called Farah," I said flatly, not taking my eyes from Stephie.

"She said to do nothing, like not right away. And then she called back. Said she thought you'd be landing soon. That I should, like, do nothing until you got here."

"Good grief," I said, "How long has this been going on? When did you first get here? When did you find her?"

"Like two, two and a half hours ago. I was late. I had to go to Klein's office, pick up the checks, go by the Bank of Tokyo. You know, the errands you usually run on Friday. I didn't get here till one, one thirty."

I remained looking down at what yesterday had been a vibrant, talented woman exuberant about her work. I noticed that she appeared to be wearing the same blouse and slacks that I'd seen her in on Thursday, but I couldn't swear to the fact.

"Bill was here when you got in?" I asked. I suddenly realized my heart was no longer racing and that I was becoming calmer. Or was this shock?

"Like I said, he's been out the entire time. Like, I tried to wake him. I mean, like, I screamed when I first found her. Ran downstairs, shook him. I think I might have screamed then too. For a second, I thought he was maybe dead also."

"So, what the hell are we going to do?" I mused out loud. "Do J&Y know?"

"If Farah knows, then at least Yoko knows."

"Terrific," I said. "Steph's been here we don't know how long—at least a few hours. Cops will figure that stuff out. They probably can tell exactly when she, well, got this way. I mean a big delay like this only makes the situation that much worse. It makes it look like we have something to hide."

"Well," stammered Maria, "like don't we have something to hide? I mean sort of? I mean, like, David, if Farah says to do something or not do something, well, like, it comes directly from Yoko. You know . . ."

I didn't blame Maria for not wanting to defy Yoko; she never had. Neither had I, and I wondered if now was the time to start. Farah might be right. After all, John and Yoko were fighting not to be deported. Then there was John's theory, "They want me out, just fuckin' because they can. They refer to me as an 'undesirable alien.'"

And, I thought, news of a murder in the workplace of a major celebrity would be headlines, maybe even nationwide, no matter the political landscape. We didn't have something to hide so much as something to protect.

I asked Maria, "Again, John and Yoko are where?"

"Something about lawyers, a meeting uptown . . . a big deal. You know, a hearing next week or the week after."

"Uh-huh," I said, "I guess it wouldn't sound too good to tell their attorney they needed to postpone some pretrial conference to deal with a murdered employee at their film company."

"Murdered?" Maria exclaimed. "Like maybe wasn't it an overdose? Or some kind of allergic reaction? A heart attack maybe?"

"Stephie's in her twenties. Or was. No, I don't think a heart attack, and you know her, she's not into drugs. I think the only thing she was allergic to must've hit her in the back of the head . . ."

"Yeah, like I thought that looked weird," Maria stammered.

Standing close to the body, but not too close, I replied, "It doesn't appear to be suicide. I mean, I don't think she hit herself."

Slowly it came to me that for the first time in my life I was looking at a dead person who wasn't powdered, coiffed, and stuffed neatly into a box for viewing. I was growing mildly nauseous.

"We've got to do something. We've got to tell somebody."

"We can't call the cops," Maria said. "Farah said that was out of the question and that Yoko would want you to deal with it."

And so I did. I walked into Edit Two, picked up the phone, and called the Bank Street apartment. The indomitable Farah Freedwoman answered. "'lo," she said.

"Hi—Farah?"

"Who else would it be? Are you at Joko? Are you aware of the situation?"

"Most definitely, and look, Farah, are J&Y around?"

"No. They're still at one of the attorneys uptown."

"Who's with them?" I asked.

"I don't know who they left with. That's not important," Farah said. She was getting more and more exasperated. "What about Steph? What have you done with her?"

"Nothing, of course," I said. "Don't you watch any television?" I was trying to keep my voice low. "I mean, you never move the body. Nothing should be touched and . . ."

"Idiot!" Farah said. "Yoko said you should handle this!"

I didn't think there was any good way out. This was a classic lose-lose situation, so of course Yoko had tasked me to make a mistake.

"Okay, fine, whatever," I said. "I guess I'll call somebody."

"Good. You better. And no matter what, do not call the police," Farah said. "Do not call the cops. Do you understand?"

Before I could say "Yes, ma'am," she hung up.

Her order was perfectly clear. So? I called the cops.

—CHAPTER 9—
WHO'S THE COWBOY?
4:45 P.M., FRIDAY, JUNE 16, 1972

"I hope you did the right thing, David, calling the police, I mean," said Maria, cautiously watching through the glass of the bolted front door. "And look, there's already newspeople out there. A couple of film cameras, everything."

A voice came from outside the locked door,

"NYPD! Is someone hurt?"

It had been the longest nine or ten minutes I could remember. I wondered what shock felt like. Was I in it? Had I been in it? Also, there was the job situation. Going against Yoko's wishes was not a good way to stay employed. Maria and I were back downstairs in our shared office. I kept glancing up at the ceiling. I could visualize the very spot where she lay, imagining a chalk outline on the plaster above. A dead body lay above where we worked. A body that had been Stephie. How fucked up was that?

I was slow to respond to the knock at the door. It opened smoothly.

"Steady there, sir. Either way, move back from the door slowly, and keep your hands out where I can see them."

That command—and it was a command, not a request—came from a tall, burly Black officer. I swung the door fully open and without a word did as I was told.

"You called about an incident, an assault?" he asked sternly. "Did you also make calls to Channel 2, 'PIX, and the *Daily News?*" he inquired, glancing over his right shoulder at the growing crowd, some of whom were attempting to follow him into the building.

"Yeah, I did. I mean I didn't. What I mean is I did call you guys, but nobody else."

"Does the victim—I assume there is a victim?" I nodded. "Does the victim require medical attention?"

"Uh, well, I don't think so. I mean definitely not," I replied.

"Well, let's just have a look."

I stepped back, following his intense eyes, which had never left mine. Without being asked, I lifted my arms from my side. The cop, more gently than I could have imagined, brushed me from shoulder to hip on both sides while his right hand rested on the butt of his gun.

Maria was right. Some newspeople had actually beaten the NYPD to the scene. Now both the film cameras and patrolmen were beginning to draw a crowd of bystanders.

In addition to the first officer, there was a scrawny, much younger second cop who looked maybe fourteen, despite evidence of a wispy mustache. He spoke.

"Hatter, so he's dead? There's a body? Is he famous?"

"Well," I said, "I'm definitely sure that he's a she, and I think, uh, know, she's quite dead."

Another patrol car pulled up on the opposite side of Broome Street.

"Christ," the younger cop said, "that's Pauly Plumski and his partner from the Fifth. Word's gettin' out whose place this is."

"And what is a Fifth?" I asked.

"Fifth Precinct—borders our territory. We're with First Precinct," the older cop explained.

Then another all-too-familiar vehicle rolled in, a light blue station wagon with a large whip antenna and the familiar Circle 7 logo on the driver's door: "Channel 7 Eyewitness News."

"Uh-oh," the older cop agreed, leaning out the door, "the circus is comin' to town. Ringling Bros. and Barnum and Rivera."

"Fuck," I said, "it's Geraldo!"

The older cop turned to his partner, "Teddy, you stay here and, well, protect the crime scene from the rest of the press."

"Not to worry." Teddy responded eagerly. "I'm on it."

"Protect this door with your life, son. If what our friend says has gone on inside, I'll call it in, secure the scene. You wait here till the ME and some detectives arrive."

A voice from the crowd shouted, "There's a body! Someone must be dead!" That was followed in rapid succession by: "Did they have a fight? Was it really brutal?" Then, "Does John have a new album out soon?"

I was thankful when the door shut behind us.

"I'm Officer Hatter—Sam Hatter—and that brave young man facing those advocates of the First Amendment outside is Patrolman Teddy Savage. First, from what you told dispatch, you suspect a crime has been committed on these premises?"

I nodded.

"And has this building been secured? I mean are you sure the perpetrator—or perpetrators—are not still somewhere on the premises?"

Again I nodded. During the time between the 911 call and arrival of the cavalry, I had accomplished at least two things. First, I kept Maria from leaving. "Like it's fucking spooky here. I mean like being in the same building as Stephie, like after finding her and all was like weird enough. But now you say she was probably murdered, and, well, like, I can't handle this and. . . . "

I had let her rattle on for another minute or so, then assured her it would be far more difficult if the police had to come by her parents' apartment and make her overly protective mother aware of any of this. Her mother or the crime scene? She decided to stick it out.

With Maria close by my side, I had had the presence of mind to check the entire building, especially the basement. There was nobody else here except for the still-snoring Bill. Later that night, rethinking my every move, I would wonder what the hell I'd have done if I had found anybody.

Officer Hatter went on, "And you are?"

I introduced myself, after which Hatter extracted the same information from Maria, now shakily leaning against the side of her desk.

Hatter and I moved through the office and into the kitchen area, where Bill had yet to abandon his beanbag chair.

"Looks more or less like a man to me. Sounds like he's alive. I assume this is not the victim." Not waiting for my obvious response, the patrolman went on, "Might I also assume that he works here, that you know him, and that his early afternoon nap is not out of the ordinary?"

"Yes, yes, yes, and you're right: he's a night person in many respects, and he often puts himself in a frame of mind to work here by napping before his day starts. His name is Bill Frost. He shoots film and edits, and if he is true to form, he'll probably still be out until five or six."

"In that case, lead the way, young man," Officer Hatter said. We went up the back staircase and into the second edit room, then into Edit One, where we both stared at the shape that used to be Stephanie.

The cop, with a growing sweat stain between the shoulders of his light-blue summer uniform, approached Stephie quietly, almost reverently. He scanned the area and made sure, I thought, not to step on or disturb anything important. He then touched his thumb and two forefingers to a spot on Stephie's neck, the carotid artery, I imagined. Why hadn't I thought to do that?

"I'm afraid you're right, son," the cop said. This poor woman appears to be dead." With that, he stood abruptly.

"Did you know her? A friend? Colleague?" With that, he held up a hand to stop the answers that hadn't quite left my lips. "Never mind, you'll have lots of questions to answer soon. But how 'bout for now you stand right there and don't move a muscle while I call this in, y'hear?"

He reached for a portable radio on his utility belt, pressed a button, got nothing but static, cursed, and backed to the barred windows to get better reception. "This is Three-Two Adam. I'm at 496 Broome, responding to a 187, and there is a body here, white female, early twenties, looks like she's been dead for more than a bit." He held the device to his left ear. "Only one entrance; it's covered. I've got two, maybe three witnesses I'll keep on ice. There's just two of us here now. We could use some backup. Need some serious crowd control outside."

He shook the radio again. More static. Then he shrugged and replaced the unit on his belt. To no one in particular, he said, "Well, they know the drill. They'll send what needs to be sent." Then, to me he said, "Let's you and me go downstairs and join your friends."

I guessed I had done the right thing. No, I knew I had. Nobody else resembling any kind of authority in our universe was around, and I really felt that if we had delayed calling the police any longer, the entire situation, whatever the situation was, could only look worse to the public.

We went down to the kitchen, where a still quite shaken Maria was sitting.

"So, is it just the three of you here, including sleeping beauty over there?" Hatter asked.

"Well, uh, there is," began Maria, stumbling more than a bit. "there's Stephie, upstairs." And at that, Maria's face began to collapse into itself, and once again, tears began to run down her cheeks.

"I'm sorry, miss," Hatter said. "What I mean is, well, is it just the three of you here along with the, uh, young victim upstairs?" Hatter turned to his left and looked down at a new figure just entering the kitchen. "Lieutenant," he said, gratefully, "good Friday afternoon."

"Wonderful seeing you as well, Sam," the diminutive figure responded.

The woman, I soon learned, was NYPD Homicide Detective Lt. Nancy Elena Maria Rosado, who introduced herself to us as simply Lt. Rosado while she quickly surveyed the room. Even for a woman she was short, not more than five one or five two.

"Officially, five feet five-eighths inches," she would tell me later. "The regs don't allow the NYPD to take anyone shorter than five feet." During that same candid discussion, I would learn the crafty homicide detective always wore some kind of footwear with lifts that gave her the extra height to remain in the department. "Between you and me, in my stocking feet, I'm four feet ten and one-eighth inches, but you keep that to yourself."

She wore a cream blouse tucked neatly into chocolate brown slacks that flowed over the tops of her customized half boots. Her badge hung on a fob from her belt; her gun was strapped to a holster on her left hip. She carried a matching brown suit jacket over her left forearm. A pair of large sunglasses had slipped down almost to the tip of her nose. She slid them on top of her head. Her ink-black hair was cut short, no nonsense. Her eyes were large, expressive, almost as black as her hair, the kind of eyes that could see right through you, even to your soul if you had one, and while they were at it hazard a guess as to what you had eaten for lunch and dinner. Taking bullshit of any kind was, I'd soon learn, not in Lt. Rosado's repertoire.

From a small notebook I hadn't noticed, the tall policeman read our names to the detective, spelling them out when necessary. Rosado then pulled an even smaller pad from somewhere within her jacket and began to take notes in kind. Hatter also mentioned that the third person, a white male in the kitchen, "is either intoxicated or under the influence of some substance, unable to be roused into consciousness."

Bill's snoring was steady and pervasive. It was pleasant, like white noise.

"There's nobody else here?" Rosado inquired. "Nobody in or near the scene?"

It was Hatter's turn to nod.

"And the vic? I assume there is a victim—right, Sam?"

Hatter paused for a moment. "Right, indeed, Lieutenant. However, I was just getting around to. . . . "

"Her name is Stephie, Stephanie Bradley. She's the assistant editor here," I said. "Looks like she's wearing the same clothes she had on yesterday, at least yesterday afternoon, when Maria and I left her to go uptown for a session. And Maria found her around three hours ago. So it looks like she's been dead for . . . "

"Enough, quite enough," interrupted Rosado. "You're quite the detective there, aren't you, big guy?"

Then, to no one in particular, Lt. Rosado posed a question. "So, who was here first?" Turning to Maria, she asked, "Did you discover, uh, Miss Bradley, miss?"

"Well, uh, yes, I guess. I got here, I mean Bill was already here, but really asleep. And so I guess I was the first to actually see Stephie, I mean to find her." She then paused. "But, like, I mean she's . . . was . . . married. So, she's not a miss."

With that, Maria reverted to more tears and pretty much collapsed into a beanbag chair that was behind her.

Nodding toward Maria, Rosado tapped her notebook against her thigh. "Do you, Mr. Johnson, have an office or a desk here?"

"Yeah, up front, facing the over-size guitar in the corner," I responded.

"Sam," she said, cocking her head toward Hatter, "take our friend here to his desk. See that he doesn't make any phone calls while I talk with Miss Anastasia."

"Ms.," Maria corrected.

"Miss what?" Rosado responded.

"No, not Miss. I'm a Ms., Ms. Anastasia."

Both cops rolled their eyes, in unison.

"Can you believe what a cluster fuck it's going to be if terminology like this makes it onto all the forms we have to fill out?" the uniformed cop asked.

"It'll never happen; it's a fad, like long hair on men," Rosado said. She continued with Sam, "When he shows up, send Quay back here."

Hatter and I moved back through the central hallway toward my desk in the front room. But before I could inquire as to what Lt. Rosado meant by "Quay," Hatter called out to a tall, slender—perhaps 170 pounds—amiable sort of gent who was signing in on a clipboard that was being held by yet another new arrival.

"Quay, I mean Sergeant. The boss is in the back room. Says you should go on back ASAP," Hatter said, pointing his thumb over his shoulder to the passage. On his way back, the newest arrival, also a homicide detective, introduced himself.

"Howdy. I'm Sgt. Jefferson Quaker Parker, homicide. I work with the lieutenant on important cases, and I assume you are a witness, a suspect, or both, and that Patrolman Hatter here has been assigned to keep you on ice."

It wasn't hard to figure out that Detective Parker was not from around here. He had a thick Southern accent—Coastal Carolina was my guess—and was, in many respects, the exact opposite of Lt. Rosado. Parker was wearing what I thought looked like a decent sports jacket, dress shirt, tie not quite tight against his neck, and standard khakis. It seemed, however, that he'd slept in the ensemble—everything was wrinkled—and his hair hadn't seen a comb in some time. From his light blue eyes and the bare but constant hint of a grin, I could tell he was intelligent, with a sense of humor not far below the surface. I also noticed, poking somewhat playfully from the left side of his mouth, a toothpick, which I would soon learn was his trademark accessory.

"What do I do now?" I asked Officer Hatter.

"Nothin' would be good. Or you could confess entirely to anything and everything and give me another reason to take the sergeant's exam again," he said. "If you're gonna confess, just keep it inside for a little bit so I can grab one of those two detectives back there to witness it."

"Confess to fucking what?" I asked.

"Oh, I don't know," he said. "To wearing cavalry boots when you probably never rode a horse, wearing faded denim jeans, possibly needin' a haircut. Or there's always assault with intent to murder. Whatever feels good to you."

I chose neither to confess nor to continue the discussion. Instead, I decided to sit at my desk, pretend to study the "End of the World" calendar, and try not to feel too scared or too weird or too anything.

Less than a minute later, the phone rang. I reached for it, but Hatter held out his hand and shook his head. "Uh-uh. Let it ring or go to service. The lieutenant said no calls. That means in or out."

I knew the call was important, and I was pretty sure that no good could come from it. Our phones had four incoming lines and a fifth for intercom, each with an individual number, although incoming calls would roll over to the next available line if the preceding was already in use. When the fifth, then sixth ring begged to be answered, I could see the only light fluttering with each shrill bell was the last line, the dreaded line four. When it rang independently, that meant a call directly from someone at the Bank Street apartment, usually Farah or Yoko. Ain't this super indeed.

"We don't have a service. Can't I just get this one?"

"Nope, like my mama always said, 'If it's important, they'll call back,'" Hatter observed.

"That's an understatement," I responded.

"Hey, man, like no need to rush! Like I'm barely awake, you know?" The voice of Bill Frost came drifting through the hallway followed by Bill himself, guided by the tall sergeant, who unceremoniously deposited him at Maria's desk across the room.

Detective Parker stood in the middle of the office, hands on hips. "Hattah," he drawled, "the ME should be along directly. And indeed, you are correct: we have a dead body right upstairs. Watch this one as well. I gotta tell y'all, for fifteen dollars in Confederate War Bonds, I'd arrest all three of you yahoos, put you in the lockup over at the First, and adjourn my ass out to a steak dinner."

"That so?" asked Hatter.

"Indeed," said Parker. "The Lieutenant recommends we round up all three of these characters, take 'em over to the precinct and conduct interviews."

"It looks like my entire Friday night is fucked royal," Parker stated emphatically. "Then again, that girl upstairs seems to be havin' a far worse Friday than any of us."

"Good point," agreed Hatter.

There was a pause in the conversation, and I caught Bill's eye across the fifteen feet between my desk and Maria's. "You more or less clued in on what's happened or happening here?"

"More or less," Bill responded. "Enough to know it's a fucked-up deal and that I may have chosen the wrong time or place for a nap."

Less than five minutes—and two more unanswered phone calls on line four —later, Maria joined us, following her discussion in the kitchen. A flurry of additional NYPD personnel had streamed in through the front door. Three more uniformed cops and two additional official-looking types carrying cases of equipment were then followed by two more in different uniforms carrying what I felt sure was a stretcher.

Lt. Rosado was the last to arrive from the back room, peeling off a pair of surgeon's-style gloves as she entered the front room. "It appears she's been dead a good while, Quay," she began, "but the ME should give us a decent idea as to the time of death." She gave me a look, recalling my guess at that info, then continued: "How are things out front?"

"Ugly. Crowd's gettin' larger," Parker responded. "But there are three more uniforms outside to guarantee an acceptable level of disorder. We shouldn't have much trouble gettin' these three into cars and over to the precinct."

"Hey, you can't do that," Maria called out from where she stood, near my desk. "That's crazy. You don't know what you're doing!"

"Don't worry," Parker said. "I've been chewin' picks since I was a boy. Only had one accident: my sophomore year in high school when I slid into third on my stomach, but the scar doesn't show much anymore."

"I don't think she means your toothpick, Detective," I said. "I think she means why are you guys taking us anywhere?"

Parker looked at me over his left shoulder, grinning. "Look, Cowboy," he said. "This will be one of the highest-profile cases in New York since the time Mayor La Guardia shut down Minsky's, and it'll go a lot better on everybody if we do this by the book."

Rosado was staring down at the small, Moleskine notebook into which she was writing. "Uh-huh," she said. "Let's go back to the station, where we can have a friendly and productive discussion. Best not stay here." And then, looking up, she said, "And who's a cowboy?"

"He is," Patrolman Hatter said, grinning. He pointed toward my feet, which were now being studied by all three of New York's Finest.

"Cowboy, I like that," the lieutenant said. "Well, let's all just saddle up and trot down to Old Slip before they discontinue room service."

Bill smiled and looked at both Maria and me from across the room. "I think they're maybe kidding about room service," he said.

"You think? Whatevah!" Maria said.

Glancing out the door, Parker said, "There's at least a half dozen reporters and such out here, *Daily News*, *Post*, someone from WINS. It's a mess."

Indeed, the frosted glass panes in the front window that declared this to be Marwood Press did reveal an eerie glow, contrary to the late-afternoon hour, a false dawn, the result of an army of battery-operated "sun guns" carried by a technician adjacent to every TV film camera in the street.

Parker opened the inner door and, along with a very bleary and shuffling Bill, went out into the street.

"By the way," Rosado asked, seemingly of no one, "who called the TV people? I mean, some were here before you, right Hatter?"

Hatter nodded, "I think it's Lafayette Radio's fault. Anybody can buy a damn scanner. I liked it a whole lot better when we could just talk among ourselves."

"Yeah, right," Rosado said, snapping shut her notebook.

"Okay, people, it's showtime," Parker quipped, putting on his best smile for the gathered forces.

From behind me, Lt. Rosado chimed in, "Quay, you take the stoner and hitch a ride with Hatter." Then, to me, she said, "Cowboy, you and Ms. Anastasia can ride with me."

We moved out the front door—I realized none of us had locked up. But then again, it appeared that Joko Films would remain a crime scene for some time to come, under the best security available, constant police presence.

Maria, Bill, and I moved down the steps toward our assigned vehicles, Bill with the much taller Parker and Patrolman Hatter, Maria and me with the lieutenant and another uniform. A sea of questions . . . flashbulbs. Maria clutched my right arm in both of her hands.

She whispered excitedly, "You think we'll get our pictures in the paper? Or on the news?"

"No doubt," I chimed back at her. I could hear the promos now: "Murder suspects taken from Lennon/Ono production company. Film at eleven!"

Getting in the back of Lt. Rosado's unmarked Plymouth Valiant, I sighed, "We are so fucked! Stephie dead. Against Farah's order, I called the police, and now three of us are being trundled off to the police station."

"No one answered Yoko's phone calls," Maria noted, "but hey, you did have the meeting this morning with the Democrats, so you can kinda tell John 'bout that good news, right?"

Oh, yeah. I'd almost forgotten about the day's other event, a rather minor failure in the big picture now before us. And then a great feeling of sadness overcame me. We were leaving Stephie alone.

I'd had other plans for the weekend. This was my fourth baseball season living in New York, and I was getting accustomed to the plight of an out-of-town sports fan. My Reds appeared infrequently on Saturday afternoon's *NBC Game of the Week*. And listening to them on radio was a challenge nearly all the time. As a result, I became fixated on each of those magic twelve days every season when they played the New York Mets. This weekend, the Mets were in Cincinnati, and I had planned to be situated in front of my Sears Silvertone on Friday and Saturday nights and on Sunday afternoon to watch the boys in red (or, on my screen, dark gray) continue to thrash the Mets, something they'd been doing on a regular basis for nearly a decade.

Instead, I was spending several hours shuffling from room to room, answering questions and feeling constantly ill at ease within the confines of NYPD's First Precinct station in Manhattan's southernmost section, Old Slip.

"So, I genuinely assume it's safe to say this is the very first time you've been in a police station for any reason save for the guided tour you might have taken when you were a Boy Scout, am I right, Cowboy?" Sergeant Parker kept up the unctuous banter while he escorted me from deep in the bowels of the First Precinct shortly before nine o'clock Friday evening. My new nickname was apparently going to stick. "We thank you for your cooperation, for answerin' all those questions. I'm surely hopeful you had no place else you had to be on this fine evenin'."

"Oh, not to worry. I'd hoped to catch the ballgame on TV, but the great thing about baseball is there's always another game tomorrow," I replied as he held open the thigh-high swinging gate that separated the backstage area of the station from what I thought of as reception.

"Don't think the Yankees play tonight; double-header tomorrow, and besides, they suck. Now, on the other hand, my Atlanta Braves— yeah, they're startin' slow but . . . "

"Yankees? No way! Hoping to watch the Mets lose to the Reds. My Reds," I said.

"Well, sorry anyway, both for the inconvenience and the fact that you root for an inferior team." Then, changing gears, Parker continued, "Standard warning: don't take any lengthy trips without giving us a heads-up. We'll be in touch, and you should be able to go back to your office if you need to on Sunday, maybe Monday for sure. Take care, Cowboy. Beat the Mets! Everybody else seems to be doin' that anyway."

It was then I saw—seated uncomfortably amid an early Friday night crowd of the flora and fauna of local eccentrics waiting to lodge any number of major and minor complaints and friends and relatives of the recently arrested—a very out-of-place Maria Anastasia. Bill Frost was nowhere to be found.

"You oh-okay?" was all Maria could muster when she walked over to give me a stiff embrace near the sergeant's desk.

"Yeah, fine, you?"

"I'm all right. Apparently that lieutenant, she got some kind of early report from a doctor or someone that said Steph was definitely killed—God, I hate that word—like late last night or early this morning. I had her call my mom to check where I was from early evening until this morning when I went to work, and that seemed to satisfy her, the lieutenant I mean. However, I still gotta deal with my freaked-out mom when I get home."

Here Maria launched into a thick, heavily accented Anglo-Italian patois, which she used either to parody "wise words" from her mother or convey sarcasm. "So, Anna Maria Anastasia, my baby, whatever have you gotten yourself into? I mean, what do I say to your grandmama, your Uncle Tony? Not to mention the relatives on Staten Island? Those wannabes on your father's side who already think they're better than us . . . "

Maria heaved a deep sigh, then showed me a slight smile, and we walked out the front door.

"Sorry you're gonna get it from your mom. Think she'll be really upset?"

"Whatevah."

"I went through the same routine. Apparently, detectives went to my house on Staten Island and talked to a couple of my roommates who confirmed I rolled in around eleven last night. Then Ian . . . "

"He is?"

"Another roommate. He said he saw me briefly in the kitchen before I headed off to my flight at LaGuardia. Then you backed up where I was from when we left Stephie till I split from the Plant at around ten."

"Yeah, you didn't miss much. I was home by midnight." Brightening a bit, she continued. "Like, say, does that mean I'm sort of part of your alibi? That's cool."

"I guess. Better still, I think that might mean the cops don't suspect either one of us."

"But what about Bill?" Maria inquired, her large brown eyes resting on mine, seeming to demand that I have an adequate answer.

"Don't know. Nobody says anything. I sure as hell hope he remembers where he was overnight, not to mention that it might be nice if someone else acts as his alibi."

"But don't they . . . "

I interrupted. "We know he couldn't do something like this, but everything has to be based on proof. Bill has to prove, or circumstance has to show, that he had nothing to do with it. Look, I'm sure it's going to work out for everyone."

"Except for Stephanie," Maria said almost to herself.

"And there's one other unanswered question."

"Which is?" Maria inquired.

"We know none of us did it. So, well, who the fuck?

"Yeah, who da fuck?"

Now, we were walking rather awkwardly arm in arm down the front steps of the station house. Maria was indeed gorgeous, but even though I was only a few years her senior, I always thought of her as a much younger little sister. In spite of her tough New York exterior, outer-borough accent, and aptitude at slinging the occasional profanity with the best of us, Ms. Anastasia somehow brought out the protective gene in most of the men she met.

Double-parked on the other side of Old Slip was a familiar sight, a black limousine bearing the logo of our car service. A cardboard placard was lodged in the driver's side window with "Anastasia/ Johnson" scrawled on it.

"You were able to call for a car?" I asked as we stepped over the curb heading for the limo.

"No," Maria replied. "It's been sitting here for nearly an hour. I checked with the driver, and he said dispatch had sent the car at the request of a Miss Friedman—Farah of course."

"We probably shouldn't burden her with the fact that her last name was butchered in the process," I said.

"You think he'll drop both of us at home?" she asked as we slid inside the car.

"Dunno," I responded. "I mean, I'm only a few blocks from the ferry, and I could . . . "

"Instruction I got was to drop the girl at her home but to deliver you, Mr. Johnson, to the Bank Street address," the driver interrupted.

Maria made a loud but unintelligible noise as she climbed into the back seat.

"I mean the young lady; I'm to take the young lady home," the driver corrected himself.

"No way. I'm going to Bank Street too," Maria ordered.

After ten or fifteen minutes weaving through the warren of streets that meld Soho and Greenwich Village, the car glided to a stop in front of 105 Bank Street. It wasn't alone. There was an NYPD cruiser and a semiofficial-looking unmarked car parked partially on and partially off the sidewalk directly in front of the building J&Y called home. Of course, the media was there; gaudily branded vehicles from Channels 2, 4, 5, and 7 clogged traffic on the other side of Bank.

"Whoa," commented Maria. "It's like they planned it, I mean lining up in numerical order!"

All this activity had of course brought a few dozen locals out of their apartments to gawk at the Friday-night spectacle. Maria and I hustled down the two steps and pushed the buzzer next to the steel-reinforced door.

The buzzer buzzed; a metallic voice called out from the speaker above it: "We see you, push the door." We did and were admitted into a space roughly four by six feet with an overhead light and a somewhat bulky video camera situated near the ceiling, similar to a second exterior camera observing the front-door area. The space resembled an airlock, a small room that often separated on-air facilities such as TV and radio studios from the rest of the building for purposes of keeping extraneous noises from an open mic. The outer door shut and clicked, indicating it was locked tight. Only then could another button be pushed from the inner room releasing the locks on the interior door and allowing us to enter the inner sanctum of the one Beatle (and Yoko, of course) who loved to call New York City home.

The space we entered was one open area, approximately forty feet deep and extending from wall to wall on the ground floor of the building. A small desk, usually occupied by a security guard, was to our left, just past the inner airlock door. An array of bookshelves down the right-hand side of the space led to two armchairs for guests and, at the end, a small kitchen: a counter area, two-burner cooktop, large refrigerator, sink, and dishwasher. One of the burners on the stove featured a flame tamer atop a very low gas jet on which sat a large cracked ceramic teapot. The scent of vile English Breakfast tea was constant. Unwashed mugs, a couple of dirty plates, and assorted silverware lay in the sink.

There was a pecking order at Bank Street, beginning of course with John and Yoko and descending directly to Farah Freedwoman, then cascading downward, and a bit chaotically, through a never-ending array of assistant secretaries, houseboys, and other hangers-on who had somehow talked their way onto the Lennon-Ono staff. The least of these was usually tasked with washing the dishes. Yoko believed she headed an entirely egalitarian workforce, so no one was allowed to give orders. Therefore, little was ever accomplished in an organized manner.

At the very back of this large room was an old circular oak table five feet in diameter, on which sat the latest IBM Selectric typewriter— today's was bright red—two telephones, scattered papers, and more mugs of burnt and partially imbibed English Breakfast tea. We all drank the stuff, even me, who didn't like tea of any kind. Because, well, John loved it.

"Mother," he would call out, "Mother, put the kettle on. We have thirsty people here." He usually called Yoko Mother, though I don't think she really liked it very much. Of course, she never put the kettle on, poured tea, or brought it to any thirsty people, merely nodding at someone to hop to the task.

Completing the counterclockwise tour of the outer half of J&Y's apartment: a little-used fireplace in the middle of the left-hand wall; more bookshelves; scattered, mismatched file cabinets; and another, more formal seating area suitable for four or five guests who might be waiting for an audience.

Left and right walls were exposed brick. The tin ceiling was low, not quite eight feet high. The floor was hardwood, recently polyurethaned, with a small area rug in front of the fireplace.

Maria, bless her heart, nodded toward Farah, who was situated, throne-like, behind the bright red Selectric.

"I'll just do these dishes," Maria said.

Clever, I thought. *Why didn't I think of that?* I could hide in plain sight washing and drying cups and teaspoons, then tidy up with a broom; do some light dusting, and, with any luck, vacuuming or sweeping out the fireplace grate when John Lennon's second wife came striding into the room. Maybe, just maybe, she would mistake me for one of this week's batch of houseboys. I was not looking forward to confronting anybody, especially Yoko, with the fact that I had been the one to call in the cops.

There was another ground-floor room in the apartment, approximately the same size, separated by a long hallway on either side of which were, oddly, two identical bathrooms. Closer to the kitchen was a third, smaller bathroom, with only a toilet and sink, and across from it, some cupboards and closets. A full-size American flag, with the star field visible at the upper right, was nailed to the top of the doorway adjacent to the kitchen and shredded into fifteen or twenty strips, acting as a more-or-less antiwar faux-beaded curtain. At the end of that hallway lay the entrance to John and Yoko's bedroom.

"Go on in, they're all waiting for you," Farah spat out.

I turned to say something to Maria, but Farah stopped me. "Just you," she said. "Since she's here, Maria can finish up the washing."

I parted the flag, which always left a pleasant, light feeling when I entered the hallway as the various strips fluttered onto and around my body. For nearly three months now, I had been thrilled each and every time I walked through this shredded banner. Was defacing it this way a federal offense? Most times I strode eagerly toward the bedroom door. Every other time I'd been admitted to the bedroom, on probably a dozen or more occasions, the door had either been closed tight or left wide open. Tonight, it was slightly ajar, and it was John's unmistakable voice that called through when he heard my footfalls on the wooden floor.

"Back here," he said. "We're in here. C'mon back." Where the hell else would they be?

The oak door swung open.

John and Yoko's bed was large, a California king, I assumed, though it might have been an original, crafted just for them. It was massive and sat high above the floor, a good two and a half or three feet. John enjoyed sitting cross-legged on the near side of the bed facing another seating area, this populated by a half dozen low rattan chairs. A person sitting in one of the chairs had no choice but to look up at John. I wondered periodically if it was coincidental, the result of some subconscious desire, or overtly intentional that J&Y gazed down upon their visitors while doing business, just talking, getting high, or otherwise holding court.

Tonight, most of the chairs were already taken. There were two men and one woman I assumed were NYPD detectives. A uniformed patrolman stood near the door to the hallway, and of course, just my luck, seated in rattan and grinning from ear to ear was Geraldo Rivera himself. How the hell had he gotten in?

John, who mounted and dismounted the bed by hopping up or jumping down, leapt to the floor, snatched a cup of the vile tea from the bedside, and thrust it toward me. "Here," he said, "it might be a bit cold. Have a sip and let's talk."

I took the proffered mug, put it to my lips, and pretended to swallow. Then I situated myself on one of the two remaining chairs. I was generally mindful not to wear a thin shirt or one of my less substantial dashikis on a day when I knew I'd be visiting the apartment. The roughly woven fiber of the chairs—which smelled oddly like hay—penetrated flimsy cloth. Often, I'd enjoy watching first-timers sit almost at attention, staring up toward John while trying desperately not to reach around to scratch as their backs and backsides reacted to the prickly seats. Tonight, I perched carefully on the front of my seat so as not to be skewered.

"These three here are actual detectives," John said, waving his arms toward the two men and one woman who had badges hanging off their jackets. "The bizzie by the door, he seems to be window dressin'." John indicated the uniformed officer, whom I might have referred to as a bobby if I were trying to be British. John preferred Liverpool slang; coppers, he told me, were always way too busy to help everyday people.

"And of course you know Gerry."

Gerry—or as he was really known—Geraldo. John referred to him as such probably to piss him off. Soon, I would find out how easy it was to get under the skin of WABC-TV''s brand-new "ethnic" reporter, whose good looks, mane of thick, flowing brown hair, and handlebar mustache would be his primary brand almost forever. Rivera nodded toward me briefly, then continued his uninterrupted worshipful stare up at John.

"So," said John, "it appears we're in the midst of a case of foul murder, and that dear girl, Stephanie, is the victim. A tragedy."

"Yeah, obviously," I responded, searching desperately for a place to put down the mug of English Breakfast tea. Finding no uncluttered area, I grinned, turned to Geraldo and offered him the cup. He smiled broadly, gratefully accepted it, and actually began to drink the brew. *Serves him right*, I thought, *for gate-crashing*.

The discussion wore on. The cops continued relating what precious little they knew in typical cop speak: "The victim, early to midtwenties Caucasian female, was found deceased in front of a Naugahyde-covered couch some eight and a half feet from her workstation."

For Christ's sake, I thought, they knew her name, knew her age; couldn't they simply say they found twenty-four-year-old Stephanie Bradley on the floor, the apparent cause of death a blow to the head with a blunt instrument? Then again, if common sense ruled, why would they go to the police academy and learn to speak like automatons? And why wasn't Lt. Rosado here? Sexism? Or could it be racial discrimination? Or maybe, just maybe, one detective crawling all over this case was actually out trying to solve the crime.

After twenty or so minutes of useless banter, the cops reviewing the same questions I had dealt with back at the precinct, and John's insisting that nobody at Joko "knew a fuckin' thing, nor would they do anything disgraceful," the small group of New York's Finest took their leave.

John nodded to the departing authorities gracefully and then ever so slightly turned his head toward Rivera. "I surely hate to fuckin' hold you up, Gerry. Don'tcha need to be on the air at eleven or so to tell all of New York City about the crime spree at my, uh, our film company?"

Geraldo took the broad hint, finished the tea without once making a face, and followed the cops through the oak door and down the short hallway.

We just sat there for a moment. I was enjoying the little bit of silence, the sense of calm that usually occurred in John and Yoko's bedroom after some sort of momentous gathering. So much, or so it seemed, of what had gone on in the world over the past ten years had whirled about him, and this spring was no different. He was amazingly calm, and that sense of—was it contentment?—seemed to affect all of us around him at certain times.

"More tea?" John asked. "You look knackered!"

"Thanks, no," I replied, "I couldn't drink another drop." I then sat more or less stock-still, thinking I should probably ask what he wanted me to do. But I was learning that patiently waiting for John's next thought or directive was far better than either suggesting a course of action or asking a question when you didn't know what the hell was going on in the first place.

Then Yoko stirred. She had a tendency to sit bolt upright on the far side of the bed, often surrounded by pillows of various sizes and shapes, aware of the gathering but not really taking part in any, or much, of the conversation. She appeared to be calmly staring into the massive, thirty-one-inch converted French television, which was built into the bed frame at its foot. The set, which had been converted from the European SECAM system to the American NTSC, was a focal point of the entire room. I don't think I was ever in the bedroom for any reason that it wasn't on, generally with the audio turned down or muted.

"Don't you see, I mean . . . what we want?" she began. At this point, John turned quickly to his right to look directly at Yoko, who stopped talking for just a moment.

She turned to her left slowly and looked me straight in the face.

"You see, I have been doing some numbers and have talked to friends since this entire affair has, um, you understand, come to my attention, and I, I mean we, feel you should try to keep, you know, this mess from getting any messier."

"But Mother," John stated, "he's not a fuckin' detective. The lawyers are going to be fuckin' up the post when they hear about this. There's the hearing next week."

Yoko interjected, "Exactly. What I mean is, you know, we need to keep this close in. After all, for some reason, you trust the boy."

I'm twenty-six, I thought, *and yeah, while John is older, nearly thirty-two, obviously approaching "middle age"* . . . Oh, fuck it. At least she wasn't armed. It looked like I'd walk out of this screwy day in one piece and still employed.

"All right then, it's good. David, stay close on this. Try to find out what the coppers know, what they're doin', and of course keep us in the know. Can ya do that?"

I nodded, somewhat reluctantly. Then another silence ensued. John and Yoko were both fixated on the telly, Channel 5, the ten o'clock news. Bill Jorgensen was staring back at the Beatle and his lady, delivering, silently in our case, the headlines of the day. John glanced at me. One is never dismissed from the bedroom. It was just made subtly obvious that it was time to leave, as the next event was about to happen.

"Go home. Have Farah call you a car. Get some sleep. We'll discuss that Democratic Party thing you did this morning later on."

He turned back to face the screen. The top stories were scrolled on with state-of-the-art Chyron computer graphics, yellow with heavy, dark-drop shadow. I could just make out one headline about the Stockholm Declaration on the environment and then saw a reference to the "celebrity murder in Soho." John rummaged through his bedclothes for the remote.

"Oh, sorry," he said. "I saw the on-screen a moment back. I think your ball club lost to the Mets."

Before I could react to that additional sad news, Yoko turned to me and said in a very quiet voice, "Oh, David, you know I, well we, think you may have made the right decision, to call in the authorities."

A perfect end to a perfect day.

—CHAPTER 11—
YOU'LL NEVER GUESS IN A MILLION YEARS!

8:50 A.M., SATURDAY, JUNE 17, 1972

After leaving the Bank Street apartment, I decided not to take John up on his offer of a ride home. I had to clear my head, so I wandered deeper into the Village and grabbed a burger at the Belly Button on Greenwich before hopping a cab to South Ferry. A little after midnight I trudged up the back driveway and climbed the two flights of brick steps that led to what was, officially, the sun porch of my large rental house in St. George, on the northern shore of Staten Island. The house stood atop something called Fort Hill, first used by the British as they'd massed in the summer of 1777 before chasing General Washington out of New York altogether. Military strategy always suggests you take the high ground. Indeed, from the second and third floors of our Tudor, even with some mature trees, you could see the whole sweep of New York Harbor, from Liberty to the Verrazano Bridge and out to sea. High ground, that's what I needed right now, some perspective—and some distance from Stephie's murder. Not for the first time, I was glad circumstances had led me to live in the farthest flung of New York's boroughs, but even at this remove, and after a couple of beers from the fridge, it seemed impossible to get any distance at all from the week's events. In my own room on the second floor, I fell asleep, or rather passed out, still in my clothes.

Almost instantly, the phone rang, eight, maybe nine times, which my exhausted mind incorporated somehow into a bad dream, a steam locomotive running parallel to a high-speed car chase.

I woke and felt for the phone, finding it just as it stopped ringing.

Then I yawned, stretched. Where was that damned answering service anyhow, the one I'd hired to pick up after four rings? I lay on top of the comforter studying the ceiling and staring at the phone. It rang again.

"Hello," I croaked. On the other end, a breathless phone operator identified herself.

"This is Richmond Answering; you'll nevah guess who called you!" the operator gushed.

"Wait a minute," I countered, "I shouldn't have to guess . . . aren't you supposed to tell me?"

"I mean I'm sure it was him. It sounded like him. You know, the accent and everything," her breathing was rapid. "I mean, you'll nevah guess in a million years!"

"Let me take a shot," I said. "Could it have been John Lennon?"

"Oh gawd," she exclaimed, obviously disappointed. "You're right. Howdja know?"

I yawned, "Not a lucky guess. I happen to work for him." Big mistake.

The operator—said she was Gloria—tried to cover her headset mouthpiece while shrieking, "He knows him! He works for fuckin' John Lennon! Can you believe?"

There was a rustle at the other end of the line. Had Gloria fainted?

"Hello, sir," an older, cigarette-ravaged voice picked up, "I'm so very, very sorry. Gloria is new, and nobody bothered to tell her that box 217, your box, is kinda special for us. Thank you for understanding. Indeed, Mr. Lennon, the former Beatle, ya know . . . "

"Yeah, I heard," I said.

"Well," she continued, "he called at seven nineteen and again exactly nine and one-half minutes ago and requested you call him back immediately. He said you knew the number. After the second call, I authorized Gloria to use the multiring callback to make very, very sure you got this message promptly. The gentleman, well, I think of them all—John, Paul, George, and Ringo—as lovable mop tops, but my husband, Vito—he works for the city—not so much . . . "

Okay, on second thought I might have to reconsider living in Staten Island. I thanked her, told her I hoped Gloria had recovered, cleared the line, and dialed one of the numbers for the Bank Street apartment.

"Good morning, this is, uh, the apartment," a small voice said at the other end of the line. I was relieved as always when anyone— positively anyone—answered the line at J&Y's place who wasn't Farah Freedwoman.

"Yes, g'morning. It's David. John wanted me to call and . . . "

"Yes, Mr. David," the small, confident voice said. "I think Mr. Lennon just went back to bed for a bit. And he said when you called I should tell you to, let me see, he wrote it down, 'Get your'—is that effing?—anyway, the gist is that you should get in here pretty quick. You know, I think his handwriting has probably suffered, not that I saw samples of it from the past, but I'm sure since he went to school in Britain he probably had good teachers, but I imagine he's been asked to give out autographs so much the past few years that, well, like I'm sure he has . . . "

Everybody who got near John became a rambling idiot.

"Excuse me. I don't know if we've met. If you or anyone expects me to be in Manhattan before noon, I'd better hang up and get going."

"Okay, sure. I called the car company, and somebody should be at your place like shortly. See ya!" Blessedly, she hung up.

I glanced out the balcony door. A sleek late-model Cadillac, nonstretch, was crawling up the drive. I changed my shirt, brushed my teeth, and splashed some water on my face; then I gathered up my wallet and watch and crept quietly through the still-sleeping household and out the door to the car.

In the back of the limo, I managed to think clearly for the first time since the previous afternoon. Someone, someone I knew and worked with, and really liked, had been murdered. Murdered right upstairs from where I worked every day. No wonder Maria wanted to leave yesterday as soon as possible. I wondered, and not for the first time, if anyone would want to come back to work on Monday. Would I?

In the clarity of a new day, I finally began to focus on the question of who had murdered Stephanie Bradley. I'd read enough crime novels and watched far too much television to know right off the spouse is always the first suspect. I didn't know Stephie's husband, but he sounded like an asshole to me. What was his name? Jeffrey? Only a few days before, she'd claimed I'd like him, a real "dreamboat;" but how did someone who preferred to discuss car mileage to hanging with Stephanie still claim her love? Had to be some kinda stiff—also more than privileged—attending both Columbia and NYU, then landing a job at JWT through a father who could pull strings. Still, it was hard to conceive of a suspect I'd never met. My attention veered to Sam next; where the hell was he anyway?

"He does this. I mean just seems to disappear a day or so at a time," Christine had confided some weeks earlier. I'd called their apartment looking for "the Great Director" one afternoon when J&Y

had announced an impromptu visit. Sam had not been in that day, nor had he called.

"I don't know where the hell he goes, and truthfully, if it weren't for the twins, I'd find it hard to care. He says he's editing. Working sometimes overnight with John and Yoko, constantly supervising changes."

Christine had sighed with a great deal of exasperation. The pause was so long I wondered if we'd been disconnected.

"You know, David, once, back in March I think it was, it was like the third or fourth time in two weeks he simply hadn't come home or called late to say he wouldn't be home, and, well, I lost it. I began to scream at him, to ask if he gave a damn about his boys, not to mention me. But he just said he and Stephanie had to meet with John and Yoko even if it meant going to the recording session to discuss scene changes that couldn't wait. Before I could respond, he hung up. I was livid."

I'd gotten used to that from Christine. I knew what Sam had told Chris just couldn't be true. Stephie had never been to Record Plant, and Sam was hardly ever there either. Finally, John had a firm rule about never discussing other business when he was either rehearsing or in session. I responded to Christine anyway.

"What did you do?"

"I left the boys in front of something on TV; we had already eaten pizza. I phoned Broome Street, no answer. Then, enough bullshit, I took a cab down there. The place was dark, security gate padlocked. The cabbie waited for me at the curb, and we headed up to Record Plant. May Pang—Yoko's assistant, hanging out at the front desk—recognized me; she said she hadn't seen Sam either. When I inquired if perchance Stephanie Bradley was there, she asked, 'Who's that?' Well, I was pissed, and when he wandered in the following day, I confronted him. You know what he said?" Her voice rose, and she didn't wait for a reply. "He was angry with me for checking up on him. Said I should never do that again; I might embarrass him."

As the limo emerged from the Battery Tunnel, I mulled over that and other conversations I'd had about Sam. I didn't like him much. He was pompous and didn't treat me, or really anybody, very well. But John, and especially Yoko, seemed to like working with him. Stephanie had been totally taken with him, defending him when either Maria or I got the least sarcastic.

Could Sam be a killer? Or was I thinking that simply because I disliked him? On the other hand, it had to be somebody, so why not start with Sam?

—CHAPTER 12—
IF YOU'RE GOOD, I WON'T EVEN HAVE TO CUFF YOU

10:35 A.M., SATURDAY, JUNE 17, 1972

"Hey there, you must be Mr. David," a small, tinny voice over the Bank Street apartment intercom answered my buzz. After more buzzing and opening of the two security doors, I found the source of the voice, barely five feet tall, ginger hair with a spray of freckles set off by granny glasses. The boss's current look was catching on.

"Yes, yes, indeed, you are he. Or should that be him?" she went on. "Anyway, you're Mr. David. See here, I have this notebook I've put together with snapshots of all the people who might visit so that I can recognize them when they show up on the video camera outside, although sometimes the images are blurry—you know, sometimes it's hard to see. People wear hats. Last week, someone stood outside the door with an umbrella, and I couldn't see a thing. Often people just turn their heads away from the camera. I don't know whether they're shy or up to no good. I've got to be diligent, got to be careful. I've got to be . . . "

"You've got to," I interrupted, "at least tell me if John and Yoko are around."

"Oh yeah, of course. They're probably still asleep," she said. "I came in about eight as always."

"So you're just here on weekends?" I asked.

"Like yeah, for the last month or so. I mean, like, I'd even come here on Christmas Eve and New Year's for free to watch the door and answer the phones so I could say, like, I was here, that I got to meet them, that I was able to work with them, be of use—you know, perform any little task, to make things more better."

"More better?"

"Yeah, more better, you know, things can be good. Then they can, like, be best and sometimes even better. So more better is even better than good or best. My mom always says that I should make things more better whenever and wherever I can. Dig?"

"Clear as a more better bell," I said.

Just a kid. She wore overalls, the kind with straps that crossed over her back, and beneath that a soft, rose-colored baggy shirt that had a busy pattern of white flowers everywhere.

"Nice shirt," I said for no reason at all.

"I got it secondhand, someplace over on Bleecker. None of my stuff is new. It''s all from the people." she said.

I figured she meant the "people" were representative of something like the movement that was underfoot to stop the war, legalize pot, elect George McGovern, and change the world forever. She probably shopped at some sort of collective, or from a basement sale at a leftist church where the proceeds might go to benefit the rumored underground railroad spiriting draft-age males out of the country to Canada, where they could breathe free, no worries about being called upon to kill the Vietcong. I wasn't far off. Later that summer, walking down Bleecker, I saw a secondhand clothing store called The People.

The shredded-American flag curtain suddenly broke my reverie, fluttering as John emerged, dressed in his light green robe, belted at the waist, and his own round glasses.

"Where ya been?" he barked. "I see ya met what's her name. Keep it down; Mother''s still nappin'. Let's talk at table."

He apparently hadn't slept much. The demise of Stephanie and the visit by police and Geraldo had completely unraveled the previous night's plans.

"You know, I thought for a moment we were going to have to throw Geraldo out; bloody man wants to talk and talk and never seems to wipe that fuckin' silly grin off his face. You think that mustache is real?" John asked.

"I guess so," I responded. "Why wouldn't it be?"

Mugs of the dreaded tea appeared in front of each of us, delivered by the freckled assistant.

John continued, "I mean, whether it's the bleedin' network or just local, I see they have makeup folk even for the news readers, powder, lipstick, fixing the hair, a real showbiz approach. Don't know, but I suppose it's unlikely someone glues on Gerry's mustache on a daily basis." He took a long, satisfying draft from his mug and sat there looking at me.

"Look, John," I began. "I've done more than a little thinking about our conversation last night. I don't really know the first thing about investigations and such."

"Nonsense," he said firmly. "First, you're a bright fellow. Also, I know you read those trashy crime novels. I saw a couple books, one by that horsey guy, Dick Francis, and—what was it?—*The Laughing Policeman* on your desk at Joko. Something tells me you've got more than a basic working knowledge of crime and detection. What about Conan Doyle; you've read him, I guess?"

"Yeah, all of them, I think. I mean, Holmes is . . . "

"Pardon, David, that was rhetorical. I don't need you to be Sherlock. Just need someone a little more anonymous than myself, no offense. Now, you know, especially with how the authorities are treatin' Mother and me, I have little or no use for them. I'm not leavin' you or anybody out there on the dangle, but I . . . I mean we, all of us, need to get on top of this thing. No one expects you to solve the bloody murder; just keep an ear into the situation. Let us know what's goin' on, and if we might expect a surprise or two, make a heads-up. For fuck's sake, for all we know the fuckin' FBI or CIA killed that poor girl while tryin' to bug the studio or illegally search and seize the premises."

Bug the office, search Joko Films, maybe. But seize the premises? Pretty far-fetched, I thought to myself. However, John did watch an incredible lot of television.

"But John," I began.

He extended his right hand to signify a stop while holding out an empty mug with his left toward the omnipresent kettle of tea.

"No buts. If this is to come to a quick solution, we've got to fuckin' be involved."

Here John took another pause, I assumed to further collect his thoughts.

"Let me see, David, now did I mention to you my talk with Dan and his ever-present sidekick? Took place yesterday afternoon before Yoko and I headed up to the lawyers."

"Uh, no," I said. "What did he or they have to say?"

"Well, happy they weren't. Indeed, we didn't think there'd be any work for either of them. Just that maybe you and Sam could chat them up, maybe give one or both a lead, with the Maysleses perhaps. But Danny said you were a bit abrupt, and Sam simply refused to see 'em at all."

"Not totally the way it came down," I said. "I spent the better part of a half hour talking with both of them, at least talking to Dan while the other guy more or less grazed through my desk drawers. As for Sam, he wasn't even there."

"Sounds reasonable," agreed John. "They're both on edge. I believe there's a not-so-hidden agenda, one that Yoko and I are doin' nothin' to encourage, mind you. But I was concerned at somethin' that the Ball fella said."

"Which was?"

"He said somethin' like, well, let me recall, 'Mebbe that whole batch a' spoiled Yanks over there need, like, a wake-up call. Mebbe if a couple a' them had a good knockin' about, that would wake them up proper,' or somethin' along those lines."

"That's chilling," I said, "especially considering what happened to Stephanie."

"Didn't take it seriously then, and I don't much think he meant it. Nor do I think the puffed-up fella has the nerve to have done anythin'. Just you should keep it in mind. Keep it to yourself. And let me know what you think when you've had time to turn it over in your brain."

"Okay," I said, drawing out the word, "more grist for my mill."

Standing abruptly, John accepted a fresh mug, then stretched, standing on tiptoe, and emitted a small groan. "Well, you'd best be off and scout around that mill. See what grist you can dig up. And, by the by, how do you feel Maria took everything yesterday? I mean, she's a brick, but havin' someone you work with, a colleague, done in so tragically—well, I'd be surprised if there wasn't some sort of reaction. Keep an eye on her, David, and don't hesitate to cut her some slack."

He took two steps toward the flag-draped opening, then stopped suddenly. Half turning, he said, "Same goes for Bill Frost. In fact, let me know when the coppers cut him loose and if he's good to go startin' Monday. On second thought, you may need some additional help down on Broome Street. Oh, but worry not. I'll not be sendin' Danny or his chum to ya. Let's talk later. Now, go snoop."

With that, he disappeared behind the strands of the shredded banner. Suddenly, the coveralled assistant was next to me, removing my untouched cup.

"Already had too much tea?" she asked quietly. "My mother never uses this stuff. Says good ol' Lipton, like in those really big bags that can brew up an entire pitcher, just Lipton is good enough, especially for iced tea. In fact, did you know that my family can go through three, maybe four pitchers of sweet tea in just one . . . "

"Well, good for all of them and for you. Not to mention Sir Thomas Lipton. But you heard John. I'm off to do whatever he thinks I can do."

"Sir Lipton? I mean, was he sirred? Or is that sired? Or maybe that comes when the queen or somebody puts a big sword on your shoulder, ceremony, stuff. My dad and uncle were both in England during the war. They went to Buckingham Palace . . . "

She was still talking when I entered the airlock on my way outside. However, with the inner door snapped shut, there was only a few seconds' hesitation before I could hear the lock being electronically disengaged, signaling the young redhead hadn't missed a beat in order to buzz me out.

Then, another Saturday surprise: leaning up against the same scuffed Plymouth Valiant that had ushered Maria and me to the police station was Homicide Lt. Rosado. To honor the weekend, she wore stonewashed jeans, slightly flared, over polished black boots. Above the waist, she sported a nearly matching, abbreviated jeans jacket over a bright red blouse, setting off her olive complexion and piercing dark eyes. I wasn't even up the two steps to street level when she levered herself off the side of the car, grinning slightly.

"Well, Cowboy, long time no see. How's your Saturday so far?"

"Nice to see you as well, Lieutenant. Since you asked, I was roused way too early, though I still think I can make it back to watch the Reds-Mets. On my way, I thought I'd . . . "

"Good to hear," she interrupted, "but we need to talk. I've got questions for you. I need you to walk me through the daily routine over at Joko. In fact, I thought we could talk down there. Quay's on site, and I want to check with him to see if—and what—the techs have come up with. Hop in. If you're good, I won't even have to cuff you."

—CHAPTER 13—
BETTER TO BE LUCKY
THAN GOOD

2:10 P.M., SATURDAY, JUNE 17, 1972

Lt. Rosado, Sgt. Parker, and I were in the back room near the kitchen area at Joko. Being back was hard to put into words. Creepy? Weird? Just plain sad? A whirl of all three? In this building, right upstairs, someone had taken the life of Stephanie Bradley. Now it appeared that people whose job it was to figure these things out had been combing over the building from top to bottom for the better part of twenty-four hours. Of course, I wanted to find out what they had discovered, if anything, both to quench my own curiosity and to report back to John. I knew this was no game.

"Look," Lt. Rosado said, "I'd like to put a lid on this pretty quick. I mean, basically, I like your boss. He's more than cool. Seems right-minded with a great many decent ideas. But this little killing staged here yesterday, or the night before, is gonna dominate headlines for a few days, and then speculation about whether he's involved or not, I mean, he doesn't need this shit, right? Nor do you. And when you come to think about it, neither do I!"

The three of us were seated on stools around the counter, less than two hours after she had snagged me at the Bank Street apartment. Before I could inquire, she continued, "Don't ask. I'm a talented detective. Besides, it wasn't hard to figure out where you were; it only took a couple calls."

Someone—probably the sergeant—had scored all three New York dailies, now scattered about with the lunch Rosado and I had picked up on our way to the office. Front page below the fold and in tasteful type, the *Times* declared, "Woman Found Dead in Loft of Lennon Film Company," with "Possibly Murdered" as the subhead. The *Daily News* led with end-of-the-world-size type right below the banner, "OH NO! GIRL FOUND MURDERED IN LENNON LOFT." Yoko was gonna love that one. Plus the "Lennon loft" reference made it look like there'd been a crime spree at J&Y's apartment. Finally, The *Post* led with a sleazy treatment of a mob hit in Queens, but one page in featured a full spread regarding Stephie's demise. There was, in my estimation, a less-than-flattering photo of Maria and me leaving Joko yesterday afternoon. I might have to think about upgrading my wardrobe a bit.

"So, Cowboy, tell me: what do you think?" asked Rosado before she took a last bite of a corned beef-and-coleslaw deli sandwich. Parker swiped her pickle.

"Think? About what?"

"Well, I suppose I could ask your thoughts on the upcoming election, but seriously, David, what do you think I want your thoughts about? About this murder. You remember, right upstairs, yesterday."

I paused to collect my thoughts. "Okay, it looked to me like Stephie was hit on the side of the head and probably tumbled or was pushed off the couch onto the floor. There was a small blood stain on the seat of the couch as I recall. And since it looks like the blow was right above her left ear, wouldn't that mean the, uh, killer, who probably approached her from behind, was likely to be left-handed?"

Rosado glanced meaningfully at her partner while wiping her fingers with a napkin from the bag. "Not bad," she said, "but what if Mrs. Bradley was lying on the couch on her right side? The blow could have come from either the right or left hand of an attacker. Also, if she was aware and awake when the attack took place . . . "

"Wait a minute. What do you mean 'if she was awake'? I don't ever recall Stephie crashing in the edit room, you know, napping or whatever. Why wouldn't she be awake when she was hit?"

Another look passed between the two detectives, and Parker commented, "Well, you know, autopsy results aren't final. There are all kinds of labs and other results that need to be considered, but . . . "

Rosado jumped in. "Look, David, when I asked you what you thought, I didn't want you to do our job. But you work here. You knew her. So who could it be? Who do you think would kill Stephanie Bradley?"

Well, I thought to myself. *before talking with John this morning, I felt sure Sam could have been the culprit, although I have no idea what his motive might have been. Then there's that violent little diatribe by Socrates Ball—about how some of us down at the film company need "knocking about." Also, here was a shred of a motive. Maybe Ball might be thinking that a scandal of some sort might be manufactured from this mess, and it might be the final straw that caused John and Yoko to leave New York and the country. In spite of John's protestations about wanting to stay, the decision might not be wholly his and Yoko's to make. Maybe, just maybe, a murder investigation on top of immigration issues could mean that Ball and Richter could be gainfully employed once again at John's Tittenhurst mansion. Pretty thin, but then Socrates seems pretty unstable.*

"Are you in there, Cowboy?" inquired Rosado as she snapped her fingers in my direction.

"Oh, yeah, present and accounted for," I responded. "And, well, I guess anyone associated with Joko could be considered a suspect." I then paused for a second and looked Rosado squarely in the eye. "Even me, I suppose."

A slight grin found its way onto Rosado's face.

"Well," she began thoughtfully, "I suppose you, Miss Anastasia, and your snoozing friend, Bill Frost—we sent him home early this morning in a cruiser—could all be considered. But I think not. There's also her husband and her boss, neither of whom have turned up yet. Let's see, she worked directly for this Sam Heintzelman, a colleague of yours I assume?"

"Yeah," I said, grateful there was, after all, only one Sam Heintzelman.

"Went to his apartment this morning; his wife and kids—cute kids, by the way, twins, right?—haven't seen him for almost two days. Let's see, wife says that his being gone overnight, sometimes for a day or two, is not unusual." The lieutenant glanced up from her notebook and looked directly at me. "Though I could tell his wife was not thrilled, you know? So we got a couple suspects, both missing and unaccounted for."

"Whew. Didn't know Sam was still missing. And you say so is Stephie's husband?" Rosado nodded.

"But what about Bill? I mean, it sounds like you, well, cleared him, which I think is right. I mean, now that I think about it, there's absolutely no way he . . . "

"I don't think he did it either," Rosado interjected. "Too much of what he says makes sense, while the story he's trying to tell—or make up—makes no sense. Also, he let us do a thorough examination of everything he was wearing: nothin' there. There's no hint of any blood splatter. Not to mention it would take a pretty cold killer to do the deed and then take a nap in the next room."

Parker jumped in, "Ya know, it's damned difficult to strike somebody with a great deal of force, especially on the back of the head, and especially if the victim is much shorter than her attacker, without gettin' some blood, bone fragments, brain matter, or somethin' on your clothing. Your buddy Bill was spatter free."

"And, well, anyway," Rosado said, "he just doesn't strike me as the killer type."

He didn't me either. Bill was a lover, not a hater. If you doubted that, all you had to do was find a copy of the acetate pressing he made from his demo album. Would anybody who recorded such songs as "A Day on Butterfly Pond" and "She Served Me Psychedelic Cream Cheese" be capable of killing Stephie? I didn't think so, and even without treating herself to those sonic delicacies, Lt. Rosado felt the same.

She continued. "What I'm needing you to do is pretend it's a normal day, just another day at the film company, and walk me through what happens. Who arrives when? What do they do on a typical work day? Who hangs out with whom? You know, lunch, drinks after. What happens pretty much on a regular basis?"

Who said it's better to be lucky than good? I had just stumbled into all the information I was liable to need had I had any sleuthing ability whatsoever. However, I was going to have to tell this wonderfully cooperative cop there were never, ever two days alike at Joko Films.

—CHAPTER 14—
YOU GUYS ARE FOOLERS
3:20 P.M., SATURDAY, JUNE 17, 1972

"So everyone pretty much comes and goes as they please?" Rosado asked.

"Well, not exactly. We all pretty much put in hours as needed. Understand, this business is a series of brief, sometimes boring days, not much to do, and then you get a project dumped on you, and it could be two, three straight weeks, including weekends—ten-, fifteen-, even twenty-hour days . . . "

"I more or less understand," Sgt. Parker mused. "It's just like police work, with the exception that we never have those brief, boring days."

"So unless you're out somewhere shooting, which you say is only a few days each month, this old building, just the two floors, is more or less where all the so-called magic happens?" Rosado quipped.

"I guess that's one way to think about it," I said. "I mean look, everybody thinks that making a movie or a film is all about lights, camera, action, you know, locations and stuff."

"Please just slow down when you use complicated technical terms such as 'stuff,'" Sgt. Parker interjected. "I mean, I'm just a simple country boy, I seldom have time to go to the moving pictures."

Yeah, right, I thought. I went on. "I mean, so much of any film, which after all is just storytelling, is like writing a novel or composing, initially thinking about what you want to say. I mean, what you want to convey to an audience. I know we look awful flaky sometimes, but a great deal of thought goes into what is going to be shot. Then, after the relatively short time we spend shooting anything, the actual hard work begins . . . "

"I assume you mean the editing process—what goes on upstairs," Rosado cut in.

"Uh-huh." I glanced toward the stairs to the second floor, still barred by yellow crime-scene tape. I wondered if any of us would ever want to go up there again. "Look, the process doesn't actually involve, as my father is fond of saying, 'honest work with heavy lifting,' but we do work. Sometimes Sam and Bill, and of course Stephie, will . . . er . . . put in several of those long days in one or both of the edit rooms, scanning over scenes, inserting shots, taking them out. I mean, sometimes it really is exhausting or baffling, and it often becomes a group effort."

"In what sense?" Rosado inquired.

"Well, almost everybody, sometimes even Sam, loses perspective. You know, looks at a problem or a scene or even a chunk of footage that covers only a few seconds. You do that enough, sometimes you have no idea if it all holds together. There have been nights when all four or five of us have gathered around one of the flattops looking at only a minute or two of edited footage. Then we discuss it, debate it, and pretty much collectively determine whether the scene works or not. You guys must do the same thing. Don't you often get lost in the middle of a case and then need to reach out and knock around some ideas or theories with others, just to see if you're remotely on the right track?"

While neither officer responded, both took time to look at me thoughtfully, and it seemed I'd caught the slightest nod of agreement from Lt. Rosado.

Being a fan of crime fiction, I assumed sharp detectives have to be keen observers. And it was obvious to me that Rosado and Parker were two of the NYPD's best. Parker watched me mostly out of the corner of his eye while sometimes glancing at Lt. Rosado. Was he looking for affirmation or silently passing on cues in a private language?

The lieutenant, however, seldom took her eyes from mine. I felt she was softening a bit, her face becoming less studied and more, well, human. She was a bit scary: no-nonsense, button-down, direct, and generally all business. Staring back at her, I realized a silence had filled the room.

"Midwesterners! You guys from out there always tend to puzzle me, Cowboy," she said. "East Coast people, New Yorkers especially, we tend to be no bullshit bullshitters. I leave interpretation of Southern folk to my partner, though I find they tend to be relatively open, friendly and forthcoming, save for the residue of racism."

"Well now, Lieutenant, my mama's cousin JW—and you only met him that once—well, I had no idea how he felt about Puerto Ricans until he said what he said. I'm still embarrassed by that."

"It wasn't you I was talking about, Parker, and with any luck, neither of us will ever see JW again." Turning back to me, she went on. "Then there are the West Coast people, Californians. Thank Jesus, not many of them commit murder in this town, so I don't have to deal with 'em much. I mean, seriously, your West Coast types are definitely flakier than my morning raisin bran. But you Midwesterners, I think you guys are foolers."

"How so?" I asked.

"I think you're either one way or the other. I mean, here in New York someone gets pissed off, blows away their girlfriend or a neighbor, shoots a family member on a Friday night, you know about it. It's out there. And when they're caught, they deny any knowledge or participation until years after sentencing, and what's more, everybody in the neighborhood lies their asses off, tells totally different stories, and after the trial, each one tells Channel 7 they were completely shocked, had no clue . . . "

"But literally, everybody knew about everything all along," Parker broke in. "We knew it, they know we knew it; it's kind of an understanding."

"In the Midwest," Rosado continued, "out there where everything is flat and allegedly straightforward, your average, garden-variety murderer may knock off his—or her—entire family over time, even the hired man, the rural mail delivery guy, a traveling encyclopedia salesman. And prop their bodies all around the dining room table, laid for Sunday dinner, then sit at the head observing the entire mess till some poor deputy wanders along 'cause someone down the road is missing a Sears catalog and the phone bill. Only then do the authorities discover there's a serial killer loose in the county, and after word spreads, everyone who ever met the perp even once confesses they knew evil was in his heart all along."

"And your point?" I asked.

"My point exactly is you guys tend to wear your hearts on your sleeves and your faces. And because those feelings appear to be genuine, out there for all to see, well, it's easy to overlook the obvious. Like I said, you're foolers. I think you personally tend to be a straight shooter, Cowboy. I think you don't like lying, though we all do lie in great or small ways, and I'm pretty sure you're not going to lie to me or Parker in an extreme fashion. Am I right?"

"Yup, sure are, Lieutenant."

"So, you didn't kill Mrs. Bradley, did you? Not that I think you ever had the opportunity, or a motive. But most importantly, you have no idea who did kill her, do you?"

"Saved by the truth," I responded. "No way. Not on either charge. I couldn't imagine killing Stephie—or anybody—and I really have no idea who might have, Lieutenant." But maybe I was a fooler. A little bit. I had my own theories, but I wasn't ready to disclose them, not yet anyway.

"Well she sure as hell didn't commit suicide and then hide whatever was used to bash in her own skull," Parker added.

Rosado stood, walked over to the kitchen counter and rummaged around in a bakery bag I imagined the sergeant had brought in earlier.

"What, no doughnuts Parker? I mean, how do we reinforce this young man's stereotype of a New York City peace officer unless one of us eats a honey glazed in his presence?"

She threw a slight smile my way, continued to poke around in one of the bags, and came up with what, as a Midwesterner, I would call a "sugarcoated French twist." She studied it for a moment, then took a moderate bite out of one end.

"Good cruller," she commented, after swallowing the chunk of pastry. "You guys have crullers back in, where is it, Ohio?"

"Well, we wouldn't call it that. We also have running water, paved roads, and—I understand from the monthly packet of letters the Pony Express delivers from my folks—electricity is within a month or so of coming to suburban Cincinnati. We're practically civilized."

"Yup, you're right, boss, he is a wiseass," Parker remarked dryly.

"Sure enough. But I like you, Cowboy. Most importantly, I've decided to trust you. And that means use you. My guy on the inside."

She then ambled back to where Parker and I were seated and took another nibble of cruller.

"With that in mind, let's seriously concentrate on your colleague, Sam Heintzelman."

"Okay," I managed to squeak out.

"Just where is he? Or where do you think he is? Like I said before, his missus claims this is not unusual, although he has been MIA for the better part of three days and nights. Can you shed any light on this?"

"Not really. I mean, let me be clear: Sam and I aren't, well, what you would call close."

"You don't like him much, do ya?" said Rosado.

I paused for five, ten seconds, which only seemed like a half hour. "Not really. Does it show?"

"I'm a detective. Mayor Lindsay pays me and Quay to detect, to think, and come to conclusions—eating doughnuts is just a sideline."

"Okay, no, I don't like him much. I never have."

"You've known him longer than the few months you've worked here?" queried Parker.

"Yeah. Back in Ohio."

"He's from Cincinnati also?" This was Parker.

"Well, originally, as I recall. But I met him only when I went with Bill up to a . . . "

"That's Frost, right?" asked Parker.

"Yeah. Anyway, went with Bill for a weekend up to a film festival in Yellow Springs, you know, Antioch College. That's where Sam was going to school at the time."

"At that time?" injected Rosado. "Does that mean he went to more than one college?" "As near as I can remember, I think he spent a couple semesters over in Bloomington, at IU, and then did some student teaching down at Western Kentucky. He floated a bit; don't know if he ever graduated from any of them."

"So, you and Bill meet Sam at this Antioch place?" asked Parker. "You hadn't met him before but had Mr. Frost?"

"I'm pretty sure Bill knew him. They acted like buddies, but there was always an undercurrent of something between them. You know, rivalry, animosity, whatever."

"And you? What about you, Cowboy?" Rosado said. "How and where did you develop negative feelings about Mr. Heintzelman?"

"Pretty much instantaneously. I mean, he's, well, full of himself; pompous. A genuine blowhard and relatively mean-spirited on top of that."

"Don't hold back," said Rosado. "I think it's safe to say that you never liked him, correct?"

"Totally safe," I said. "I think Bill and I went back to Antioch together once because of Sam's being there. I took a rain check the last couple times he went up."

"Antioch. That's not a big school," said Parker. "But the name, there's something familiar about it."

"Of course, it's more infamous than famous. There's a saying about it and the town: 'four square miles surrounded by reality.'"

"Oh yeah," said Parker, "very liberal, very chic . . . very artsy-fartsy."

"More or less," I said, "and I don't know what his major was, if anything. Sam pretty much ran the film society, which, in my estimation existed mainly so he could run his own short pieces before whatever Bergman or Antonioni film they'd show on a Saturday night."

"So Sam's not a good filmmaker? Then why was he hired by John and Yoko?" wondered Rosado.

"He has a good eye. A good sense of composition. He's great behind the camera. Occasionally he has some good ideas. He just wants to, well, be everything all the time," I said.

"He doesn't know his limitations is what you're saying?"

"Spot-on. That and, from what Bill told me, he sees himself as a major-league ladies' man at the same time. Screwed pretty much every girl he saw."

"And," said Rosado, now slowing the pace of her questioning toward a methodical end, "do you think that continues to this day, Cowboy?"

Here I realized my own prejudice could get in the way. I found Sam so disagreeable, so arrogant that I simply assumed he was more than reprehensible as a husband as well. I often wondered what Christine ever saw—or still saw?—in him. Still, I answered, "Dunno. Possibly. Bill says he just up and disappears, a day here, a night there, has done so ever since Bill came east to join him more than a year ago. Wherever he has gone in the past, maybe that's where he is now?"

"Not exactly a masterpiece of deduction, but sure, could be," said Rosado, snapping her notebook shut. She nodded toward Parker, who stood and began to move with her toward the front office and the outside door.

"Goodbye, officers," I said.

Over her shoulder, Rosado commented to Parker, who was less than two feet behind in the hallway, "Midwesterners also tend to be overly polite. They feel a need for closure at every opportunity. Get used to it, Quay."

Then, to me she said, "Seeya, Cowboy. Stay out of the upstairs edit room till Monday earliest. I want to review crime scene reports, make sure we don't need to go back into the murder room. Quay or I will call you and let you know it's okay to take down the tape."

I glanced again toward the stairs to the second floor, criss-crossed with bright-yellow tape with the bold black words "Police line. Do not cross." Just like in the movies.

—CHAPTER 15—
KEEP A SHARP EYE OUT
6:10 P.M., SATURDAY, JUNE 17, 1972

The front door clicked shut behind the detectives. As if on cue, the wall phone in the kitchen insisted I answer line four immediately, which I did.

It was the yet-to-be-identified-by-name weekend assistant.

"Mr. David," she began, "glad I caught you. Mr. Lennon would like you to come by again. Told me to find you wherever, and, well, like, not to brag, but I saw you and that lady cop you were talking about—that was her, wasn't it?—get into her car when you left, and I just assumed you were more than likely heading back to Joko, and so when . . . "

"I assume there's a car outside?" I interjected.

"Well, yes. Well, I called the limo company and . . . "

Hating the fact that I was about to imitate Farah Freedwoman, I hung up.

• • •

I spent less than an hour with J&Y, mostly with John. "Brilliant," he interjected at least four or five times during our conversation. Glad he thought so, but I felt like a fraud.

"Both coppers, I mean detectives," I be sgan, "opened up a lot easier than I ever would have thought. I didn't really do any detecting, just mostly listened and let them tell me what was going on."

"Stuff and nonsense!" John insisted. "You're doin' exactly what Mother and I hoped would be possible, and even quicker. It's that trusting face of yours. And you tend to look people right in the eye. Again, exactly what we thought. Just stay on things, keep a sharp eye

100

out, and let us know what's goin' on. Fuckin' brilliant!"

As per usual, Yoko was seated on the far side of the bed, appearing, best I could see, to be going over some music charts. I knew, however, she wasn't missing a word. "And, you know, what about Sam?" she interjected. "Where is Sam? David, please, if you have any idea where he is or how to reach him, you know it must be done." All this while she kept her eyes steadily on the stack of papers in her lap.

"Uh, no. Nobody really knows. The lieutenant . . . "

"Lieutenant? Is this the woman who is heading the investigation?" Yoko asked.

"Yes, Lt. Rosado, Nancy Rosado. I'm sure she wants to talk with you, both of you. You'll like her, I'm positive, and she's really sharp," I said.

John chimed in, "Good. Let's make that happen. Now, has someone been in touch with Sam's wife, with Christine?"

"That's what I was going to say. The lieutenant has talked with her a couple times, and all she or any of us knows is that Sam hasn't been home since, well, before the murder. No one has seen him."

"I'm sure it will all come out. It will turn out that Sam is off doin' somethin' about nothin'," said John. "You let us know the minute you hear of his whereabouts and that he's safe."

It was only about half past six when the steel-reinforced faux-wood red door closed behind me, leaving me once again on the Bank Street sidewalk. What to do? So little time of late, or so it seemed, was my own, unplanned and without consequence. Had it only been yesterday I'd flown to Washington? Once more, I'd failed to bring John up to date with all that had not happened there. Beating Nixon would have to wait.

I walked east, into the heart of the Village. Of course, my Reds had played in the afternoon while I was entertaining Rosado and Parker. Pausing at the newsstand near Seventh Avenue and Twelfth Street, I grabbed an early-afternoon *Post* off the stack and gazed at the back cover trying to learn if they'd beaten the Mets. Had Wayne Simpson cinched it? A gravelly voice from inside the kiosk insisted, "This is not a lendin' library. Youse should put down a dime and a nickel!"

I glanced up and into the booth, seeing no one but hearing the gruff sound of a man clearing his throat. He was considerably shorter than Lt. Rosado, staring up and back at me—timeless, or at least somewhat less than a hundred years of age.

"C'mon, what's fifteen cents to youse?" Then he stepped up onto a platform that allowed him to maintain a level of eye contact with customers.

I slid the paper back onto the stack, using the heavy iron disk with the well-worn legend *New York Herald Tribune* to keep the papers from blowing away.

"All I did was glance at the back page," I protested. "You know, just wanted a baseball score."

"Youse coulda asked. Woulda told ya they beat Texas 2-zip. Ya know, it ain't right that teams should name themselves after whole states. I mean, they play in Dallas. They should call themselves the Dallas Rangers. Maybe Dallas-Fort Worth somethin'. But not the whole state! And ain't there some sort of team in Houston?"

"I hate to agree with you, but I do. However, note that all these teams that misidentify themselves, the Minnesota Twins, the Cal Angels, the Rangers in Texas, they all play in an inferior league. I'm interested in real baseball."

Before I could launch into my defense of the National League, the news dealer, now leaning forward, straightening his stack of early-edition Sunday *New York Times*, glanced up,

"Poor devil! Tell me youse roots for da Mets. Might give ya the rag free, outta pity."

I shook my head.

"Aw, no! Don't by Gawd tell me youse roots for Cincinnati. That ain't right if you live here! And ya do, don'tcha? But you didn't always, I can tell . . . "

Before I could admit it, he went on.

"You're in New Yawk. Pick a team—we got two—hell, use ta have three. Pick one, stay behind it, register and vote Democratic, complain about the next ConEd rate increase. But, if youse wants my opinion, and I'm sure ya don't, stick with the Yankees. They'll get good again soon. The Reds and the Mets? Fuhgeddaboudit! That thing in '69 was just a foible. And the fifteen cents? Fuhgeddaboudit that too. Have a nice fuckin' day."

I dropped thirty-five cents in his change dish, slid out a three-day-old copy of this week's *Village Voice*, and moved on. Glancing toward the back of the paper, I walked uptown a bit farther west, just in time for the 7:20 showing of *Play It Again, Sam* at the Waverly.

Emerging a little over two hours later onto a crowded Sixth Avenue, I was halfway tempted to grab a bite and come back to the venerable old theater for the midnight showing of *Woodstock*—would have made my third time—but I decided instead to check out Village Oldies on Bleecker. Nothing caught my eye, though I lost myself for almost an hour flipping among vintage Jazz albums, used and on sale for ninety-nine cents, and the latest rock releases.

Next, I dropped into the Dugout for a burger and a frosted mug, disappointed to find nothing of interest at The Bitter End next door. Hell, it was nearly eleven. I began to search for a cab; none to be had, so I jumped on the No. 1 at Christopher Street heading for South Ferry but missed the damn 11:30 boat by less than a minute. The ferry schedule, usually twice an hour during weekends with as many as five boats an hour during the weekday rush, went hourly each night starting at half past eleven.

But the familiar trip never failed to offer me a calming period. There's time to think and then there's wasted thinking time. The South Ferry Terminal is a study in various shades of seafoam green, supplemented by decades of neglect. I cataloged these augmentations.

By contrast, each boat of the fleet of "world famous" Staten Island ferries is relatively pristine. All the boats are painted "ferry yellow'" with cobalt blue trim and the legend "Marine and Aviation Bureau of Ferries" on the stacks in bold type. It was the *John F. Kennedy* I finally boarded at nearly half past midnight.

Ferries are eternal. For one thing, the bow and the stern are identically shaped, rounded to fit into whichever slip the boat is headed for. Once you are aboard, there's the clink and squeak and the casting off, followed by one or two long whistle blasts.

The walk uphill through St. George on this spring evening was lonely but a good way to work off the beer and the burger. Several dozen steps through Borough Hall's grounds put me further uphill on Hyatt Street, which I passed under the closed marquee of the local movie palace. Another slight upgrade at the corner where the Civil War era Brighton Heights Church raised its copper steeple, then two more upward stretches of darkened streets and I was home. At my leisurely pace, the walk from boat to back door had taken almost as long as the trip across the harbor.

Fumbling for my keys, I realized that not once during the hour I had spent on a hard bench in the Manhattan terminal had I thought about Stephie. Now, journey complete, moving through the darkened first floor of our shared home, climbing the stairs to my second-floor room, I could think of no one else.

−CHAPTER 16−
SO, SUSPECTS?

11:15 A.M., SUNDAY, JUNE 18, 1972

I slept late that Sunday. At least until Liz, my ex-girlfriend and these days a housemate, unceremoniously threw parts of the Sunday *New York Times* on the bed beside me, as well as yesterday's *Daily News*.

"Super picture," she quipped. "I guess you're in the middle of this?" She pointed to the "Ono/Lennon Loft" headline.

"Well," I said, "I mean, I didn't kill anyone."

"Seriously," she said, "I didn't think so. I mean, you're not exactly the killer type."

"Should I take that as an insult or a compliment?"

She continued, "But it does involve Joko, and that means, to some extent, you gotta cover your Beatle's ass."

"Thanks for the insight," I replied. "Now if you'll clear out of here for a second, I'll get up and cover my own ass."

"Nothing I haven't already seen. I'm sure it hasn't changed much in the last two years. Good God, you Ohioans are so hung up on modesty. Get over it!"

A native New Yorker, the only child of divorced parents, Liz had just turned twenty-four. Her mother's third marriage, this time to an investment banker, had been a shock.

"It happened one weekend when I was stuck at boarding school," she'd told me. "I never even met the guy until she introduced him as my stepfather. Can you believe it?"

Liz had grown up mostly on the East Side. Home was a prewar building chock-full of classic New York "sixes" at the corner of Seventy-fourth and Fifth. Knowing that a mere six rooms was far from prestigious, her stepfather acquired two adjacent units and knocked down dividing walls, allowing Liz to brag she now lived "in a converted New York eighteen."

Her mother had slated her for Juilliard or the Berklee School of Music, but Liz, a talented violinist, totally rebelled, announcing one night at dinner she'd been accepted at the College-Conservatory of Music, the University of Cincinnati.

"Good lord," her mother gasped. "Is that a state school? Oh darling!"

From behind his *Wall Street Journal*, her stepfather muttered something about basketball schools.

We had met during my senior, her sophomore, year at the College-Conservatory. An advanced string student, she had little use for rock 'n' roll, folk music, film, or even much of the twentieth century. I was a radio/TV major and a disc jockey on the college station, but somehow we became an item, accumulating some history, nothing too serious.

Despite the fact that she more or less qualified as an adopted Midwesterner, Liz dropped out midway into her senior year to follow her loser boyfriend, Travis, back to New York. Several years later, hearing that she was in town, I got in touch.

"Good to hear from you," she'd begun, "but I'm crazed. Need a place to live, not in Manhattan though. Brooklyn is a dump. Can you believe I actually checked out a place in Jersey City just yesterday?"

When I explained I'd taken out a lease on a big old house in Staten Island, we discussed her taking a room.

"Well, whaddaya think? Can we hang? I mean, like, cohabit as friends?"

I thought for more than a few seconds. "I don't see why not. I mean, you're still with that Jack—I mean Travis, right?"

"To some extent, and let's not get started on Trav. I know what you think of him."

So we didn't discuss Travis but did discuss living arrangements and sharing the rent, and we negotiated how many shelves she could dominate in the shared refrigerator. "Just one," I insisted.

She arrived a few days later with a U-Haul that contained several suitcases, her great-aunt's chest of drawers, and three violins. Travis, living in a loft in Brooklyn and detesting Staten Island, thankfully stayed away.

"Is there anything left to eat?" I asked Liz while paging through the papers she'd brought. Sunday breakfast, which had gradually evolved to more of an extended brunch, had become one of the few meals regularly shared by the entire household. Sleeping in, I assumed I'd more or less missed today's event.

"There's still coffee, no help for you. Of course Jack made eggs and scrapple; undoubtedly there's some of that left. What does anybody see in scrapple?"

"Don't know. I hate the stuff," I said. "It's a Philly thing. Then again, Jack spent some time in Philadelphia."

Jack O'Leary occupied the knotty-pine-finished basement apartment. An accomplished carpenter from Northern Kentucky, he'd tried a couple of semesters of liberal arts at Temple University in Philly but dropped out. Then he saw my ad in *The Village Voice*, "Rooms to Rent," a couple of years back. I had worded the ad "Lonely, lapsed Midwesterner seeks same to share large, rented Tudor mini-mansion overlooking NY Harbor in fashionable, downtown Staten Island. Repair skills a plus." Of course, everyone knew Staten Island was the least fashionable borough. Jack arrived less than a week later in a Dodge van, a rolling workshop that he now drives all over the island, Brooklyn, and sometimes Manhattan, creating one-of-a-kind kitchens, libraries, and guest bathrooms for the needy rich. His business boomed. Meanwhile, every cabinet hinge, crank window, and ceiling fixture in our house functioned perfectly.

While I'm on the subject of housemates who are lapsed Midwesterners, the other member of our mismatched foursome was Ian Thomas, an Ohio native from Dayton. Ian was the brains of the outfit, though Liz seldom yielded that point. He had a photographic memory and penchant for pedantic details of any kind.

"Did you know that besides being the home of the airplane and the cash register, Dayton is also the birthplace of the stepladder?" he might say over dinner. The three of us, or more if there were guests, often looked at him blankly. Eventually someone will admit that no, we did not realize the stepladder hailed from Dayton, wondering silently how we've been able to get through a day without that knowledge. Ian was seldom amused. He's in the middle of a career in market research at a Midtown Manhattan ad agency.

Liz, on the other hand, held several part-time jobs: at an antiques store ten minutes from the house on foot, in the Village at a bookstore, and at the local Jewish Community Center, teaching music to children.""

"Why don't we flee the scrapple and head on down to the diner for a sophisticated brunch, something like an overstuffed cheese omelet?"

I suggested.

"Well, you know my one guilty pleasure is Velveeta. God forbid my mother ever finds out," Liz replied.

"Omelet, side of bacon or sausage, some greasy, underdone home fries, maybe even a pancake or two."

"Sounds like health food to me," she said. "And oh yeah, I meant to ask, did your sister ever catch up to you in town? How is it I didn't know you had a sister? A brother, yes. How many other family members have you hidden from me over the years?"

"My sister?" I asked.

"Uh-huh. She's gorgeous. Little if any family resemblance, although I've heard that blondes and redheads—you know, recessive genes— aren't uncommon in the same family."

"Um, well, no, my 'sister' did not catch up to me. How did you find out about her?"

"She just arrived yesterday, middle of the afternoon, came up the front steps. She has a terrific little Audi; why does it have Maryland plates? Had a suitcase. I simply assumed you knew she was coming. I showed her to the loft on the third floor, and then she was off in search of you."

"So she's up there now?" I said, pointing to the ceiling.

"No. Don't think she made it back last night. I got the impression she didn't know New York. then again, none of you guys do your first few weeks here."

I was playing along, stalling for time. I didn't have a sister. Only a younger brother who, last I checked, has no interest in what I'm doing in New York.

"So she still has red hair?" I went on, faking it, for some reason.

"Yeah," Liz said, "And she's hot! Long red hair down to her ass, charming freckles. Come to think of it, she has your eyes."

"She's staying on the third floor?" I asked.

"Where else?" she said. "I mean, you're family. We only have the one spare bedroom, and how sick would it be to suggest she stay in here with you. I think there are laws against that!"

Stalling had gotten me somewhere. I now had an idea who the Maryland redhead was.

"Possibly," I said, wondering privately if there are any laws, on or off the books, that deal with sibling impersonation. Then again, if she was who I was sure she was, you could add the fact, accurately reinforced by Liz, that she was hot.

Liz eventually left my room to give me time to shower and dress before walking with her down to the St. George Clipper, a local greasy spoon one block south of the St. George Ferry Terminal. We slid into a booth opposite one another near the front plate-glass window.

Liz started talking while reading directly from the "Breakfast Anytime" portion of the menu.

"So, suspects? How many you got? Employees? Friends of hers? The husband? I know you, David. In true Hardy Boys' fashion, you've begun to amass data and calculate who could have done this."

She abruptly closed the thick, encyclopedic menu and joined me in ordering an omelet and the sides we'd dreamed of less than an hour before. Sure. Why not? Might as well start bouncing ideas off someone.

"Okay," I began, "on the employee front, there's Sam . . . "

"Whom you dislike," Liz noted.

"More than a little. And there seems to be no one else at Joko under suspicion. But there is this guy that dropped in out of nowhere from the Lennons' place in England, semitough guy named Socrates, who just seems to threaten people from the get-go. And of course the husband is always a suspect, but I'm sure one of the two detectives mentioned he was out of town for the whole thing."

"And who do you like for it?"

This forced me to contemplate. "Sam, I guess, and he's among the missing. However, with no motive anyone knows about. I've never even met Steph's husband, so I can't hazard a guess. Sam and Stephie seem to get along." And not for the first time, I thought perhaps they got along a bit too well.

Smiling, Liz then mused, "And so the Beatle makes you his detective?"

"Well, sort of . . . "

"I love it. However, you once told me—we were in bed, I think—that the murderer is never really obvious. At least in a well-crafted mystery."

Blushing slightly, I had to disagree. "Yeah, Liz, but this is real life. This actually happened. You know, I think real murders are seldom well crafted."

And with that, we simply sat across the partially sticky table and looked at each other. I never could tell what she was thinking, in bed or out.

By midafternoon, I was at last in front of the Sears Silvertone, taking in most of the last of the Reds-Mets three-game series. Because of the weekend craziness, this was the only game I'd been able to catch, and, my luck, the Mets started Tom Seaver, who subdued the Reds 2-1. Without much to distract me, thanks to the Reds' lackluster performance, Liz's questions kept running around in my brain; I didn't have any answers.

—CHAPTER 17—
THIS IS INFINITY

9:40 A.M., MONDAY JUNE 19, 1972

By morning, the only thing I knew was that my supposed sister had not returned for a second night. As I was concerned about the whereabouts of the girl I assumed would turn out to be Katie Steigerwald, I spent a few minutes skimming through her suitcase and hanging bag on our third floor. Hey, I was now a detective; I had a right.

This told me what I suspected. She was indeed Katie. Her name was plastered on every label and surface. It looked as though she avoided her surname as much as she wished future audiences might. Her suitcase was full of musical charts, notebooks with lyrics scratched in pencil and pen, and a half dozen reel-to-reel tapes, not unlike the one I had trucked home from Washington that Friday afternoon. Her luggage tag showed she lived in Chevy Chase, a fairly upscale neighborhood near the nation's capital. Having spotted more than one piece of clothing with the University of Maryland logo (Fighting Terrapins), I was happy to know that another member of my family had attended a state school. Having satisfied myself as to my new-found sister's identity, though still a little unclear on why she had arrived for a family reunion, I headed into Manhattan.

On my way across the harbor, I suddenly wondered if anyone would be at Joko at all this Monday morning. I wasn't looking forward to reentering the Broome Street premises without either Lt. Rosado or Sgt. Parker.

As it turned out, I was not alone at Joko and hardly the first to arrive. The padlock and gate were wide open.

Bill had called in Sunday night, said he was going to be "under the weather." Sam was still missing, and of course Stephie wasn't coming in ever again. Nevertheless, gathered in the kitchen, where a pot of coffee was unnecessarily brewing, were the rest of the "staff" of Joko Films: Maria and a new recruit, the weekend warrior from the Bank Street apartment.

"Morning," Maria said. "This is Infinity. She's working here now."

"Infinity? Your parents must have had long-range goals."

"Actually, it's Mary Josephine, but, like, I mean, how possibly fucked up would it be to go around calling yourself Mary Josephine right now? I mean, we all need names that, like, leave an impression. Mary Josephine? Really? I mean, like, Mary Josephine means, when you first hear it, little-girl shoes. You know, high-polish patent leather, shiny black."

"Okay, Infinity it is," I said.

"Yeah," this other new redhead in my life went on, "my college roommate at Southern Illinois was already using 'Blissful,' and, like, I mean, most of the cosmic and astrological names are so very overused. Besides, I want to be known as someone who knows no limits."

"No limits," I said. "How nice for you. Can you answer phones?"

"Doesn't Maria do that?" Infinity responded. Behind the girl and to her left, Maria turned and wrinkled her nose. "I mean, when I got this promotion—I mean this is a promotion, right?—Farah more or less told me that I would be yours and Maria's assistant, doing really important stuff. Nothing like typing, answering phones, getting mail, or running errands. You know, just important things."

"You know, I think one of the important things we all might consider," Maria stated, "is moving this circus someplace else."

"You mean the entire film company?" I asked. "Why? And most importantly, where?"

"I mean, like, it's creepy. Upstairs, behind that tape stuff, Stephanie was, like, killed. So we're supposed to come here, do what we do, just like every other day?"

She had a point. I had lain awake last night imagining what it would be like walking back into 496 Broome. I knew it was safe, but Maria was right; it was a bit creepy.

"Look, whoever did this to Stephanie, well, for sure they're not here. They weren't here when you discovered her on Friday, and they're not coming back. Don't you think Stephie would want all of us to keep on? You know, carry on, finish *Imagine* and do the films J&Y envision?"

A rousing halftime speech it wasn't, and it was followed by silence. A sad kind of calm seemed to be settling on Maria. It was our new recruit who spoke.

"Well, like, for sure. We all have to carry on. I mean, I'm not quite sure what goes on here, but it's gotta be pretty important. I mean, if John and Yoko think it's worth staying in the country for, if making these films means so much to them, how can any of us, like, abandon it? I mean, we all have to stick together, make it all more better."

"More . . . better?" said Maria.

"Don't get her started," I said pointedly.

Thankfully and right on cue, the phone rang. All three of us stared at the wall unit near the kitchen counter. It rang a second time.

Maria said, "Could one of you get that? If it's the newspapers or someone, I just can't cope."

Infinity busied herself refilling the sugar bowl, obviously one of those important tasks, so I grabbed the receiver from the wall.

"Joko Films," I said.

"Hey, yo, man . . . or guy. Is, like, John there?"

I had given up on the various versions of "John who?" I had tried the first few months and now just answered, "Nuh-huh."

The caller wasn't put off that easily. "I mean, I can hang on the phone while you get him. I mean, no bother."

"Look, man," I said. "We both know he doesn't work here. We both know I'm not going to put you through to him wherever he is. We both know you're about the eight millionth person to call here, pretend to be cool, and expect to be put through to John Fucking Lennon."

"Man, cool it. No need for profanity. We're both God's children. I mean, like, are you aware that the world could come to an end this summer?"

With Stephie's murder, a chunk of my world already had.

—CHAPTER 18—
HEY, BRO, WHADDYA KNOW?
10:25 A.M., THURSDAY, JUNE 22, 1972

Bill was dressed in his professional best this Thursday morning: leather pants, paisley shirt with puffy sleeves, and leather vest with brass buttons, all stacked atop a pair of Frye boots with extraordinarily high heels. He held a paper cup in his left hand, which probably did not contain coffee. Whatever it held, the cup reminded me somehow of Stephie, "Of course . . . I keep forgetting you don't like coffee!"

Bill nodded to me and continued back toward the stairs to the second-floor edit area. "Still no word from Sam?"

"Nope, and dammit, nobody seems to know where he is, even Christine," I replied.

"Yeah, she's been here the last two days lookin' for him," Maria chimed in. "Wouldn't it be more efficient or whatevuh if she just called and asked one of us whether Sam showed up?"

Pausing to reflect, Bill added, "Yeah, it's like she has to see for herself he's really not here, I guess."

"Also, she's all the time droppin' by more baked goods, muffins, cupcakes, and then there's the jam. Even pokes around lookin' for empty jars and stuff."

"Well," I said, "to borrow a phrase from my favorite Italian-American, 'whatever.'"

Maria pulled a face and pretended to type something. Bill ambled upstairs.

The first half of the week, I reflected, had passed pretty quickly. The edit room had officially been released as a crime scene midday Monday. I wondered if whoever passed out titles at Joko would start referring to Bill as our new assistant editor. Maybe, just maybe, things were beginning to get back to normal.

• • •

Meanwhile, back home, things were anything but normal. Not till Wednesday had I finally set eyes on my new-found "sister," on the sofa.

"She's been there since I got home," Liz had volunteered. It was ten p.m., an early night. I stared down at Katie's red hair, spread out over the couch cushions, her bisque doll's face in repose.

"Were you two close as kids?" Liz asked.

"Not much. You might say we only just started to connect."

"You mean reconnect."

"What I mean is we have only begun to get to know each other—as adults, you know—recently."

"She's younger than you, right?" Liz asked. "By how many years?" I didn't even begin to know Katie's age, so I continued to bluff. Not sure why, but it was sort of fun.

"Just a few years, but enough to make a big difference when you're really young; not so much, you know, now."

I needed to change the subject, claiming I had to check the answering service and make a few calls before I turned in. Seemed I would have to confront my "sister" in the morning.

"Didn't I put a couple of beers behind the yogurt on the second shelf, which, as I recall, is supposed to be mine?" I asked of no one in particular.

"What a gig you have," Liz said as she trailed me into the kitchen. "You work for the most famous man in the entire world, crazy hours, and yet you look and act as dull as you did a year ago, when you were at the agency."

"Thanks for that," I said. "I think you're superinteresting also."

"Well, not really dull," she said, "just not charged up about the entire scene. I mean, I think your Beatle is a bit overblown. In twenty, thirty years, no one's even gonna remember him, the three other guys, or any of their frivolous music. But even I have to admit he's a pretty big deal right now."

"Never can tell. I mean, last I checked, people still cover some of the stuff that Bach and Beethoven wrote, and that was, what, two, three hundred years ago?"

"Give me a break," Liz said with a great deal of exasperation. "Those are the masters you're talking about, not rock 'n' roll."

Having completed my fruitless search for purloined beer, I grabbed a can of Coke and headed upstairs. Communal living definitely had its drawbacks.

The following morning, it was still difficult to catch up to my new fake relative. As I passed through the kitchen, grabbing a Pop-Tart and a glass of milk, I discovered Liz putting the finishing touches on a piece of cinnamon toast.

"I think she's going to like it here. She's out early this morning looking for work. You know, we might have a new, semipermanent roommate. Another woman! Wouldn't that be neat? You could really get to know your sister. It seems to me you have a lot of catching up to do. Oh yeah, she left you a note."

"Dearest Brother," it began. "Isn't Liz terrific? Thanks so much for understanding my quick visit. Mom and Dad send their love, of course. And I'm off to the city to meet with a guy I scored with over the weekend, who thinks he can get me some sort of intro gig at the Village Gate. Do you ever come home at anything resembling a regular hour? L. gave me your office phone and address, so maybe we'll catch up there later. Thanks for whatever you've done with my tape, you're the best! XOXOXO (sisterly), Katie."

For some reason, the phrase "scored with" had created an ever-so-slight pang at or near where I stored my jealousy. Also, I was overwhelmingly uncomfortable with the prospect of Liz and Katie becoming close. Liz had already spent more time with my "sister" than I had the entire time we were "growing up together" in two different parts of the country. And why was I so damnably concerned with trying to extend or cover up Katie's lie about our family connection?

I folded the note and slipped it into my pocket. "Did you give her a key?" I asked Liz.

"One of the spares of course. She is your sister." With that, I left for the ferry.

When I arrived at the office around 11:30, no one else saw fit to answer line one, so I picked it up. "Hey, buddy," a somewhat familiar voice on the other end spoke out. "Sorry I haven't been back to you earlier. How did John like the tape?"

It was that little dweeb from the DNC, Peter something. Sometimes I didn't mind people trying to use me; sometimes it grated. He rambled on about how I should try to get another meeting with his boss. And no matter what, come down sometime soon to the District, where we could—oh joy—hang out. He didn't think there was much chance that anyone in marketing and communications needed the use of our film company, although it was a super offer. Meanwhile, had I heard about the big-deal burglary over the weekend at their office building?

"A bunch of guys were arrested, like maybe ten or twelve; the *Post* has been giving it a good deal of coverage. You read about it up there?"

"No, and I read the *Post* nearly every day, at least Dick Young's column in the sports section."

"I mean *The Washington Post*," he interrupted. "A real newspaper."

"Nothing about a burglary up here," I said. "We have a real newspaper here as well, and if it had been important, I think the *Times* would have mentioned it."

He rattled on breezily, in a manner that suggested we had been best buds for years.

"I don't suppose you've seen my singer? I mean, she disappeared over the weekend. No one seems to know where she went."

For some reason, I held back. "Sorry, haven't seen her," I said. "It's always crazy up here. J&Y are in the studio, we're cutting something in the other room upstairs, and, uh, my sister's been in town and I've been pretty busy."

"Far flaming out," Peter said, for no reason at all. "I mean, you just mention them so naturally. Just like John and Yoko are part of your everyday life. So cool!"

"Indeed very groovy," I agreed.

"So if Katie does show up, tell her to call. I think she might have forgotten that Bix has her and the group booked on a ten-day Norwegian Caribbean cruise gig—third billing, in the big room—out of Miami sometime in early August, I think. It's an important career move."

"And what is a Bix?" I asked.

"Bix, you know, Buddy Bixley, up-and-coming promoter and talent rep here in the District. Her manager. Sort of my partner and, uh, well, Bix is also kinda Katie's boyfriend."

"Interesting. I'll keep an eye out for her," I said.

"And hey," Peter added, "didn't something happen up there? Wasn't there something like a murder or something at one of Lennon's companies? Is that where you work?"

"Gotta go," I said. "Important call coming in." Indeed, line four was flickering.

"Hey there," I said, answering it.

"Is that the way you answer a business phone?" Farah Freedwoman asked. "Maybe you clowns over there don't respect the fact that Yoko and John provide all of you good livings while that business venture barely brings in enough income to justify the square footage. You're college educated, supposedly somewhere. Did you ever take any business courses?"

"What do you want, Franny?" I asked, just to piss her off. She hated being called Franny. "Just give me the bad news, or whatever. Besides, when line four rings all by its lonesome, I know it's one of you, so there's no need to be formal."

"Simple decorum," she spat out. "It's just simple decorum and proper."

"Proper and simple. I'll make a note of that for future reference."

Farah snorted. "Yoko tells me to tell you she needs to know where Sam really is, no kidding."

"He's still MIA."

"Oh come on," she said. "You're probably just hiding him to be spiteful."

I truly think Frances Miriam Friedman assumed that the heavy rain now pounding the windows at the front of the building, not to mention the torrent of garbage-laced water that probably sloshed over her sandals as she crossed the street to go to work that morning, was all evidence of the spite God was leveling directly at her each and every day. Her burdens were legendary, and her ability to both enumerate and complain about them seemingly endless.

"When Sam shows up, believe me, Franny, you'll be the first to know," I said. "Anything else?"

"They've canceled the session tonight at Record Plant. Yoko has voice problems."

I bit my tongue, threw away at least four good one-liners, and asked the divine Ms. Freedwoman to pass on the concerns of all of us at Joko Films to Mrs. Lennon and our hopes for a quick recovery.

"I will," she snapped, "although I don't think you're being genuine. And don't call me Franny." With that, she hung up.

And then, with little or no fanfare, Kathleen Elaine Steigerwald, at last, walked through the front door.

"Hey, bro, whaddaya know? By the way, your door's broken," she said airily. She was even taller than I remembered, the long fall of red hair adding to the effect. Clad in a pink tank top, loose-fitting bell bottoms, and sandals, she carried over her left shoulder a rawhide bag with fringe on three sides and a large brass clasp that more or less matched her belt buckle. In her right hand was a partially collapsed, smallish umbrella that featured a Cincinnati Reds logo that I'm pretty sure I had misplaced last summer. How had she found that? Only three or four steps shy of Maria's desk, she stood there expectantly. I was still composing an answer when Maria burst in.

"Hey, whatevah!," she chirped. "You must be David's sister. Been hearin' about you from one of his roomies. Welcome to New York! You here long?"

If Liz was right and I was so damn dull, how is it everybody was interested in, or at least knew, most of my business? Maybe Liz was putting out a newsletter, "Harborview Highlights" or "The Weekly Commune," with gossip about the four—or now five—of us sharing a house on Fort Hill.

"Don't know how long I'm here," Katie responded. "Kinda up to Davey. Did you know he doesn't like being called Davey? He had a Little League coach used to holler at him as he was striking out. He'd yell, 'Davey, dammit. Davey, learn to hit the curveball, wait for it, don't swing at everything so hard.' He hated that."

How did she make up this stuff? She was mostly right. I did hate being called Davey and I never could hit a curveball, but my Little League coach was my father, who'd pointed out that football might be my better sport of choice. Good grief! This woman had an overactive imagination yet was spookily accurate.

I stood up and, looking directly at Katie, said, "Hungry? Have you had lunch?"

"Starved. Never thought you'd ask."

Still with the big smile, she went on, "Is there any place local? Let's go out, grab a bite, and catch up! The rain's almost stopped."

—CHAPTER 19—
LOVERS AND KILLERS
12:55 P.M., THURSDAY, JUNE 22, 1972

Of course I headed toward the nearest—and only—appropriate place in our part of Scho, the Spring Street Bar. Not without second thoughts. It still seemed a bit spooky, considering that the last time I'd eaten there was lunch only one week earlier with Stephie. In fact, if not for the rain, I would have searched for a cab and headed up to the Village, but here we were.

"Nice. I mean, really, a nice place," Katie said.

In spite of the hour, we pretty much had the bar to ourselves. I chalked the sparse crowd up to the weather.

"It feels new?"

"Brand-new," I said. "Opened around the first of the year. But who cares? What I do care about is just where did you come from? And why are you suddenly staying at my house? And how and when did you become my sister?"

We'd ordered drinks: me, a draft beer, and Katie, a Bloody Mary, which the same uninvolved waitress of last Thursday was setting before us.

Unfazed, Katie continued, "I've always liked the way you beat around the bush: small talk, chitchat, concern about my welfare, not to mention Mom and Dad."

She sat there grinning, pleased with her performance.

"Look . . ."

"No, you look," she interrupted. "I mean, like, what was I supposed to do? You liked the demo. Peter said you loved it, even before you promised the contract, and then I sort of thought I'd hear from you that afternoon. Peter said he thought you'd call. He was really excited. I mean Bix was a bit put off, but he'll get over it."

The grin was fading, but her eyes remained fixed on me.

"Contract?" I said. "And when did I offer Peter this contract?"

This brought her up a bit short. "Well, I guess that afternoon, you know, last Friday. You did tell him you were going to put us under contract to Apple. I mean you did, didn't you?"

"I work at a film company!"

"Yeah, but I mean I saw, you know, like an Apple notepad on that girl's desk, and like Liz says you really work for John Lennon. I mean you do, don't you?"

Her resolve seemed to be waning. Her flawless complexion was showing red blotches on both cheeks, competing with the light spray of freckles, and all at once she seemed ready to tear up.

"There is no contract, is there?" she finally said. "Peter's full of shit, isn't he?"

"Well, no, and probably," I said. "That is, Peter is probably full of it. Actually, I do work for John and Yoko, and I do love the demo, honestly. Your voice is clear and wonderful, but the tape is still in my saddlebag, back at the office. I haven't had a minute to even tell John or anyone about the tape, let alone play it for him. It's always crazy. Then there was this murder, you know."

Her posture changed dramatically, shoulders slumped, elbows on the table. She picked up her drink and took a long pull.

"Should have known with Peter," she said. "He always has some sort of scam going. I don't really care. Hope I never see the short fuck again. He's not my only manager, you know."

"Big shock. Tell me, probably the main part of your career he really wants to manage is south of your belt buckle, am I right?"

"Big time." she spat out. "Fuck him. Well, not fuck him, well, screw him." She sighed, caught me with those liquid eyes, and finally said, "You know what I mean! To hell with him."

I took a big gulp of Rheingold draft, which reminded me to ask the bartender if and when they anticipated getting some real beers on tap. I stared at her for what seemed a long time. In less than ten minutes, she'd gone from elated to more than a bit depressed, deflated.

Changing the subject, I asked, "Well, what are your plans for the summer? Are you heading back soon? I mean, you do have a group, a band, and I guess there must be other gigs, bookings."

Sucking the last bit of tomato ice melt through the cocktail straw, she glanced back up at me.

"Back to where? Home? My mom's new husband is a disgusting jerk. He hits on me all the time. Mom's insecure about that, not to mention we've never really gotten along. I'm out of the dorm, don't know whether I'll go back to College Park for my junior year—school's bullshit anyway. I have no fucking summer job, and now I've got to tell the band and the few friends I spoke to on my way out of town that there is no Apple Records contract, no studio session to look forward to, and, well, shit."

She looked around for a waitress, signaling for a refill. "It's my fault. I do this all the time. Mom says I'm too—what is it?—impetuous? I hear from Peter that there's a contract, that he thinks we should hear back from you shortly. Let me tell you, after I heard that from him, I stayed inside the rest of the afternoon and evening staring at the stupid fucking phone, willing it to ring. Twice my mom got phone calls, and I practically had to beg her to hang up, to not tie up the line. So then what do I do? Saturday morning I jump in my car. Blitz up to New York, find you to thank you, and, well, to start a wonderful new life. It's all my fault."

The fact that Katie had mentioned nothing about the cruise line job—that magnificent career move about which Peter was so proud—I thought was interesting. As a result, I genuinely felt no responsibility to mention to her that this Bix was looking for her. Also, some time or another I had to find out how she did find me in New York.

"Well," I said, trying to be light, "I didn't know Mom was upset with you, not to mention I forgot that she and Dad were divorced. They are divorced, aren't they? Mom would never be a bigamist."

"Four and a half, maybe five years," she said. And then a small trace of a smile played back over her lips. "I think you were probably away at college when it happened."

"Yeah, I kinda miss Dad, you know, chucking the football around in the backyard; him wanting both of us to help wash the car on Saturday mornings, season tickets to the Redskins."

"No yard. We live in a condo. My real dad's a GS-14 at Treasury in accounting, hates football, by the way. And the chauffeur usually washes both cars, although I've never seen him do it. Mom has all the money, kept what balls Dad had as part of the settlement. I haven't talked to him in more than three years."

"Gosh, seems like we had two different fathers," I said.

Her grin returned, she nodded.

"And while we're talking family," I continued, "why this sister act?"

"I mean why not? It was like spur of the moment. When Liz said you weren't home and didn't know when you'd be back, I just went with it. Sorry, I guess . . ."

"Okay," I said. "So Liz mentioned you met some kind of a promoter who thought he might get you stage time at the Gate. Anything there?"

Again, her smile faded. Speaking directly to her freshly delivered Bloody Mary, she replied in a small voice, "There was nothing to it. All he wanted was, well, you know. I definitely will not fuck my way to the top of anything."

I stared at her for nearly a minute, then sighed.

"Look," I said, "I'll talk to the rest of the guys in the house. I'm sure you can stay on Staten Island for a while until you get things together. After all, what's family for?"

She glanced up. Wiping a tear off her left cheek, she said softly, "You don't have to do this. I mean, don't get me wrong, I'm most definitely going to take you up on it, but you don't gotta."

"I don't gotta, but I wanna. So there," I said. We clinked glasses to seal the deal.

Just then, the two other brand-new women in my life came through the door, one after the other.

"Boy, it's good the lieutenant came along when she did," began Infinity. "I was like leaving, and the padlock back at the office stuck, but she fixed it. Then, just before I left, this reverend guy called. He said you have his book, and I think he wanted to enter the end-of-the-world competition. Is it a competition or more like a lottery? Well, anyway . . ."

It seemed as though Infinity would continue for some time in her usual nonsequential fashion, but Lt. Rosado interrupted.

"Cowboy, tell me, why would your buddy Sam be out of the country?" she asked. "Looks like he left on a flight from JFK, one of those overnights to Paris last Thursday."

This was important and brand-new information, such that it actually caused Infinity to stop talking for a moment. She achieved a thoughtful look and then, turning to Rosado, said, "Wow! Thursday, you mean the same night that, well, Stephanie was, well, brutally murdered?"

"Brutally murdered? And who's a cowboy?" Katie wondered aloud.

We moved to a larger table, and I introduced Lt. Rosado to my "sister." Infinity excused herself to search for the restroom. Nodding toward Infinity as she scurried off, Rosado said, "You know, she sometimes comes off stupid, that one. However, I don't buy it."

My wonderful sister produced a Diners Club card from somewhere in her tasseled bag. "It's Mommy's," she said. "I don't abuse it very much. I see it more as a way of keeping the family together. Lunch is on me."

"While I'm on duty," the lieutenant said, "of course I can't drink, and I can't allow any of you to buy my lunch." With that she signaled the waitress and ordered a gin and 7Up while menus were passed around, adding, "Good thing I clocked out early today."

Infinity returned. We ordered and made a modicum of small talk. During a lull, I looked at Rosado and asked, "When did you find out Sam was out of the country?"

"My secret," Rosado replied.

"Well, can't you get Interpol or Sherlock Holmes or someone to pick him up over there?"

"First, we have no definite reason to pick him up anywhere, no proof he was directly involved in any way. Also, we didn't think he left the country originally. After all, his wife—" she flipped through her ever-present notebook—"it's Christine, right? Anyway, she thought some kind of family emergency might have taken him back to Ohio. This apparently is not the first time he's disappeared for a few days. Again, have you seen that kind of pattern before?"

"A couple of times. And I think that he and Chris, well, let's just say they don't have a traditional marriage."

"They're married?" Infinity jumped in. "I didn't know he was married! Well, I mean..." Her cheeks reddened, and she suddenly became quiet.

"Do you know Mr. Heintzelman well?" Rosado asked.

"I've known him just once, a couple weekends ago," she responded, unwittingly speaking in the biblical sense.

"From what I've gathered," Rosado continued to me, "your friend Sam seems to have known a great many women. Were you aware of that, Cowboy?"

"I try not to be," I answered. "Let's face it, everything's changed. I mean people are a lot freer."

"Either that," exclaimed Rosado, "or they're more reasonably priced."

At that, our food came. Lt. Rosado had several more questions, and I could offer little if any information. I didn't know many of Sam's other friends, girlfriends, whatever they were called. No, he didn't brag about these conquests to anyone at the office; don't know what he said at home. Yes, he did seem to smoke some pot on occasion. Who didn't? I didn't think any of his behavior was reckless, just far too arrogant.

"Look," I said, "so he likes to get laid. I hear as a fad, it's spreading, pardon the expression."

"Expression pardoned. So, how long had he been sleeping with Ms. Bradley?" Rosado asked.

Well, there it was. For all my avoiding even thinking about Sam and Stephie, apparently the good lieutenant had sniffed out what many of us thought might be true.

"And her husband, let's see, Jeffrey, he was conveniently absent as well, until day before yesterday. Did you know he came back?"

"Yeah. In fact, he called Joko midday Tuesday, pretty much upset, wanting to know what any of us knew about the situation. Isn't the husband, I mean, the spouse, one of the first people you guys suspect?"

"He says he was in Cleveland," Rosado went on, ignoring my question. "Client meetings on Friday, flew to Colorado early Saturday, more client meetings. Since he had more meetings in Denver on Monday, he decided to stay over, didn't even hear his wife was dead until someone from his office snagged him at some country club midday Monday."

"Wow! You're kidding?" Infinity warbled. "You mean like everybody else in New York knew Stephanie Bradley had been killed like days before her husband? I mean he must have stayed pretty out of it for all that time, you know, not to talk with anyone, not to hear anything."

"Good point. You would think a loving husband who hadn't heard from his wife since he left town on Thursday would check in more regular," Rosado noted.

"So," I said, filling a sudden silence, "is it safe to say you guys have maybe two suspects, the husband and the lover?"

Putting down a half-eaten slice of pepperoni-mushroom-anchovy pizza, Rosado replied, "Playing detective again, Cowboy? I didn't say either was a suspect. In fact, too many people have access to that building. Only people I feel are totally in the clear are your stoner buddy, Bill, you, and Ms. Anastasia."

"Yeah, but I heard Mr. Frost was there, I mean right there all the time," Infinity volunteered. Helpful kid.

"Of course he remains a person of interest—God, I love that term—but I don't think he had any idea of what was going on or had gone on. The ME has placed time of death between seven and ten p.m. Frost has a pretty good alibi for that time; we're still checking it. Anyway, I don't like him for it."

The lieutenant stared at me; a small smile found its way to each corner of her mouth. "And of course you, Cowboy, are more or less accounted for Thursday night, but tell me, at any time, were you and your assistant editor involved in any extracurricular activities?" she asked.

"Well, what do you mean by 'extracurricular?'"

"Were you also sleeping with Stephanie Bradley?" the lieutenant asked in point-blank fashion.

I blushed involuntarily and then took in a deep breath. Katie's left hand found its way to my right knee beneath the table, squeezing gently, and, I assumed, supportively.

"'No, no way! I mean, I think I might have suspected Sam and her, but I never . . .'"

"Enough, Cowboy," the lieutenant said, snapping shut her notebook. "I didn't really think so, just wanted to see how you'd react."

With that, she abruptly stood, bent over, and took one final sip of her gin and 7. She thanked Katie for lunch; then, to no one in particular, she said, "The biggest problem we have is logistics. Everyone who might be a viable suspect seemed to be out of town, or it looks like they were. It really depends on when everybody's airplane left for wherever. And while all of you had access, well, you fall into the category of 'lovers.'"

"Lovers?" said Katie.

Still standing, the lieutenant leaned in over a corner of the table.

"There are only two kinds of people, especially the kind I come across in my business. There are lovers and there are killers, though one does not necessarily have to be involved in either act. Lovers are basically nice folks. Probably would be vegetarians if they had to kill what they ate. Then again, your killer types, well, they have the capacity to do the deed. Right here, right now, I see a table of lovers, not a killer among you. Consider that a compliment."

With that, the lieutenant left, leaving me with more than a bit to think about.

—CHAPTER 20—
PATTERNS ON THE FLOOR
8:32 A.M., FRIDAY, JUNE 23, 1972

"Hey," piped Katie without provocation, "it's our anniversary."

We were situated in one of my favorite ferry spots, leaning on the wooden rail on the front port side of the *Governor Herbert H. Lehman*, which, on a long blast of her horn, was just easing out of Slip Three in Staten Island, bound for South Ferry.

If boats and ships are always referred to in the feminine, why does anyone ever name them after men? I wondered.

"Anniversary? Based on what?" I asked. If this Friday meant anything to me, it marked one week since Stephie had been found on the floor of Edit One.

"It's been one week," she said. Then, glancing at her watch, she continued, "In fact, in two hours and twelve minutes, it will be exactly one week since we met. Therefore, happy anniversary!"

What was it about Katie? Yes, she was talented, smart, and undoubtedly sexy, but what was actually going on inside?

"It's neat," Katie continued. "Don't you think it's very cool that like every morning on your way to work, you go past the Statue of Liberty?"

"Cool indeed."

Katie, who had a 10:00 a.m. interview at the Village Gate, was keeping me company on my way into town. Though she'd chosen not to sleep with the alleged "promoter," he had done her a solid by passing her name on to the Gate's assistant manager, who apparently was in need of a part-time bartender. If she got the job, it meant she'd be with us for a while. I was suddenly aware that this possibility did not disappoint. Among other things, Katie was, well, whimsical . . . a one-week anniversary indeed.

"So, is it always the time to go back and forth?" she inquired.

"Something like 22, 23 minutes."

"So, in twenty-three minutes or less, can you tell your favorite sister exactly how you landed this job?"

I could and I did, recounting the afternoon the previous December when I'd been running a lunchtime errand from the youth marketing agency I worked for, my first job in New York.

"Hey, yo, David! Dave Johnson, is that you, man?"

It had been at least three years since I'd seen or heard from Bill Frost. Though we were both from the radio/TV department back in Cincinnati, Bill's time at the university had been strictly avocational: four majors in five years while editing and reediting what we all thought to be more or less random footage he and Sam had shot.

He was that day in Times Square as I remembered him, never without a slight smile, bright if unfocused eyes, and a hearty demeanor with hippie overtones.

Standing on Seventh Avenue, Bill explained to me that he'd been in New York less than six months. "You remember Sam Heintzelman? You met him a couple times up at Antioch."

Apparently, Bill and Sam had been working for a couple of people on "experimental" films, way-out-there stuff that was hardly ever seen. However, now they had this project, something really big, possibly feature length, that their boss wanted to see on network TV.

Easier said than done, I'd thought.

"So," I continued with Katie, "I went to a screening that night, and the little rough cut Bill had talked about turned out to be an early version of *Imagine*. I was blown away, both by the film and, of course, by the two people he and Sam worked for."

"John and Yoko?"

"Uh-huh. Six, seven months later, *Imagine* continued to change. I was hired in late February, and we've just begun to schedule screenings, get some interest from advertisers."

"Amazing," Katie said. "Kind of like being discovered in a drug store."

"Sorta."

"Well, with luck maybe I get discovered today too! A little less glamorous, but I'll take a few shifts at the Top of the Gate in the meantime—that is, until you play my tape for somebody."

The *Lehman* was bouncing gently against the pilings in Slip One at South Ferry.

"Anyway, I'm meeting this guy at ten, and I'm catching up with an old girlfriend from U of M for a late lunch. Would you mind if I came down to Broome Street and hung out for a couple of hours, just to kill time?"

"Fine by me, but a quick question; how long do you want to keep up the brother/sister act?"

"Oh wow, I meant it more as a goof, and now it's taken off. Let's just go with it for a while . . . our little inside joke. Whaddaya say?"

I said I didn't mind.

With that, Katie and I disembarked and headed for the No. 1. The local was its usual rush-hour self, jammed, hot, stuffy, and noisy, no time or place for discussion. As the train pulled into the Canal Street station, my stop, I shouted in Katie's direction over the air brakes, "Remember, take this just two more stops, to Christopher Street. Then follow that map Liz sketched out for you. Good luck, break a leg, whatever."

She smiled, nodded, and, leaning forward, gave me a peck on the cheek. Wasn't there an old saying, something about a tie game in football? Some old coach had been quoted, "It's like kissing your sister." Well, being kissed by your sister, real or otherwise, wasn't half bad. Overall, better than a tie.

I walked the four blocks over to Broome Street. The security gate was locked. There was a growing pile of the usual detritus: bouquets (four); assorted envelopes and boxes containing audiotapes; scripts; some minor gifts (a couple dozen); a large, portrait-shaped package wrapped in brown paper; and a nearly empty bottle of Four Roses, indicative of the neighborhood, not an offering from a fan.

I left the flowers, shoved most of the packages through the inner door, and set the "artwork" on the floor: a watercolor picture of John lying on his back, staring up at the sky. Amid the clouds had been glued most of the *Imagine* album cover. I gazed at it absently, then propped it on Maria's desk and wandered off.

What sunlight was able to penetrate New York City's almost chewable air was casting shadows through the frosted panes on the front of the Marwood Press building. It created patterns on the floor of the reception area, which cascaded down the wall to our desks. This incredible workspace always seemed to be alive to me even when everything else in the building and on the street was quiet. But today, no phones, no chatter, and no playback upstairs. In many ways, Stephie had been the life of the place; I missed her.

—CHAPTER 21—
A CUP OF CHOCOLATE
12:13 P.M., SUNDAY, JUNE 25, 1972

It was a Sunday in New York—well, okay, in Staten Island. In what had become a minor tradition, I placed the A side of Peter Nero's *Sunday in New York* on the stereo. We weren't quite through the title track when the phone rang in the kitchen, and Ian called out, "Phone's for you. I think it's that new kid from the office, you know, Ecstasy, Amnesty, whatever she calls herself."

I grabbed the phone only to hear "Look, tell that guy, the one that just answered the phone, first, I'm not some kid. I mean, like, I turned nineteen in April. And tell him my damn name, okay? Who would ever call herself Amnesty? Like, it's limited. The word has no range. I mean . . ."

"Infinity! Whatever can I do for you?" I said, directing her chosen name as clearly toward Ian as into the phone.

He shrugged and continued to open a package of Kraft macaroni and cheese. "Breakfast of fucking champions if ever there was one," he muttered, no more a fan of Jack's scrapple than Liz and I were.

Infinity, meanwhile, on weekend duty at Bank Street till Farah could find a replacement, sounded both harried and urgent.

"Like first, John and Yoko are out for a walk . . ."

""By themselves? On the street again?" I was astounded.

"Yes, by themselves. They are adult people, you know. David, you, Maria, Farah, all you guys are way too protective of J&Y. But that's not why I called. That detective, that woman, Ronzoni or something . . ."

And she complained about "Amnesty"?

"Rosado," I said, "Lt. Rosado."

"Well, anyway, she called here looking for anyone who might have heard from Sam. Like, I have no idea, and neither do J or Y, I think. You're not, like, hiding him, are you? She really wants to know when he shows up. I think, like, he's gonna be a major suspect. Wouldn't that be cool?"

"Infinity," I continued, "I hate to interrupt these notes for your memoir. Is there a reason you called, aside from letting me know John and Yoko are on the loose, while Lt. Rosado continues to look for Sam?"

"Gimme a sec. Yeah, hmmmm . . . " I heard her snap her fingers.

"Of course. John said you should come over right away. He's got something he needs to go over with you. Well, anyway, you should get over here. Anyway, I called a car."

Through the kitchen window, I beheld a limo idling in the back drive.

"Way cool, Infinity. I'll be there in about an hour."

I grabbed my jacket, saddlebag, two mouthfuls of egg, and a piece of toast, passing through the dining room.

I'd grown to enjoy the nearly unrestricted use of limousines; in fact, I'd begun to take them a bit for granted. All of us pretty much went to and from anywhere on John and Yoko business in one of the sleek chauffeured cars. Still, more than two hours later, I was fidgeting in the back seat of this one. Rain had driven many weekend New Yorkers back from the shore early, so the traffic on the BQE and into the Brooklyn Battery Tunnel was slow as molten tar. A city bus had broken down in one of the two inbound lanes of the tunnel, backing traffic up all the way to the Verrazzano Bridge. I was pretty sure I could walk that distance in way less time, even with a stop someplace for a perfectly normal breakfast.

It was nearly 3:15 when we pulled up in front of the Bank Street apartment. I hadn't even touched the buzzer on the left side of the door when I heard the snap of the electronic lock. Infinity must have been staring at the video feed, awaiting my arrival. I passed through the airlock and into the outer room to find her dressed in her usual coveralls and flower print blouse, sporting a brand-new pair of Birkenstocks—and anxious.

"They're in the back. He's been wondering every few minutes for the last hour and a half where you were. And oh yeah, they got back just fine, thanks for asking."

"Did you think to call the limo service and have them radio the driver to make sure we weren't having too much fun in beach traffic?"

"Whoa, great idea! Thanks! I'll remember that in the future. You know, my overall goal is to become even more efficient, more tuned in each and every day. Now that you're here, though, I'm gone. Seeya tomorrow."

The future for Infinity, I assumed, was a period of time stretching out nearly ninety minutes in all directions. I moved deeper into the apartment, through the outer room and toward the shredded-flag entrance to the inner sanctum.

The oak door was wide open. Yoko sat on the bed farthest from the door, with her back to it, hunched over the telephone. John sat cross-legged facing the massive French television, watching intently with the sound turned off. He held up his left hand in a "stop" gesture, whispered "shhhh," and continued to watch. I squatted in one of the rattan chairs and waited.

"Can't fuckin' believe it," John said, crawling toward the end of the bed to shut off the set.

It was unusual for John to shut off the TV. Many of us privately referred to the set as his hearth, where he warmed himself in the glow of whatever fare New York TV stations had to offer.

"What can't you believe?" I asked.

"Whatever the fuck I was watchin',' whatever it was."

He began to search under a pile of pillows, then patted his front shirt pockets. "There it is," he said, leaning forward to grab a piece of paper from a shelf unit beside the bed.

"Sam has done us the favor of surfacin'. He's on a BOAC flight that gets into Kennedy; fuck, it's landing now," he said, glancing at a small clock on the same shelf. "I told the driver to bring him right here."

"You do know the police are anxious to talk with him?" I said.

"Ain't we all? Makes good sense. The little one outside—does she really call herself Infinity?—mentioned there'd been another call from them, before Mother and I took our walk. Best we speak to Sam before the coppers."

"Do you know what he's been up to?" I asked.

"Yeah. Jonas, you know, Jonas Mekas, called early this mornin' from a small town somewhere, I think in Bavaria. He had taken Sam to some minor film festival or screening somewhere in France or Italy or wherever. Sent Sam home on a plane as soon as they heard about Stephanie's murder. Didja know it made the fucking *International Herald Tribune*?"

"No, but I'm not surprised . . . "

"And," John went on, "what have you learned new? I mean the coppers must have a viable suspect now, someone other than one of our people."

"Not really," I mused. "I mean Jeffrey . . . "

"The husband?" John asked.

"Yeah, of course Jeffrey is at least under suspicion. The spouse always is."

The receiver at the other end of the bed clicked into its cradle.

Without even turning around, Yoko said, "You know, I do not think that the woman's husband, this Jeffrey, is to blame. I feel—people and I have talked—it may very well be, you know, that it is someone who wants to bring down bad karma onto us all. It is quite logical a husband would be suspected, but I do feel, you know, that it is much deeper than the obvious." She now turned fully to her left.

She looked directly at me, "David, as you have been following this matter for over a week, do you feel, do you have faith in the police officers working on this case? I understand it is a woman, and I think that would be a great advantage, you know, considering the victim."

This was a first. Yoko was actually seeking my opinion on something.

I hesitated for only a moment, nodded, and said, "I think she is more than competent, Yoko. She is dedicated, experienced, and, well, amazingly inquisitive. For example, she has gone over and over with me all of the people at Joko, what they do and . . . "

"This is good," Yoko commented. "Continue to keep us informed, you know." Yoko then smiled somewhat agreeably and picked up a magazine that apparently had been lying in her lap all the while.

"Let's get some tea and wait outside for Sam," John said, stepping down from the high platform that held the bed.

Oh joy, more English Breakfast tea, and late in the afternoon, boiled as many times as it had been, thick enough to cut with a knife and fork.

I was, however, more than pleasantly surprised.

"Heat's gone off 'neath the tea," said John as we moved into the kitchen area near the cooktop. "The little one, she probably turned it off to save the pot. Week or two back we come in after a session at the studio, past three, to find that Farah left a full pot on the flame, so the tea dried right up and the pot cracked. Had to toss it."

Gently touching the bright blue ceramic pot, John rattled around in the cabinet near the fridge and announced to my unparalleled joy, "But we've got chocolate. We can brew some cocoa."

Now, sitting comfortably at Farah's table, John methodically stirred a mug of rich, oversweetened hot chocolate and said almost to himself, "Missed much of this as a boy. Don't get me wrong—I wasn't abused, just not, well, looked after as much as I'd have wanted. You might say I wasn't used proper."

There were at least a dozen things I wanted to ask. Like anyone, I was fascinated and curious—and to have these personal moments? It was hard to stay restrained. Did Julia, his mother, never make him a cup of hot chocolate? Or maybe Aunt Mimi did, and that might have made him miss his mother more? Or during the war was there no cocoa, no sugar, so nobody could make him a cup? I've had a lot of tea with John, but somehow this was different. Not only was the thick sweet chocolate not the dreaded overbrewed English Breakfast tea, but even better I realized this had been made by John for just the two of us. I took another small sip, wishing it would last a long time.

John continued. "It's the simple things; sometimes they're very comforting. Do you not agree, David?"

His question made me think. "Well, I want to say of course, and for me, that would be true. But I'm almost constantly aware just how many people seem to make their lives unnecessarily difficult, you know, in pursuit of—what they think they need."

"Agreed. Now take our current situation to hand. For some reason, some sick mind chose to erase Stephanie Bradley from this earth. Whoever it was must think they had good reason; but just think how difficult this one senseless act has made all our lives, includin' the killer's. I've grown to understand that violence is never a solution to any problem, anywhere." With that, John took a long and what seemed like a very satisfying swallow of chocolate and changed topic.

"Now, David, we may have a few minutes before Sam pops in, and I do want to talk to you about somethin' more or less, private. It's about Danny and his sidekick."

"Socrates Ball?"

"Indeed. Not worried about Danny, he'll catch on somewhere. It's the other concerns me."

"How so?"

"He's a bit worrisome, has a temper, more than a short fuse. I don't want he should pop off, you know, cause trouble. We've enough already."

This made me wonder, and not for the first time, if Sock Ball had already caused some kind of trouble.

"I know there's no place for them at Joko, not really, but could you think of something?" John asked.

"What about your place in England? You could suggest they go back . . ."

"Oh, I don't know," John mused. "It was cozy there for a bit, Yoko and I learning to live together for the first time. And Dan, well he was an important part of it. You know, helped with everythin'. Made the place run smooth. Made our lives a bit easier. Worked himself like a dog, which is why we agreed to bring on Ball when Danny suggested it. Anyway, he, both of 'em, I think, got too used to the situation. So when Mother and me decided to leave for New York, it was a bit of a blow, don'tcha know."

"I understand. I will look around, I'll make some calls . . . "

"Good. It's a big, excitin' city . . . somethin' 'll gobble him up."

With that the buzzer sounded, indicating someone was just outside the door. A check of the video feed found Sam staring wearily up at the lens and, for once, not banging on anything to gain entry.

—CHAPTER 22—
NO EMOTIONAL ATTACHMENT

8:10 P.M., SUNDAY, JUNE 25, 1972

In an unusual nod to economy, Yoko insisted Sam and I share a car home. We had talked with John and Yoko for nearly two hours, and Sam had been in rare form. He'd appeared wearing his riding boots, into which were stuffed a new pair of khaki corduroy jodhpurs. Above the stylized pants, he wore a blousy, cream-colored shirt he referred to as an English riding garment.

"I think they work well together," he said, catching me eyeing his outfit as we entered the car. "You must understand, of course, that everyone in Europe is wearing khaki this summer"—Sam pronounced the color as "car-key," a brand-new affectation to join the others.

On his arrival at the apartment, he'd provided his alibi right off. He explained that Jonas Mekas happened to have called him the previous Thursday afternoon, the day Stephie was killed. The founder of Anthology Film Archives and a major figure in the film community, Jonas had offered Sam the opportunity to accompany him and a few other friends for two weeks visiting some minor festivals in Italy, France, and Germany.

"Great product! Great work at these festivals," Sam told us.

"Super. But didja not think about possibly checkin' in? Callin' your wife, the office, anybody?" John questioned.

Sam, whose large, flowing walrus mustache and deep, slow-paced baritone seemed to make his pronouncements that much more ponderous, took his time, as usual, in answering.

"Well, as I think about it now, I was more or less moving on instinct, letting my gut and artistic sensibilities drive me. However, of course I did make arrangements to head back to the States as soon as we read about the murder. An old paper we came across two mornings back. Ghastly! Unspeakable!"

We were in the bedroom; John looked over his shoulder at Yoko, ostensibly reading a book propped up on her lap.

"Mother, you took the call from Jonas. What exactly did he have to say?"

"Yes, well, you know Jonas; he's very sensitive, was very upset, you know, to hear about Stephanie. However, there had already been, he said, you know, a bit of an issue between Sam and some of the others in Jonas's party. Apparently, there was one of those, you know, discussions about best movie ever made, which one was best."

Here, Yoko paused, and Sam saw an opening.

"Well," he began, "I did state, and I stand by this assertion, that Jodorowsky's *El Topo* is among the best, if not the finest, films ever made."

The bedroom remained silent for the better part of thirty seconds. John continued to stare intently at Sam while Yoko returned to her reading, a slight smile on her face.

"*El Topo?*" John began. "What about the likes of *Casablanca, Citizen Kane,* and almost anything by Bergman or Fellini? It's no wonder Jonas sent you packin'."

Clearing his throat, Sam retorted, "Well, after all, *El Topo* is an Apple release, and I just simply thought . . . "

John held up his right hand in the familiar stop-sign gesture. "To quote the lovely Maria, whatever."

Somehow, it took another hour to find out that Sam claimed to know little if anything about Stephie's demise, was upset that everyone was concerned he had not checked in, and, most charmingly of all, was concerned that the entire affair had disrupted almost all activity at Joko.

"Don't worry. I'll get everything put back together there in the morning. Get everything back on an even keel. I'll look into things and report back to both of you as soon as I have a complete grasp of the entire situation," Sam promised.

Yeah, right, I thought to myself—*just what we need.*

• • •

Sam and I rode on in silence for nearly forty blocks heading for his apartment uptown. He might have been miffed, having to share a town car, but I was not thrilled that for every block north we went, we'd have to double back so that the car could take me south to Staten Island. More or less Sam believed he was our boss, not that anyone had stated that, but he was the oldest, had worked for John and Yoko a few months more than Bill and then Stephanie. Clearly, he had a higher opinion of himself than anyone else in the place.

I surprised myself by breaking the silence, "So, how long have you been sleeping with Stephie? Is that the reason you hired her in the first place?"

He stared straight ahead and, amazingly, said nothing for nearly three blocks. "That's a rumor, a tragic rumor," he declared.

"Really," I said.

Again silence, and then, "Well, anyway, not often, and there was no emotional attachment."

"Emotional attachment? To the rumor or to Stephie?" I asked.

He turned and stared at me, licked his lips, and took in a deep breath. "David, what I did or didn't do with Stephanie is, well, was of little importance. It's nobody's business. If you continue to banter this about, it will only look bad and reflect poorly on many others: John and Yoko, the company, the entire Apple organization, and that's not to mention how it might affect Christine and the boys."

With that, the car came to a full stop in front of a rather nondescript postwar midrise apartment house. Sam, without further comment, began to unfold his tall frame from the back seat.

"Daddy, it's Daddy!" came a shrill cry from beneath the awning, which ran from the apartment's front door to the curb. It was Robbie—or was it Ted? Anyway, one of Sam's boys came running toward the car and launched himself at our director as soon as he stood on the sidewalk. The other boy ambled up more slowly, hands thrust in pockets, beside his mother, who was carrying a small bag of groceries.

"Hey, Sam," was all Christine said. Then, leaning down to peer into the back of the car, she offered me a smile. "David, how nice of you to see Sam all the way home. Without you, I wonder if he would have found us at all tonight."

She then took another half step toward the car, leaned in through the open door, and said, "Is it true what Bill tells me, that John has asked you to try to help catch Stephanie's killer?"

At that, Sam's meaty paw came into view, settling on his wife's left forearm. "That's nonsense, complete silliness. John is just probably using David as some sort of sounding board, baby doll. He's a gofer, just does odd jobs, don't know why we hired him, or keep him. I'll let you know everything that's going on after I get a chance to sort things out."

At that, he slammed the car door. Sam, his two boys, and his reluctant wife strode toward the building's entrance. I genuinely believed, however, Christine was nobody's "baby doll."

"Your place in Staten Island, sir?" the driver inquired.

"Definitely."

"Bridge or tunnel, sir?"

—CHAPTER 23—
HAS EVERYONE AROUND HERE BECOME AN AMATEUR DETECTIVE?

10:35 A.M., MONDAY, JUNE 26, 1972

The front office was full. Katie was sprawled on the Joko reception couch with *The New York Times*. She had landed that part-time bartending gig at the Gate and, for the moment, taken up residency in the house. This morning, she'd come in with me for another interview later that morning, with a promoter who said he could get her some stage time at The Bottom Line. I was at my desk, and Maria, at work nearly on time, was at hers.

The recalcitrant front door opened, and Sam and Bill strode in together. Sam was upset, demanding of anyone who heard him, "Why is this hard-ass bitch detective hassling me and my family? Do you know she called Christine nearly every day over the past week and a half? Came by the apartment, maybe twice or three times, even talked with my kids. That's police harassment, plain and simple."

"Sam," Maria responded, "don't you think it might have something to do with the very fact that you were missing for ten days after a murder in your office? I mean, you are one of the staff, and all the rest of us have spent a lot of time with Lt. Rosado. Like, she's nice. You may even like her!"

Sam reddened slightly above the collar of his cerulean-blue shirt, another of his English riding garments. He was wearing the same jodhpurs and riding boots from the previous night. Above all, I knew Sam did not see himself as "one of the staff."

"Gaddamnitallltofuckinhell," he spat out. "Doesn't she know I've been out of the lousy country?"

"Y'know, Sam," inserted Maria, "you just might find out Lt. Rosado knows a lot more than you think." Turning to me, she went on, "Fact, didn't she and that other detective call this morning looking for Sam again? Whaddidya tell him?"

"The truth," I responded. "That Sam flew in last night and would, more than likely, make a guest appearance this morning."

Right on cue, the front door opened, smoothly this time, and Sgt. Quay Parker strolled in. Sam or Bill had not slammed it properly.

"You know, y'all oughta get this latch fixed. Ms. Anastasia, Mr. Frost. Hey, Cowboy." Parker drawled. With that, he hesitated, as he noted Katie peering over the top of her newspaper. The detective grinned, rolled his toothpick to the other side of his mouth and simply nodded her way. He then directed his attention to Sam. "And this must be our world-famous globe-trotting di-rec-tor."

Sam had been in the process of trying to fire up a Gauloises. He seldom if ever really smoked, just placed such items in an available ashtray, empty film can, or coffee mug in such a way that the Gauloises's white-winged logo was prominently displayed.

Parker glanced at me again. "Looks like the gang's all here, Cowboy. The lieu is runnin' a bit late. But she should be in directly."

"Lieu?" Sam asked. "Is that the chick detective?"

"It is," Parker drawled, "and if you don't want to be forced to eat that foul-smellin' cigarette, you'd best drop the chick part when Lt. Rosado arrives. By the way, should you be curious, my name is Sgt. Parker, homicide. We both have been looking forward to meeting you, Mr. Heintzelman."

With that, all four foot eleven and a quarter inches of the good lieutenant strode through the front door, carrying a large bag of pastries with grease stains.

"New doughnut place down the block. Well, not exactly down the block, but close," she said to us all. ""Everybody here?"

"Everyone but Infinity," Maria volunteered.

Sam, being nearly two weeks behind in Joko roster moves, looked at me quizzically.

"Who here is a cowboy and what or who is Infinity?" he asked from within a cloud of blue smoke.

Bill, who had been silent to this point, piped up, "As I recall, infinity is the state or quality of being infinite. It can also be a figure greater than any assignable quantity or countable number . . . "

Maria continued, ""Well, she answers phones, is usually late, works weekends for J&Y at the apartment, and, like, I think you probably know her."

"In fact," I inserted, "you definitely know her—as Mary Jo."

Remarkably, Sam said nothing, but his eyebrows and mustache rose upward as one.

Cutting through the banter and Gauloises haze, Rosado looked at Sam.

"We need to talk, Mr. Heintzelman. Obviously, Sgt. Parker and I have several questions."

Bill was already heading upstairs for a nap in Edit Two, and Maria was settling in at her desk, having for some unknown reason threaded a blank piece of paper into the carriage of her barely used typewriter. I noticed that this most recent Selectric had a terra-cotta brown or pink hue.

"Well, why don't you guys set up back by the kitchen? Let me see if there's coffee on, or maybe I could put on a pot," I said.

"No need," the lieutenant retorted. "Parker and I are going to take Sam—we can call you Sam, can't we, Sam?—over to the precinct for a talk in private." Turning to our director, she went on, "After all, you have an awful lot of explaining to do, and I want to be sure we treat you properly. I have three black coffees, two crullers, a jelly-filled, and a batch of Boston creams to see us through the morning."

To my amazement, Sam shambled quietly toward the front door. On his way, he noticed Katie for the first time.

"Who the fuck is this?" he demanded.

Looking up at Sam, Katie responded, "David's sister." She went back to reading.

"Well, fuck me runnin'," Sam retorted, then exited, followed by the two detectives. Over her shoulder, Lt. Rosado called back to me gaily, "We'll have him back to you by afternoon, Cowboy, good as new. I assume if any work gets done around this place, he might be directly involved."

"More or less," Maria said, mostly to herself.

Moments after the door closed, Katie peeked back over the top of her paper and winked in my direction. I was more or less amazed. The line about being my sister had tumbled out without hesitation. Was Katie completely embracing her fabrication? Or did she simply slip in and out of any lie seamlessly?

Roughly three hours later, Sam attacked the door to reception, only to find it, for once that day, closed and locked. Rather than dig all the way into his pocket for his keys, he chose to pound on the outside of the door, demanding attention and admittance.

"Yo, hear something out front?" Maria said, keeping her back to the door while smearing Wite-Out on whatever she had just typed.

"Could be a delivery," I said. "We expecting anything?"

"Open the goddamndoor! I fuckin' mean it now," someone sounding remarkably like Sam was saying. There was silence for about thirty seconds. The door swung open, admitting first Infinity, key in hand, then Sam and his attitude.

"Hey," Sam queried. "How long has she been workin' here?"

"Man, are you loud," Infinity interrupted. "What gives you the right . . . "

Maria came to her rescue, standing abruptly and heading quickly for the door.

"Infinity, we need to do some shopping, some food for both here and the apartment. Get your skates off and come with me right away," she coaxed.

"Fuckin' Infinity my ass," Sam declared. "Look, yeah, I know her as Mary Josephine."

"Know her indeed," I commented.

The women left almost immediately, and Sam strode over to my desk. Glancing to his left, he said, "Where'd your sister go?"

"Job interview," I replied.

"She here long? When'd she show up?"

"Don't recall, Sam. Do you have a point?"

Sam shrugged. "You know, I think this fuckin' chick detective believes I had more to do with Stephie's murder than, well, anybody. Did you have a part in putting that idea in her head?"

"No way, not me. However, let's see, like Maria said, the fact that you took a red-eye out of JFK that Thursday night, maybe even after Stephanie was killed, and haven't been in touch at all for ten days, and—in addition to fucking Infinity—you were doing the same with Steph, I mean, why would anyone think that's suspicious?"

"Has everyone around here become an amateur detective in my absence?" Sam thundered. "I mean, I'm gone for less than two weeks, and I come back to a film company without an editor, with precious little progress on anything. Everybody seems to know all my private business, and now I think the cops think, well, maybe I'm a suspect. We have to talk, you and me. Let me go wake up Bill and look at some of the stuff we shot last month. Stay here till I come back down, ya hear?"

He hadn't disappeared up the back steps for more than ten minutes when line four rang and a higher authority demanded that I head over to Bank Street. Saved, by of all people, Farah Freedwoman.

—CHAPTER 24—
A TERRIBLE INCONVENIENCE

"So, after that call from Farah, you run over to the apartment to make nice, and, like, Jeffrey was already gone? I mean, like, that's a drag."

Maria had just come in from some sort of important errand up at Apple for J&Y.

"A drag it was, but at least it got me out of the office and away from the 'Great Director.'"

We were back in the kitchen at Broome Street. Infinity had nearly climbed into the fridge, digging out science experiments disguised as leftovers from the back shelves. Maria and I were supervising.

"But he was there when Farah called you yesterday? I mean, how did he know to find the apartment?"

"C'mon!" a small, muffled voice said from within the fridge. "Everybody knows. I mean, like, nothin' is really a secret in Manhattan." Infinity paused, stood up, and dumped a half-full container of ancient coleslaw, a carry-out carton of what might have once been chicken chow fun, and a partially eaten slice of cheesy pizza into the garbage can.

"Everybody knows where everybody lives. I can find Dustin Hoffman's place blindfolded, can tell you exactly where Dylan hangs. I know that apartment on the East Side that's Alice Cooper's, you know, where he keeps his snake."

"Gross!" said Maria. "Enough with the snake."

From deep inside the refrigerator, Infinity continued, "I mean, like, I know the guy who walks Allison Steele's dogs. Then there's a brownstone in the Village where Geraldo and his wife fight. And then there's . . . I mean, like, jeez, the cops didn't put anything back where it was supposed to be after they, like, searched the place."

"Yeah," Maria agreed. "I think somebody lifted my carton of vanilla Dannon. I only had two or three spoonfuls."

Then she sighed, turned to me, and said, "But, so you got to Bank Street and Jeffrey had split, but why was he there in the first place?"

"Well, Farah said that he wanted to talk to J&Y. She thought he wanted to ask them about Steph's murder—like they could tell him something he didn't already know. Then he rambled on about picking up her personal effects. She said he seemed to be agitated, like really nervous."

"And all this time she kept him standing outside, talking through the intercom?" asked Maria.

"Apparently so," I said. "Anyway, by the time I got there—it was less than fifteen minutes —he was gone. He did leave a business card stuck in the doorframe, note on the back asking someone to call him at home."

"So did you?" Infinity inquired. "Like, you shoulda called him right away. I mean, everybody I've talked to—and some of my friends are really smart and have read mystery books and everything—everyone says that, like, the husband is always—what did they call it? A preliminary prospect?"

"Primary suspect," I corrected. "And at the very least, a person of interest. And yeah, I called him last night. He said he'll stop by this afternoon, so I brought down that box of stuff that you guys put together from Edit One as well as that film can where Steph kept her real valuables. I checked with Lt. Rosado this morning to make sure she didn't mind that we gave the stuff back to Steph's husband."

Again, from deep inside the fridge, "Whoa! Creepy!"

"What's creepy about Steph's husband wanting to come by?" asked Maria.

"What's creepy is how this orange fuzz stuff just kinda grew all over this half-eaten can of tuna—I think it might belong to Bill—in the back of the third shelf. If you blow on it . . . "

"The shelf or the tuna?" I inquired.

"If you blow on the tuna, like the fuzz stuff moves, like on its own. It might be alive. That's creepy!"

"Agreed," I said. And with that, I heard a loud rap at the front door just as line one began to ring.

"Maria, could you get the phone? I'll answer the door; it's probably Jeffrey." She did, I did, and it was.

I'd wondered exactly what Jeffrey would look like. I'd never met him, but I knew I wouldn't like him. I was also sure he would arrive clothed in something from Brooks Brothers, his hair neatly combed, and the rest of him rather buffed, if not polished. He did not disappoint. For some reason though, I was surprised at how tall he was.

Stephie's husband, her widower now, V. Jeffrey Bradley III, was a bit more than six feet. He had relatively broad shoulders and carried himself quite well, a fact I found annoying.

He followed me to my desk, and I sat, reaching to the floor for Steph's things. Not surprisingly, he exuded a sense of superiority, evident as he hovered above me while I cleared two hatboxes and a crate of what appeared to be designer shirts from the client chair adjacent to my desk. Seated, he directed his remarks to me, but I felt he was mostly talking to himself.

"Well, anyway, you just don't have any idea what a terrible shock it was to hear what I heard that Monday afternoon. There I was, just putting on my golf shoes in the locker room at the Cherry Hills Country Club—great course in the foothills, just outside Denver. Have you ever played there? Classic course; it's hosted several championship tournaments. Anyway, there I sat with two of the executives from one of the agency's hottest prospective clients and a senior account exec from the LA office, and this fellow comes rushing in, panting and breathing hard for all he's worth, to say there's a call for me from New York in the pro shop. He said it sounded urgent. And one of the other fellows said that it had better be, as it took nearly two weeks to secure the tee time. And, well, it was the call about Stephanie. You can imagine how upset I was."

"Shocked, I am sure," I said. "And then there's the fact that it must have taken such a long time to organize the foursome. How terrible for you!"

"Oh, we did have to let some other fellows play through. We were late for our original start, I mean. I had to have a quick chat with my dad and then of course I called Stephanie's parents. Terrible thing!"

"You mean you went off and played golf anyway!" I asked, incredulous.

Maria, who had been eavesdropping from her desk across the room, ripped a piece of paper from her Selectric with such force, I feared for the machine. Jeff Bradley rattled on.

"After all, Coors Brewing could become an important client for the agency. That Joe Coors is a heck of a fellow! The right politics. And to be totally truthful, I didn't feel it was my place to share with any of the other fellows anything about a personal problem. Not professional. Besides, Stephanie had been dead for a few days; whatever could I do about it?"

"You seem to be bearing up quite nicely," I went on. Jeffrey beamed at the perceived compliment.

"Here's a box. All of her personal effects are either in here or the film canister," I informed him. "I checked with the accounting people uptown. They said . . . "

"What's in that can?" Jeffery asked, interrupting seamlessly. "It says 'negative' along the side. Isn't that work that should stay here?"

"Uh, no," I said. Steph kept the negative stickers mostly as a joke, a warning to keep prying fingers away from her stuff. And besides, this is a 35 mm film can, more than twice the height of one for 16 mm film. It's just a few odds and ends."

"Clever."

"Anyway," I continued, "people uptown will compute Steph's final pay, any vacation days due, stuff like that. We can messenger it to you . . . "

"Not to bother. Just tell them to pop it into the mail. I'm sure they have our home address. I mostly wanted to drop by personally to meet with someone—anyone—in this organization and convey to them how sorry I am this entire messy affair happened. I do hope the Lennons—there has been a bit of publicity I've seen—aren't too upset. You'll pass on to them my concerns?"

"Yeah, well," I said, searching for the proper words. "Look, of course they're upset, not at publicity. I mean a woman, a person who worked for them, was killed, right here, upstairs, at her job!" My voice was rising, and I felt a flush in my cheeks.

"Good point!" Jeffrey said, standing now and moving smoothly toward the door. "I guess things this end are all tied up. I'll have Naomi—that's my girl, I mean my secretary—send for these things. Did I mention there will be a service, kind of a remembrance, but it's not yet scheduled? I assume many of you would like to attend, but we didn't get Steph's body back until yesterday, and that's thrown everybody off stride. We'll keep all of you informed."

"A terrible inconvenience," I said, speaking directly to the coffee mug.

"Yes, and we were just considering planning a family. Well, what can you do?"

Jeffrey shot his cuffs, checked the crease in his pants, and smiled agreeably at a spot over my head.

"I'll be off. Just wanted to, you know, drop by and achieve some, well, closure."

I stared at his hand, which was thrust in my direction, leaving it dangling in the open for more than just a moment before finally taking it. It was like grasping a fist full of tapioca, clammy and soft, and inconsequential.

"By the way, do they, the police I mean, have any leads? Any indications they might have shared with you?"

"I assume you've made the acquaintance of Lt. Rosado?" I said, freeing my hand.

"Oh yes. That discourteous Hispanic woman. And her suspicious-looking redneck partner. Yes, we had a chat, a brief one. When I was able to prove that, indeed, I was on a flight from LaGuardia bound for Cleveland—another important client, don't you know—while poor Stephanie was probably being . . . well, anyway, the lieutenant had little else to ask me. If only someone had found poor Stephanie that evening and rung me up when I first arrived, I most assuredly would have hopped right back on a flight. Anything new your end?"

"My end is just fine, thank you," I said. "I'm sure if anything concrete ever comes from this, any facts to establish who killed your wife and why, it might be in all the papers."

"What a remarkably disagreeable fellow you are," Jeffrey said. "Don't know why Stephanie said she liked you. Absolutely don't know why she stayed working down here. My dad, on more than one occasion, assured her he could get her on either at CBS—Dad has several good friends high up there, knows Bill Paley personally—or at the very least over at Channel 13. Mother is on the advisory board, as I'm sure you know."

"How nice for all of you," I said. "However, I think Stephie liked it here. She liked the challenge, the constant change. Most important, I think she liked that people here respected her thoughts. Here she wasn't just an editor. She had opinions, ideas. She—and they—were valued."

"Anyway be well. Again, I am off."

I heard a small sniffle from Maria's desk. Jeffrey and I stood looking at each other. The air was still. The silence, more than a bit oppressive. He nodded once, then turned, choosing not to acknowledge Maria, and strode through the front door, not bothering to close it behind him.

"What a jerk!" I said, more to myself than to Maria.

"No," she said, rummaging around her desktop for a tissue. "That is a dick! The very definition of a dick. And probably a jerk as well. Too bad he's so torn up by the loss of his wife."

"The news must have taken at least three or four strokes off his game."

"Can you imagine? Playing golf right after you hear . . . "

"For sure. Jeffrey might be the best example of why a spouse is always under suspicion when his . . . or her opposite number is murdered. It's a genuine shame his ass was on a plane that evening."

"It's a genuine shame," said Maria, "that his ass exists!"

"Good point."

With this, Maria pushed her chair back from her desk, sat upright, and addressed me directly. "I mean, like, David, so who the fuck actually killed Stephie, do ya think? You spend time with the cops, you know; what do they think? Why isn't this Jeffrey clown sittin' under a bare bulb in one of those little rooms down at the precinct place being grilled—or threatened, or being hit with a rubber hose— something!"

With that, she let out a long, disgusted breath. Suddenly, out of nowhere, she seemed on the verge of tears. "I mean, David, like, who, ya know?"

"Well," I began, "fortunately or unfortunately, it can't be that clown Jeffrey, as you so vividly call him. The lieutenant mentioned yesterday they had confirmation that Steph's hubby was on a five-something flight to Cleveland and couldn't possibly have been the murderer: estimated time of death, stuff like that."

"Yeah, well, that's a genuine fuckin' drag." said Maria.

After her outburst, we were both quiet for a minute, maybe less. I almost told her my developing private theory about Sam or even Socrates Ball, but I felt any opinion of mine was premature. Then the mood was broken.

"Speakin' of Rosado, that call right before the clown showed up was from her. She asked if you would call her back."

"Gladly," I responded. Maybe I'd find something new to pass on to John and Yoko.

I sat on hold for three or four minutes, till the lieutenant jump-started our conversation.

"Okay, Cowboy," she began, "now that we know Mr. Heintzelman was both on the planet and in the city the night Ms. Bradley was murdered, my job's become both harder and easier."

"How so, Lieutenant?"

"Well, easier because he's a suspect with both a motive and an opportunity, but—and I'm sure this won't be a surprise—he's claiming not to be involved at all in dispatching your editor."

I could imagine Sam's bellows of indignation.

"And then there's the harder part," I said.

"Yeah, the harder parts," the lieutenant continued. "Much of this case doesn't fit together, for reasons I can't share with you right now. Again—and I ask you to take a second and really reflect on this—is there anyone else connected to the film company who might have wanted Ms. Bradley dead? Anyone at all?"

With that, our rickety front door burst open admitting one very disheveled, anxious, and seemingly quite angry Socrates Ball. Without fanfare, he took a spread-legged stance, drew himself up to his full height, and then, while pointing the stubby index finger of his right hand at me, declared, "You, mate. You 'n' me. Gotta talk. I mean, for real and reg'lar like, we need to talk."

"There might be someone after all," I said into the receiver, "Can I get back to you?"

—CHAPTER 25—
'TIS A BRAVE CONCOCTION
2:10 P.M., TUESDAY, JUNE 27, 1972

"A good cup has body, stands up to a man's needs," Socrates Ball announced as he sipped his second cup of our nearly four-hour-old coffee.

Finally, I told myself, *someone really enjoys the burnt excuse for coffee offered here at Joko.*

Ball had positively inhaled the first cup, which he took black—no milk, no sugar, no kidding.

"I gotta tell you—and it's Sock—Danny calls you Sock, right?" I asked.

He nodded over the rim of the cup.

"I'm glad you like the stuff."

"Don't get me wrong, mate. It's a brave concoction, but not halves as compared to the tea when I can scarf it up at John's apartment."

"So you and Dan have been hangin' out over at Bank Street?" I inquired.

"I wouldn't say we wuz hangin' reg'lar, but Danny's keeping our oar in, just to be certain sure that when somethin' comes along, me and him are toppa mind."

Unbelievably, he now turned and poured himself a third cup, this one appearing to have the consistency of molasses, as he neared the bottom of the pot.

"Don't know how you do it," I said. "That's pretty strong stuff."

"Man's gotta pick his poison," Ball shot back quickly, "careful like." Glancing over his shoulder, he slid the empty pot into the coffee maker, then leaned back reflectively.

"Returning to the subject at hand, I mean, I'm sure the two of you know that, well, there just isn't any work here. At least nothing on a regular basis. Especially since the murder . . ."

"Enough shovelin'—I'm on t' ya. Bloke like you will just dance until his pipe wears out. Think Danny agrees. All o' ya here are just shinin' us on. Fact is, it's part of what I'm needin' to discuss—face-to-face, man-to-man."

"Okay," I said.

"Look, Davey—it is Davey, right?"

It most certainly wasn't, but he plowed on.

"Danny and I had a good thing goin' on over in Berks—John's place. Sweet digs, but you've seen much of it, all youse in that nonsensical film you're workin' on here. If they was to return, would be a great opportunity for John and the missus to get back to their creativity, relax and unwind, escape this bleedin' country, which seems like it don't want either of 'em in the first place. Don't mean this film company thing here has to stop altogether. Seems to me the makin' of the films could go on real reg'lar in Britain. Reels could be shipped over to ya to edit and show about. We don't have to be an exclusive situation. Just think it's best for all concerned. What I means is we can cooperate: shoot in England, edit here, and you sell the shit in America."

I studied him for a moment. For a peripheral ex-employee he certainly wasn't shy about his vision for Joko. His eyes were two intense and riveting coal-black pinholes punched into a wide, rubbery face like layers of sediment left one on top of the other by broad sweeps of nature. Sock Ball seemed to have been in the planning stages for millions of years. He was substantial, almost violently built.

In my heart I wished Jeffrey could be proven Stephanie's killer, but in my head, I had continually thought it had to be Sam. Now, my gut liked neither man, a fact that was taking form the longer I looked at Ball. Could it be this guy? It seemed too coincidental, but maybe that was how evil things happened. Something inside someone twists and breaks? He seemed to be forcing what I thought might be a smile.

"Look, uh, Sock, I don't know where you think you're going, but I . . ."

"Goin'? Where I'm goin', where I want to be headin', is back to Jolly Old, back to kith and kin and Tittenhurst."

"And," I mused, "I assume that means you would prefer that John and Yoko and, I imagine, Dan went along for the ride?"

"Well, Davey," Ball said, drawing out the two words as if each had three or four syllables, "that's a big part of what we need to discuss. I'm a bit concerned about Danny."

"And that is how?"

"The boy has a violent streak don'tcha know? Look, I love 'im; he's done me solid for more than these past five years, but it was me that pretty much kept him on the level during the Kubrick film."

"Is that a fact," I said.

"Truth, total. The boy, talented as he is, would oft lose it, fly out of control. I mean, them monkey suits, all that makeup, the lights, the heat. Was me, ya know, who they relied on more than a bit to settle him down. To calm the beast."

"So you've known Dan a long time, I mean, well before '2001.'"

"Not so. Met him on the set. I had been tagged along as a third grip, a best boy or whatever. Me uncle's in the union, and I would sometimes pick up a day or two on a big shoot. I think it was only half into a four-day booking that I saw Danny losin' it, and I just stepped out, told him what a great job he was doin'. We talked, and it calmed him down. I think he thought it was good havin' someone total in his corner—a calming influence, don'tcha know. But still and all, he has a violent streak, unpredictable."

"That's interesting," I said. "And your point in telling me all this is what?"

Here, Ball paused. I wondered if he was making his mind up to continue, choosing his words carefully, or both.

"Well, must tell ya, don't know where Danny was that Thursday more than a week back. You know, the night that poor girl got herself done in."

Now wasn't this an interesting turn? Sock Ball implying his "mate" had something to do with Steph's murder. I had already wondered if Sock had done the deed, perhaps to create enough of a scandal that J&Y might want to quit the city. Now, if he could implicate Dan, he just might get the grand prize: John and Yoko back to England with Ball as their prime assistant. I took more than a moment to respond.

"And you—where were you that night, Sock?"

The grin that seemed to linger somewhere between nose and chin broadened into a full-fledged smile. "Aren't you the Sherlock Holmes? Just so happens I picked up a few quid helpin' them Elephants load gear into Record Plant. Hung around out back with the van, waitin' for session to end so's we could load out in the wee smalls. In fact, thought I caught a glimpse of you and that willowy one out front somewhere's in the hallways durin' the evenin' as well. Yes, you could say we might be each other's alibis, don'tcha know?"

Well, I thought, it wasn't so important what I did or didn't know, or what I thought, but I felt at least I did have to bounce this new piece of information off Lt. Rosado the first opportunity I had. I felt I needed to keep contributing so that I could stay in the conversations.

A moment passed. Ball was leaning lazily against the kitchen counter while I perched on the arm of the leather couch. We were staring at each other. I broke the silence.

"So, to review: you think Dan might be involved in Steph's murder, while you also think it's about time for John and Yoko—and yourself—to head back to England, with or without Danny. Does that sum things up?"

He pushed himself away from the counter and stretched up on his toes for whatever reason, then began to shamble toward the doorway to the front office. "Don't know for certain sure. Just thought someone of responsibility should be in on what I know—don'tcha know."

The smile had hardened into a grin.

"Well, none of this is my responsibility," I said. "But I will give it some thought."

"You do that, for certain sure," Ball said, disappearing down the hallway and out the door.

—CHAPTER 26—
EVERYTHING WITHIN A 25-MILE RADIUS

8:10 A.M., WEDNESDAY, JUNE 28, 1972

"Thanks, brother dear," Katie said as she grabbed a mug of the coffee I'd poured her, while simultaneously blowing a stray wisp of red hair away from her peridot-green eyes. Though Katie had been part of our household, and my life, for less than two weeks, we were all becoming accustomed to her rhythms, her comings and goings, the most obvious of which was that she was up and out around seven every day for a morning jog. While she was out, she picked up one or two of the morning papers.

"I mean, both papers agree that your baseball team, the Cincinnatis, beat the Los Angeleses last night five to four and that they've moved into first place."

"That's great, thanks," I said. "And with this win, they're ahead of the hated Dodgers by half a game."

"Well that's the problem. That has to be an error," Katie insisted. "How can you lead somebody by a half game? I mean, don't they play complete, whole games all the time?"

"Don't worry, just trust me, it's possible," I said. "The next thing you'll want me to explain is the infield fly rule."

"The what?" she stammered, then paused. "Never mind. David, really, I think baseball is a silly sport. On another subject, I gotta tell you again, I really appreciate being able to crash. But, you know, I'm just hanging out until you get John to listen to my tape."

"Like I said, these things have to happen at just the right time, when he has the space to absorb, to really hear your voice."

What Katie didn't know is I carried her tape nearly everywhere. Unlike so many potential favors, this was one I wanted to deliver. I was waiting for just the right moment, when John was not hassled. I had played it for Bill, whose taste I respected, and he listened to almost three full cuts before patting his pockets in search of a joint. "Far fucking out!" he observed, followed by, "Have you seen my lighter?"

With that, she took her cup of lemon-strawberry Dannon yogurt and the coffee, gave me a peck on the cheek, and darted into the hallway.

"I'll grab a shower while there's still some warm water left," she said.

I checked the Southern Railway wall clock, determining that if I left right now, I could possibly catch the 8:30 boat and be at my desk somewhat early for a change.

An early arrival at Joko was always its own reward. I always enjoyed quiet times, just me and the sun streaming across the floor.

Maria and Infinity were nowhere to be found, and it was far too early for either Bill or Sam. But as it happened, my solitude was quickly broken; the first phone call of the day fell to me.

"Hey, man, I am just going to blow your freaking mind," a rather scratchy voice on the other end of the line insisted.

"My mind hasn't been blown in, perhaps, tens of minutes; give it a shot."

"You are just not gonna believe this, man, but I know the whole fucking world is gonna end, erupting in a firestorm like you've never."

I sighed. I was enjoying the "end of the world" calendar less and less lately, so it seemed. I remembered sadly how much Stephie had loved going over a week or two of it at a time, perched on my desk. Her favorite had been graffitied in Maria's hand, "Jersey Shore facing great peril: Mom & Dad's vacay at Bradley Beach & I get the apartment to myself."

"Look," I interrupted, "I think I even recognize your voice. Didn't you call with the Lyndon LaRouche people about a month ago? Something about a massive tsunami that would strike the West Coast, clear the Rocky Mountains, and wash completely across North America in less than a day's time?"

"Hey, not me, man. I did hear about that though, totally bogus information. Something to do with Mercury in retrograde, but my charts don't support it."

"Okay, quickly: date and time," I said.

He brightened, "Cool, like, this coming Monday, July 3, at high noon standard time, which fucking makes it one p.m. in New York. Daylight savings time completely fucks with ancient calendars, you know, man?"

"Yeah, that's gotta be a bummer. One would think the ancients, whoever they were, might also have known that civilization would inflict daylight savings on itself, don't you agree? Then again, there's the fact that if you're right, and the world does end on Monday the third, that's going to screw up the entire July 4 weekend for all of us."

The phone fell silent. Either he was genuinely thinking or so much information had been funneled into his brain he was struck speechless. No such luck.

"Whatever, man. Anyway, a lot of us can, like, avoid a lot of misery if only John collaborates with me, ya know?"

"Oh, I know, believe me, I know. Whatever does he have to do?"

"Okay, okay like great, man. All John has to do is meet me on the observation deck of the Empire State Building at, well, around 12:30 on Monday. Yeah, that should do."

"Half past twelve, Monday the third, observation deck of the Empire State," I repeated slowly as if I were taking careful notes. "By the way, man, you're in luck. That entire Monday is free for ending the world. Nothing else scheduled so far."

"Whaddayamean?" He seemed momentarily confused. "Anyway, John should be there on time and, like, bring his guitar and an amp. Nobody else, just John—and Yoko of course—and his shit and, well, maybe you if you wanna tag along to be saved."

"Wouldn't miss it for the world, this one or the next."

"So like John and I need to plug in, tune up . . . "

"What about power?" I asked. "Will you make arrangements with the building for a power drop?"

This was far from fair. This guy was way more gullible than most.

"Like, okay, I'll go over to the observation deck as soon as we're off the phone and look into it. Great thinking, man. I might have fucked up the whole thing."

"Don't mention it," I said dryly.

"So me and John, both our guitars . . . "

"You'll bring your own guitar?" I interjected.

"Like, sure, what do you think I am, crazy?"

He had me there.

He went on. "We tune up and at exactly one o'clock—high noon in the ancient writings—we both hit and hold C above high C for exactly sixty seconds. Also, one of us—I mean probably John if he wants to—then chants 'ohm' for like that entire minute."

"C above high C, exactly one o'clock, and hold the note for exactly one minute, chanting optional."

"Yeah, and then like everything in a twenty-five-mile radius, well, like everything in that whole area, is saved, ya know?" His speech was speeding up. I heard him pant at intervals.

"Okay," I said, "Just one thing. What about everything outside that area?"

"Look, man, whoever you are, I can't be responsible for the whole damn world! Gotta split now, goin' over to the Empire State; check out that power thing. Seeya Monday."

He never left a name, nor a sponsoring organization. I put the phone back in its cradle, picked up a Sharpie, moved to the first Monday on the next month's calendar. "Ancients EOW prediction, 1 PM, cataclysmic fire, ESB OD, good for one twenty-five-mile radius only."

Then line one flashed again. Maybe I wasn't so lucky. I sighed and picked it up. "Yeah, Joko Films, can I . . . "

"Cowboy, that you?" It was Lt. Rosado. She continued without any response. "Look, I gotta couple questions. Do you have anything on right now?"

"The usual, jeans, my older pair of Frye boots, this really neat dashiki that my roommate Liz found at a stall in a street fair."

"Deliver me—please!" the lieutenant said. "Tell me, do you guys have a cleaning service? Regular, maybe weekly?"

Before I could answer, she went on. "What I really want to know is when's the last time anyone cleaned the kitchen, especially the refrigerator?"

"The fridge, lieutenant? No one person is responsible, but actually, just a couple days ago, Infinity tossed out a whole bunch of stuff. Why do you ask?"

"I was afraid of that," she said. "The crime scene guys went over everything pretty thoroughly, but their notes are sketchy. Tell me, David, can you remember: did either you or Miss Anastasia take anything from the fridge the afternoon you discovered Mrs. Bradley's body, you know, before any of our officers showed up?"

"Um, no, definitely not. I mean eating or drinking anything was pretty far from my thoughts, Maria's as well."

"Well, something just doesn't seem right."

"That is?"

"Don't worry about it, Cowboy. Forget I mentioned it. Go on

about your business, and I'll try to expunge from my mind thoughts of you in a dashiki."

"Wait a minute, Lieutenant, please. There's something I want to talk with you about."

"And that would be, Cowboy?"

"Ball," I responded. "You know, Dan Richter's sidekick, Sock Ball."

"Sock—Ball," she responded, separating the first and last names with more than a moment's pause. "Gotta tell you, I have a problem with thinking of him as a person rather than a cat toy. What about him?"

"He was here yesterday."

"All by his lonesome? Or with that side kick you mentioned?"

"Just him. He went on about how cool it would be for him and Richter if J&Y went back to England; moved back to John's place in the country."

"Cool for them, but not for you, am I right?"

"Probably. There was a lot of bullshit about working cooperatively; maybe John and Yoko could make films in England, send prints here for editing. And we might be able to sell the pieces in the States—stuff like that. Pure nonsense."

"Makes sense," said Rosado. "However, your point, at least as how it relates to the case?"

"Toward the end of the discussion, he rattled on about how his good buddy Danny has a violent streak in him. He also just happened to drop the information that he did not know where Danny was that Thursday night and also pointed out that he . . . "

"Richter or the cat toy?"

"Himself, Socrates. He had an alibi as he picked up a few bucks helping the Elephants move into Record Plant for a session."

"Hmm, let's review, David. Now, at first you told me you felt certain it had to be either V. Jeffrey Bradley III or your personal nemesis, Sam Heintzelman. And now you think it might be Dan Richter? Have I got this right? Cowboy, you're running out of potential suspects."

"Hey, I'm just trying to give you whatever comes my way."

But her wisecracks did make me stop to think. The last thing I wanted to do was become a finger-pointing machine. However, I heard myself say, "Well, then there's Ball himself. Heaven knows, he's a mass of . . . "

"A ball of anger, Cowboy? Ironic!"

"Yeah, well, whatever. Seems like everybody I think of has more than a good motive. Sorry, Lieutenant. I should keep my thoughts to myself."

"Not at all, Cowboy. Keep thinking. After all, one of us just used the words 'cat toy,' 'helping to load Elephants,' and 'Record Plant' in under two minutes. Out of context, that all sounds ridiculous. But, then again . . . "

"Okay, I just thought you should know."

"Now I do. And you know something? I may bring those two in for another chat, when time allows."

"So you have talked to them?"

"Be a bit remiss not to, no? Anyway, Parker and I, so it seems, have talked with everybody south of Houston Street. So yes, we chatted with Richter and Ball, but I have to admit, neither one of us talked much to your friend Socrates. He didn't leave much of an impression. Quay was checking alibis. You? Just keep thinking."

With that, she hung up, and for once the rest of the day at Joko was boring; what a relief.

—CHAPTER 27—
DOES SHE HAVE ANY OTHER FAKE RELATIVES?

9:05 P.M., THURSDAY, JUNE 29, 1972

It was a warm early-summer night on Staten Island, a cloud or two in the darkening sky, at least half of the Big Dipper visible even through the city's glow. I was stretched out on the rickety chaise on the balcony overlooking the harbor, spending quality time with Liz and a bottle of Pouilly-Fumé.

"This is really great," I said. "Pricey?"

"It's donated! My stepdad's personal stock, one of the reasons I still do dinner with my mom in the city at their place."

"Well, thank them for me!"

"I'll consider it. So . . . the murder investigation. Anything new? What can you share?"

"Not much, really. Everybody, at least to me, appears to be a suspect, and—don't start—I know I'm probably overthinking this, but if I spend much more time considering the entire thing, next I'll have a motive for Maria while considering how Infinity might have sneaked into the studio that night."

Liz smiled, topped off my glass, and refilled her own, then leaned back against the railing from her perch on the floor, head tilted skyward.

"You always did overthink things. So let's change the subject. Katie, the real story? Who is she? Where does she come from? And why the brother-sister act?"

I wasn't really surprised. If anybody was going to see through Katie's thin charade, it would be Liz.

"What gave it away?" I asked.

"A few things, but most obvious is how you look at her—with a combination of interested adult and lost puppy."

"What kind of puppy?"

"Focus here. So tell me: when you gonna make your move?"

"God, I hate being transparent," I admitted. "Especially to you. It's that obvious, huh?"

Nodding, Liz pointed to a small half-open window one floor above. A radio was playing, and we could hear Katie talking softly, a one-sided phone conversation.

"She's right up there! Holler up and tell her to come down and join us. I'll politely excuse myself in five or ten minutes. After all, Mother did teach me to have some discretion."

We were both quiet for a minute or two, listening to harbor sounds. Then, suddenly, the radio stopped, Katie's bedroom light went dark, and I heard the muffled sounds of her descent from the third floor.

"There," Liz said, "the absolute power of concentration. We've summoned her from on high."

Starting to edge off the bench, she continued, "I'll go down and get another glass; you just wait here and lay it on Katie that at least one other person knows she's not your sister."

But before any of that could happen, we both heard Katie's footfalls on a second set of stairs, the ones leading down to the first floor. Less than thirty seconds later, the back door, directly beneath the balcony, opened and closed, and Liz and I watched Katie Steigerwald almost skip down the driveway and take a right, headed briskly in the direction of the ferry.

Standing to follow Kate with her eyes, Liz said simply, "Well, so much for that. And going to the city this late on a weeknight? I know she's not booked at the Gate till Saturday, though I did hear the phone ring ten, fifteen minutes ago. Maybe they called her in? Then again, does she have any other fake relatives in town?"

"None that I know of."

"No biggie. More wine for you and me, and you're off the hook, at least for tonight."

A few hours later, I lay awake trying not to think about Stephie, or much of anything. As for Katie, I was both relieved and disappointed. I wasn't really waiting for her to return. A good thing too—because she never did.

—CHAPTER 28—
UPTOWN, DOWNTOWN
2:10 P.M., FRIDAY, JUNE 30, 1972

I hadn't gotten a lot of rest that night, but I couldn't afford to sleep in either. An 11:00 a.m. screening of *Imagine* was scheduled for an old friend and contact, the marketing director for Fabergé. His management apparently felt the need to reach out to the under-thirty generation, and a possible sponsorship of Lennon's film had sparked their interest.

"Hey, can I bring extra people to the screening?" my friend had asked earlier in the week. "How many do you have room for?"

"Just keep it well under four dozen; that's the capacity of the screening room," I told him.

"No problem. I just want to bring, tops, three or four folks from my team, including Richard Barrie."

Barrie was the eldest son of Fabergé's owner and CEO, George, who styled himself both a businessman and a celebrity, maybe not in that order. Richard had a role in his dad's company and the title of vice president of something or other.

Well before eleven, I found myself fidgeting in a seat in one of the plushest screening rooms in the city, in the Rizzoli bookstore on Fifth Avenue. This was perhaps the seventh or eighth time I'd screened *Imagine* for potential sponsors, but this time it seemed I might have a live one. I had a small add-on audience as well, including Sam Sutherland, an old acquaintance from *Billboard*, who promised to be quiet and out of the way. Infinity had begged to come along; she could see the film in its entirety for the first time. Quite out of character, Bill had busted his ass all week to pull together a composite print, which included a few last-minute edits by Yoko, a new ending, and some additional audio mixing, including added sound effects and remixing.

The Fabergé entourage showed up around 11:15 with apologies and a bag of deli coffee and pastries, treats that were nabbed at the door.

"Whaddaya think we got here, some kinda grind house with chewing gum beneath the seats?" barked a fiftyish assistant manager who guarded the screening area like it was an extension of his living room. "Ya don't see no concession stand out there d'ya? I mean, look at these seats: better, more comfortable than Radio City, more plush than the old Roxy!"

I scrambled up the aisle to rescue my clients and thanked the territorial bureaucrat, who made a few more disparaging comments and then, no doubt, went off to his office to enjoy the coffee and pastries.

We all made greeting sounds, introductions. In addition to the younger Mr. Barrie and my buddy the marketing genius, some senior executive from brands, profoundly disappointed he wouldn't be able to get John's or Yoko's autograph for his granddaughter, was in attendance. He fell asleep ten minutes into the film, snoring gently for the rest of the hour. The remainder of the foursome was rounded out by my friend's executive assistant, definitely young enough to be his daughter. Five six or five seven, she had long natural-blonde hair, a broad smile, and lots of eyeliner; she wore a low-cut pink silk blouse. It was obvious to anyone in the room she was no family member.

From traditional Madison Avenue stock, the guy was in his late forties, with an agency pedigree. He looked over his shoulder at me, seated in the row directly behind him and his tribe.

"Didja get a look at her? I mean," he said, nodding at her chest, "as you guys would say, 'far out!'—pun intended!"

Less than two hours later, the remark was obviously still troubling Infinity as we shared a car down to the office.

"What do guys see in big tits? I mean, what?"

"Honestly? I don't really know. Face it, a lot of men are just pigs, pure and simple."

"You bet," Infinity continued, "and as for her, she was gross, I mean positively gross. Did you smell her? Like Bloomie's entire perfume counter!"

"Well, she does work at Fabergé. Anyhow, it's their business. They liked *Imagine*. It looks like they're really serious about picking up half of it assuming we can get clearance at one of the networks, and I can find another sponsor. The screening went really well."

Infinity was wearing a long-sleeve T-shirt beneath her standard-issue coveralls. On either side of the denim, the front of her shirt proclaimed, "GIV-----LAR. GI----OB, G------MN!"

I took the plunge. "What does your, uh, shirt say?" I asked, in an effort to change the subject.

She unclasped her arms and actually looked down into the space between her shirt and overalls as if she had to remind herself.

"Give a dollar. Give a job. Give a damn. Like you see on the city buses," she spat out. "But I still think she stunk up the place, and I didn't like her very much."

"You could have fooled me!" I said.

Heading down Broadway, we took a left onto Broome, passing the poultry slaughterhouse and slowing for traffic. The moment we stopped, Infinity popped the door on her side of the limo.

"Oh, I almost forgot, I've gotta go to Bank Street. Farah wants me to run some errands, probably really important."

With that, her skates materialized from her jute bag. She strapped them on and streaked off toward Broadway, partially enveloped in the omnipresent cloud of feathers that always seemed to hover in front of what all of us had named the chicken shack.

The limo covered the last block to 496 at a leisurely pace, which gave me time to prepare myself for what I could see: a pair of unscheduled and unwanted visitors standing in front of Marwood, the comedy team of Richter and Ball.

Alert and angular, Dan was standing on the top step, obviously waiting for someone to answer the door, while his sidekick leaned against the building's wall, wiping what appeared to be mustard from his left hand onto the front of his denim jacket.

"Superterrific," said Richter as I reluctantly exited the town car. "Just the chap we're here to talk to. What a time—what a time, and that poor girl. It's no wonder Sock and I have heard nothing from any of you since last we spoke."

I found it noteworthy that Richter didn't seem to know Ball had been to Joko the day before.

"In fact," Richter continued, "I was just saying to Sock, 'Sock,' I said, 'I'm sure those folks over at J&Y's film company could use our involvement more than ever now and we . . .'"

"Look, Dan," I began, but was immediately interrupted by Ball.

"Hey, Danny's talkin'. Has stoof to say. Me Mum would tell ya it's certain impolite to interrupt a bloke who's makin' a point. Idn't it so, Danny?"

Richter was taken aback by Ball's interruption, and so was I. I began again.

"Look, guys, it's not a good time. In fact, we have absolutely nothing in production right now. All of my time is spent, or should be spent, looking for sponsorship for *Imagine*, and Sam and Bill, now that we're down an editor, are kept busy screening with John and Yoko, making changes. There's just no opportunity to . . ."

"Sounds to me like we're about to be fooked with, Danny," grumbled Ball. "Thiz clown 'adn't any intention of workin' with us. 'E's a stiff, and we're about to be frozen out, certain sure."

I was more than curious that Ball was making the exact same point two days in a row, this time, apparently, just for Richter. I glanced at him to see what his next move would be.

Richter's attention seemed to be focused on something he saw over my shoulder. I turned to follow his gaze and discovered Maria sauntering down Broome, carrying a bag of groceries and wearing a smile.

"Hey guys," she said, "like, we're meeting on the street now? What's goin' on?"

"A pig's trough, a nuffin', you axe me," volunteered Ball.

"Maria," I began, "just in time. The screening was great, so we've got to really concentrate on that proposal outline for the clients. It looks good for a commitment, but we really have to buckle down this afternoon and crank out several pages—you know, a marketing proposal for them to have first thing tomorrow."

That stopped Maria cold in her tracks, less than five feet away from our group. Thoughts of cranking out any number of pages with Maria behind whatever colorful typewriter was available were about as realistic as my walking home across the harbor; but thankfully she picked up on my improvisational fiction.

"Gotcha. Like, cool."

She mounted the steps, glided past Richter and effortlessly inserted her key into the inner door. "Just let me get some of this stuff in the fridge. You say goodbye to our guests and get your ass in here so we can crank out those pages."

"You know, Sock, the more I see of this operation, well, I think it's a joke," Richter said.

"No regular hours, no reliable staff, and positively nothing has come out of this place with any creative flair or impact. I think what David is going to tell us, or try to tell us, is that they don't need us. Well, to be blunt, I think it's more than likely that it's we that don't need them." Then, taking one step down toward the street, past the Marwood Press sign, he hissed, "It's ridiculous."

Relieved that the pair were going to split, I still felt a need to defend Joko and our work, so I made the mistake of continuing.

"I'm sorry you feel that way—genuinely. The truth is we don't need a big staff, lots of hangers-on. We do just fine with a small, dedicated group."

Maybe "hangers-on" was a bad choice of words. Richter snapped his head around and glared at me in amusement, but it was Sock who reacted.

"Well, then, bloody fool you and the horse you stole from the queen's stables. Danny and I, well, we been talkin', got plans, stuff to do that'll right guarantee both John and Yoko will realize this smelly city, this New York, is no place to . . . "

"Enough, Socrates," Richter interjected. "Just settle."

"Don't want to settle, want to move forward," spat Ball.

With that, he slammed a meaty, mostly mustard-free left hand powerfully against the brickwork below the window once, then twice, and finally a third time. With every blow, he seemed to redden a little more, as if the very building were causing him pain.

Richter, on the other hand, maintained what seemed a calm malevolence. Taking in a lungful of late afternoon air, he went on. "We'd best leave David and whoever might be inside to their workday now."

"They need showin', Danny. If somethin' or someone's in the way, they gots to be moved."

They strode off briskly toward Broadway, crossing Broome to avoid a fresh cloud of feathers.

I was totally confused. Just yesterday it seemed Ball was trying to implicate Richter. Today, however, the duo seemed as one, with some sort of plan. What was apparent, if nothing else, was that both had powerful tempers.

From inside the open front door came the now small voice of Maria. "Hey, like, whaddaya think just happened? I mean, I think we might have just been threatened!"

"Perhaps," I said.

"Whoa, whatevuh," said Maria. "Now get in here and tell me what we're really doing this afternoon, after you totally explain what it means to 'crank out pages.'"

—CHAPTER 29—
COWBOY, I'D LIKE YOU TO DO ME A FAVOR

5:15 P.M., FRIDAY, JUNE 30, 1972

I was feeling pretty good about the week with the exception of the occasional visits from Richter and Ball, singly or together; the unsolved murder; and Lt. Rosado and J&Y both waiting for me to report back with anything substantive. On further review, I was a ball of nerves. I figured I deserved a break. So I thought I'd grab a bite to eat. Maybe wander over to the Gate to see if a certain part-time bartender might have picked up a Friday shift. I had called the house mid-afternoon and spoken to Liz.

"Before you ask, yeah, she came back late morning. I was on my way out to teach a class, we hardly spoke, and when I came back, she was gone. Sorry, David."

It was a little after five—Maria and I were in the process of locking up. Bill had come and gone, pausing only for a quick nap. Sam had yet again failed to show, and, of course, nobody had worked on a proposal of any kind. Was Richter correct? Was this whole business really just a joke?

"Which way you headed, David?" Maria interrupted my thoughts. "I'm goin' by Bank Street, picking up Infinity, we're gonna have a girls' night out. I'd say you could join us, but...."

"Thanks, but since I don't qualify I guess I'll have my own night out. Thought I'd go...."

"Out for a wild night with your favorite neighborhood homicide detective! How thoughtful, Cowboy!"

Seeming to appear from nowhere, Lieutenant Rosado obviously had her own agenda.

"Well, whatevah," said Maria, aiming a finger-wave first at me, then the Lieutenant, as she headed up Broome to Broadway.

Waiting just a few seconds, until Maria was out of range, Rosado stared over and up at me.

She had the strangest duality in her effect; somehow both a thoroughly intimidating countenance, but somehow also communicating with a core of kindness.

When she spoke, her voice was soft, almost conspiratorial, "David, are you aware that there is a rather major event that has yet to occur in this entire investigation? As a part-time sleuth, tell me, what really needs to have happened by now?"

A riddle, I thought, or was I being tested? To hell with it. I looked at her and just replied,

"Nope, I have no idea. Tell me. Who screwed up? Who dropped what ball?"

"Me, David."

So she wasn't infallible after all.

"Cowboy, I'd like you to do me a favor. You have plans for the next hour or two?"

"Not really, and of course anything I can do, just let me..."

"Good," she said sharply. "I'm double-parked over on Wooster..."

"Of course you are."

"Ride with me up to the Lennons' apartment, would you?"

"Sure! But you must've heard that's where Maria's headed, we could all have gone together."

"That's okay, Cowboy. Actually I wanted some time alone with you, you know—to talk about...them. How you approach them, what they're really like, just basic information."

It was then I realized what obvious thing had not occurred. Though J&Y had been visited by some NYPD detectives the Friday Stephie's body had been discovered, I now could not recall any time Lt. Rosado, the lead investigator, had spoken to them. Could it be that she was reluctant, even intimidated?

"It's not like I'm intimidated, Cowboy!"

Good grief! Was she also a mind reader?

"Anyway, just ride with me."

So that's what we did. Rosado had called into the apartment earlier that afternoon, and spoken to Farah—"A very nice, efficient person; can't understand why you don't like her!"—and had been told J&Y

were in for the evening. She could drop by any time after five or six.

We didn't ride up directly. After all, even with traffic it was only ten or fifteen minutes between Broome and Bank Streets, and with the addition of her car's portable flashing blinker and a siren blast or two, we could have made it door-to-door in under five. No, Lt. Nancy Rosado, under the guise of needing deep background, was looking for someone to tell her how to spend time with two real, very intelligent people, who happened to be the most famous couple in New York. After all, she was just an unknown public servant. As her unmarked bumped up onto the curb in front of 105 Bank Street, I smiled inwardly at the pleasure of introducing three of my favorite people to each other.

Maria and Infinity had already departed. Farah herself answered the doorbell, buzzing Rosado and me through the air-lock and into the apartment. The two women introduced each other, and it was Farah's turn to take off.

"David," she declared officiously, "I leave you in charge. Do check if Yoko and John need something ordered in to eat before you leave, won't you?"

Then Farah nodded towards the bedroom; "They're up, they're waiting for you both."

I led the Lieutenant back through the sitting and kitchen areas and noted with a bit of amusement how she raised her left hand and slowly allowed two or three strips of the shredded stars and stripes to float through her fingers, as she passed into the inner sanctum. She had been uncharacteristically quiet since we arrived. So, I introduced the three to each other.

"We've been wonderin' when we'd get the opportunity to meet the famous Inspector Rosado," John said with genuine warmth.

He was wearing his green silk bathrobe and an air of confidence I almost never saw him without. Sitting cross-legged at the very edge of the bed, he had taken the Lieutenant's proffered right hand in both of his and was, I knew, genuinely glad to meet her. Totally out of character, Yoko put down whatever she'd been intensely reading and, at first, slid, then simply crawled to John's side of the bed. Sitting next to John, she smiled openly.

"In fact," John continued, "Mother and I were actually wonderin' if David had made you up, created you from out of nothing."

"Well, um, uh, John, that is..." the Lieutenant, whose voice cracked slightly, was either at a loss for words or was picking each one carefully. "You know, I mean we both know that your David has quite an imagination, but I'm pretty sure it falls short of simply inventing an entire person out of thin air."

"Oh no, you know," Yoko began, continuing to smile at the Lieutenant, "I've told John a couple of times there was no doubt, no doubt at all, that this investigation, looking into solving this terrible crime, would be best handled by a woman. An intelligent and, I think you know, a very dedicated woman. I see wisdom in your eyes. But tell me, when were you born? And do you happen to know what time of day?"

I had prepared the Lieutenant for this question. She answered, and I watched as the conversation unfolded naturally. Yoko, of course, took notes.

They got on famously, how could they not? I was thrilled to discover that my Lieutenant went over all the facts of the case which she had shared with me carefully and thoughtfully. On more than one occasion, John, and even Yoko, had commented that this was information I had passed on.

"But now," John interjected, "it seems, we know the source, know where all this info is comin' from. So maybe David could get back to the business full time of sellin' our movies."

"Don't know about that," observed Rosado. "But there is one other thing I need to share, not just with the two of you, but with David, too."

"New information?" queried Yoko. "Possibly a break-through?"

"Not exactly, in fact neither. We have information which we've shared with no one, not even David here. It is a fact that Mrs. Bradley was, indeed murdered, but the means are far different than what was initially reported, and in fact what we first observed on that Friday afternoon."

"But Lieutenant," I broke in. "It was obvious that Stephie was struck on the back of the head."

"That she was, Cowb . . . I mean, David, however Sgt. Parker and I were quite perplexed by how little blood there was at the scene. Without getting too graphic… but, well, as you might know, wounds to the head and the face tend to bleed far more profusely, especially a wound that is fatal. This is because so much blood is sent to the head by the heart. In this case, there just wasn't as much blood as there should have been."

Not taken aback, in fact, more interested than surprised, John asked, "So what you are sayin' Lieutenant, is that our Stephanie was hit, but that is not what did her in?"

"To be direct, Mr. Lennon, Mrs. Bradley was poisoned. Fact is, she might well have been very near death or dead altogether when whoever struck her did so. Autopsy results are conclusive."

The four of us sat stunned for more than a few seconds. Lieutenant Rosado was looking at me, so I broke the silence.

"Okay," I began, "So, you keep this information to yourselves so the suspect doesn't know you're on to them?"

"That's one reason. As you can imagine, we've had at least a half dozen phone confessions over the hot-line we've set up. Each individual was carefully questioned, and all stated quite clearly that they simply beat Mrs. Bradley to death, no mention of poison or any other means. It continues to amaze me how many sick people there are, people who feel they need to confess to almost anything. As you might know, especially in high-visibility cases, we always try to keep back a fact or two from the public, the press, so, when we do speak to a prospective suspect we can tell if they're lying or not."

Another silence. It was Yoko's turn to speak. "So, Lieutenant, you and your friends have been looking all this time for a poisoner. Shouldn't this mean, however, that it is easier to narrow down the list of suspects?"

"Indeed, Miss Ono," the Lieutenant responded. There are a few stereotypical rules of engagement the press and public dwell upon. Men will use a knife, women won't. A woman might use a gun, so too will men. Men, usually bigger and stronger, will use their hands on occasion—women, even if they tower over a victim hardly ever do. And then there's the most common cliche of all, that women will use poison, that men never do."

"And is that true?" John inquired.

"Nope, not really."

Wow, I thought. *This turns everything upside down. So somebody poisoned Stephie, no telling how or when. And then I imagined them doubting whether poison would do the job, so coming back to finish what they'd started. Poor Stephanie. If only it was true she hadn't suffered, if only she had been passed out before the blow was struck. Lots of if onlys.*

We wrapped the evening without any more revelations. Out on Bank Street, the Lieutenant and I paused. What were we going to do next, I wondered.

"Give you a lift, Cowboy?" offered Rosado, breaking into my thoughts. "I'm heading back down to the First, could drop you at the ferry."

"Thanks, no. This has been a lot to, well, absorb. I just want to walk for a while. You know, clear my head. Think kind thoughts, about anything other than…."

"Know the feeling, David. It's especially hard when you're personally involved. I'm beginning to get the impression that she, Mrs. Bradley, was or maybe could have been more important to you than just a friend at work."

I turned slightly, looking the Lieutenant eye-to-eye. She was on the sidewalk, and I was a step or two below, still near the front door of the apartment. There was a silent agreement that passed between us. Then she said, "Have a good walk, and a good Fourth of July. Let's try not to have any excitement except some planned fireworks."

With that she climbed into her battered Plymouth, and I turned left, heading deeper into the Village. Now I was not so sure I wanted to go to the Gate, or look for Katie; not sure, really, of anything.

—CHAPTER 30—
NOTHING ELSE WILL BOTHER HIM ANYMORE
11:50 A.M., SATURDAY, JULY 1, 1972

"If she was here at all, it was late last night, well, early in the morning, really, and then she was probably up and out again first thing. You know, David, if you're ever gonna get anywhere with Katie, you're going to have to spend some time in the same building when you're both awake."

Liz was lecturing me about my love life, or lack thereof, sitting on a stool in the kitchen, waiting for the Melitta to drip the coffee into its carafe. I guess she knew my failings as well as anyone.

Home late, I had slept in. After leaving Lt. Rosado, I had weakened, wandered over to the Gate, and found that indeed Katie was not on duty, nor hanging around. Then I poked around the Village for a while, wound up at the Bellybutton for a late burger, and just missed the 11:30 ferry. Again.

"I kinda wondered if maybe you two had met in the city, stayed out late, maybe crashed at a friend's house, you know," Liz continued.

"So maybe she spent both nights out, Thursday and Friday," I said, "then crashed someplace, but definitely not with me."

"Poor angel," said Liz, almost genuine. "Don't get too close to that one. I mean, I like her a lot, but I don't really trust her. Do you?"

"Don't know. And since the sister/brother drama is blown, at least to you, it will come as no surprise that you're right, I really don't know her at all."

"Yeah, but you want to, or you did," she reflected.

Liz seemed capable of being definitely ex, and yet was she somehow jealous too? Pouring a cup of strong, black coffee, Liz glanced over her shoulder. "Saved by the bell, David! Get the phone! I'll just bet it's for you."

It was. Another call to duty. I should have asked for a Raymond Chandler-type deal, fifty dollars a day plus expenses. A quick shower, a glass of milk, but this time no limo. I made the one o'clock into Manhattan. As promised, an NYPD cruiser, a blue-and-white police car driven by a uniform, was waiting near the curb at South Ferry. With little conversation, we headed uptown with, I was thrilled to say, lights flashing and sirens blaring all the way. Our destination was one of the six- or seven-story prewar buildings on Park Avenue in the lower sixties.

The call had come from Sgt. Parker. "Sorry, Cowboy, no rest for the wicked. The lieutenant asked me to ask you if you'd come into town and join us at a crime scene. And no, don't ask, just come quick."

In the lobby of the building, another uniform, standing with a pudgy doorman, checked my name on a clipboard, had me sign, and told me to take the elevator to the third floor. There, yet another uniformed cop pointed to a door at the end of the hall. At the threshold, a familiar voice, with more than a little authority, instructed me to stop.

"Hold it, Cowboy. Quay, give 'im a set of booties. David, keep your hands in your pockets and don't touch anything."

Sgt. Parker quickly slid some sock-like things, booties, over my boots, then gently took my right elbow and led me down a hallway, past a living room on my left and into a bright airy kitchen space. A marble-top counter dominated the center of the space. A great deal of copper cookware was suspended above and around it. Before I could admire the rest of the kitchen, I noticed two legs, culminating in stockinged feet, protruding from behind the counter in front of me. First kneeling and now standing, Lt. Rosado nodded to the sergeant and me. She didn't smile; in fact, she showed no emotion.

"Thanks for coming, David. I really don't want to upset you, but I wanted you to, well, experience this firsthand."

The "this" she wanted me to witness was V. Jeffrey Bradley III lying awkwardly on his back, head canted away from us, paisley tie still knotted but loose around the collar. I'd only seen him once, but I recognized him right away. He looked worse this time. He was obviously dead.

"Good grief, Nancy . . . uh, lieutenant, I mean, what the hell?" I gasped.

"Good grief indeed, David. It's a busy day here in Fun City. You actually beat the ME's time, and from a totally different borough too. I'd say Mr. Bradley has been dead several hours, and, as you can see, there's no apparent reason why he should be."

What I did see was a bowl of what looked like melted ice cream on the counter, next to an open jar of some sort of topping. A spoon lay on the floor, less than a foot from Jeffrey's right hand.

"Well, do you have any idea what killed him?" I asked.

"My money is on the jam from that unmarked jar over there, blueberry. Looks and smells innocent enough, but I'm not about to taste it to find out," Rosado speculated.

"Okay, but why do you think it was the jam?"

"Because I'll bet when the ME is done with this Bradley, we're going to find traces of the same foodstuffs that were found in his wife's stomach, some partially digested blueberry jam with more than a small trace of something Smucker's never adds: arsenic."

"Yeah, right. You said last night Stephie was, like, poisoned, but you never said how it got into her."

It was then I noticed the lieutenant had dressed for a leisurely weekend, jeans and a gold-and-green short-sleeved jersey with a slogan in Spanish stitched over the breast pocket; around her neck, a small gold cross completed the outfit.

Turning again my way, she instructed, "Look over next to the sink. That open film canister, does it look familiar?"

It was difficult to divert my attention from what was left of the arrogant man I'd met with only a few days before. He looked a lot less self-impressed than the last time I saw him, and yes, on the counter at the far end of the room lay an open 35 mm film can, a thin strip of yellow tape marked "Negative" dangling from the can's lid. Two grease pencils and a roll of camera tape protruded from one end. Out of place, however, was a plastic bag, an evidence bag, I thought. Inside was a napkin bearing the legend of the Spring Street Bar.

"Yeah, I'm pretty sure that can was Stephie's secret hiding place," I said to the room in general. "We had it messengered up here a few days ago. But what's with the napkin in the plastic bag? Was it . . . "

"Did you open the can before you sent it up?" asked the lieutenant.

"Nope, I wanted to give it to him when he came to the office, but he was too busy to be bothered."

"Well, nothing much will bother him anymore, and since you asked, David, we found that napkin inside the film canister, along with a rubber band. There were small marks, indentations, in the paper that perfectly match the bottom and the lid of that jar on the counter. We measured, and that can would just hold the jar. Looks like that jam had been tucked away for safekeeping, arriving here with the rest of Mrs. Bradley's things." I noticed out of the corner of my eye that Sgt. Parker, wearing those ever-present gloves, was placing the jam jar and its lid into a separate evidence bag.

The room was terrifyingly still. I was overcome by a tremendous wave of sadness. Here I was for the first time in Steph's apartment, where she'd actually lived. Had she used those lovely copper pans? Had they shared breakfast on opposite sides of the wide counter? Where had she slept? Dressed? I realized there might never be a memorial service for her now.

Ten minutes later, standing on Park Avenue and breathing in the thick July air, I forced myself to ask, "Why did you want me here? What the hell was your purpose?"

"I, we . . . are genuinely sorry, David. Look, doubtless these deaths are connected somehow. There must be many people who knew them both, maybe disliked one or both enough to commit murder, but I have to admit it, I just wanted to see your reaction firsthand."

"You didn't think for a second I had anything to do with, well, that upstairs, did you lieutenant?"

"Well, David, you knew Mrs. Bradley, liked her a lot, and I'm sure you at least knew about her husband. He was, according to folks we talked to, before he was cleared of suspicion, more than a little narcissistic. Many said he was distant from his wife, and more than one implied he might not have been very faithful."

"Yeah, that's how we knew he was up there," jumped in Parker. "His girl, his administrative assistant, was supposed to pick him up first thing this morning for some time in the Hamptons. The doorman knew her. She had a key to the apartment, and she's who found him and called 911. She might not be the same for quite some time."

"So you see, David," continued the lieutenant, "we probably don't have an overt act of murder here, planned and deliberate; more than likely it's an act of manslaughter."

"Manslaughter? Isn't that always accidental?"

"Well, yes, and let's face it, when someone poisons someone, they don't necessarily hold the victim down. It's a sneaky crime. Food or drink is laced with, in the case of Mrs. Bradley, arsenic. The intended victim in essence kills herself, eating or drinking her death."

"There's more than one crafty defense lawyer who's tried to get a client off by sayin' just that: 'Didn't do it, y'honor. His uncle Willard or Aunt Velma done it to themselves.' But it doesn't work," offered Parker.

"Yeah," agreed the lieutenant. "Someone didn't just give young Bradley a jar of jam. Most likely it arrived all tucked away in that film canister just waiting for him to discover it and, unfortunately, decorate his vanilla ice cream with it."

"So they both used jam from that same jar, is that what you're saying?"

"Don't think so," said the lieutenant. The jar upstairs appeared to have had just one large spoonful taken from it. No, I think we're still looking for another jar, possibly the same jam, somewhere where Mrs. Bradley would have had access to it."

"Wasn't down at your place, Cowboy," Parker offered. "We searched carefully. And the day Mr. Bradley came back from his road trip, we had a warrant to go over their apartment, the fridge, cupboards, garbage . . . no hint of blueberry jam."

"So we, I mean you, are still looking for another jar of jam, possibly laced with poison."

"Bingo!" said Parker.

"And, well, isn't it weird that Bradley up there looks like he didn't even finish his ice cream treat, yet you never found any jar, open or otherwise, near Stephie?"

The lieutenant observed, "Sometimes poison takes a painfully long time to do its job, and then occasionally it hits the system like a locomotive, triggers all sorts of things inside the body. The autopsy may find that young Bradley had a congenital heart problem. You never can tell."

"Well, who's to say, but maybe the original intended victim might have been Jeffrey all along? Somebody gives Stephie some jam to take home, and then . . . "

"Thought about it, Cowboy. Doesn't make sense. Besides, there's that additional fact of the back of Mrs. Bradley's head. Nah, I think the jam was meant for your editor, and the blow to the back of her head was insurance. Young Jeffrey upstairs is likely collateral damage."

"What we've gotta find," said Parker, slowly rolling today's toothpick from one side of his mouth to the other, "is another jar of homemade malevolence. Who gave it to Stephanie? How did she get it? When did she first eat it? And where the hell is it now?"

"You see, Cowboy, the ME theorizes that Mrs. Bradley took on a goodly amount of the poison earlier that Thursday," said the lieutenant.

"And then," added Parker, "the contents of her stomach also contained a partially digested muffin, along with a generous amount of jam. We're sure the ME will find a smaller amount of the same jam in her husband's stomach as well."

For a few seconds, the three of us just stood there under a green Park Avenue canopy, glancing at one another, seeming to study the sparse traffic as it moved up and down a normally busy boulevard. Snatches of the conversation were already stuck in my brain: stomach contents, unmarked jars, autopsies. I wondered how these two people did what they did. I admired them, and I also felt more than a little sorry for them.

"You know the drill," said Parker. "Call us if you think of anything, and don't go anywhere."

Then he paused to talk to a woman I thought was a crime scene technician of some sort on her way upstairs. Lt. Rosado was already in the passenger seat of their unmarked vehicle, speaking in low tones on the radio. It was a Saturday, the start of a four-day weekend, but for these two, just another workday. Rosado interrupted her conversation, held the mic to her chest, and said quietly through the open window, "Drop you someplace, David? You okay?"

"Fine, Lieutenant. I think I'll walk awhile. I seem to be making a habit of it." And that's what I did, crossing Park Avenue to the downtown side. I didn't walk with purpose. I had no plans, but I did think, as I moved with busy people on the holiday sidewalk that afternoon, had it been just a day or two since I had told Maria I was entertaining some sort of theory? All my amateur sleuthing had centered on two guys: Sam and, of course, that Brit weirdo Socrates. Neither struck me as the poisoning type. This line of thinking led me, for the first time, to consider Christine as a suspect.

—CHAPTER 31—
XOXOXO, KATIE

"Home again, are we?"

"Indeed, home." I answered Liz without turning around. I was sitting on one of the deck chairs, feet on the railing, studying what I could see of New York Harbor through the trees from my balcony.

"And are we receiving?"

"Suppose so, though I don't think I'm good company."

With that, she came around from the right, hoisted herself onto the balcony rail, feet entwined in the fencing so she wouldn't tumble off, and sat there more or less contemplating me.

"You went upstairs? You saw the note?"

"Uh-huh, and before you ask, yes, I'm a little upset, even a tad depressed, but overall kind of relieved."

"Interesting."

The note had been thumbtacked to Katie's bedroom door. It was simple, straightforward, and, who knows, truthful?

"Bro, et al.," it began. "Sorry, but I gotta go. Pressure from DC., big gig in four weeks, need to rehearse and pull the band back together. Should John ever listen to the tape, I can be reached through my mom's home number."

A number with a 301 area code followed, then, "XOXOXO, Katie.".

"When did you find it?" I asked.

"An hour or so after you left for the city. She got a phone call, some guy with a husky voice, wouldn't give his name, insisted I bring her to the phone. He was weird."

"Weird how?"

"Well, at first I thought he might just be a breather. I said hello two, three times, asked who it was before he spoke up, asked for Katie. After some back-and-forth, I put him on hold, went upstairs, and saw her note."

"What did he say when you told him?"

"I didn't. Wasn't sure what his business was, just told him she was out, and before I could ask more, the jerk hung up. I think he might have called again three or four hours ago, not sure. How long you been here? Didn't hear you come in."

"An hour or so. I stayed in town, went to the Quad."

"What'd you see?"

"Peter O'Toole, a sneak preview, The Ruling Class, pretty good, but I wanna see it again. Had trouble concentrating. It's been a tough day."

"Sorry. Want to share?"

I went on to tell her about witnessing a second murder scene in less than a month, the questions from Rosado and Parker, then about the overwhelming feeling I had of helplessness. I confessed I felt a bit of a fraud: I was no detective, amateur or otherwise. I felt lonelier than I had in quite a while.

"'cause you found Katie had split?"

"No. Not completely. Well, maybe not lonely, just kind of empty."

The two of us sat there a while, possibly fifteen minutes, completely silent. I was grateful for her company and for the fact that she didn't ask any more questions. Eventually she slid off the railing, bent over, and kissed me softly on the forehead, saying only, "You know where I live, last door, end of the hall, if you want to talk."

I turned in a few minutes later, but I needn't have bothered. Images of Stephie curled up on the edit room floor, like still frames, kept quick cutting in my mind's eye. Then a different set of stills: the legs, torso, and the entire Jeffrey Bradley flat on his back in their kitchen. Rosado's penetrating eyes, Parker's distant, intense glances, uniform cops filling the blank spaces. There was the gurney wheeled out the back of a rather plain-looking van, passing me on its way in through the front door of the Park Avenue building. And then I saw again the small open jar of jam on the countertop. If there was another one, where was it? Most disturbing, I feared I knew who might have made it. Chris Heintzelman swam in from the left, staring right at me, ironic smile, feigned innocence. Wasn't she scavenging the fridge? Did I dare mention this suspicion to Lt. Rosado? How many suspects had I already gone through? Would she believe me? And what would she think? An hour or so before dawn, I finally fell asleep.

—CHAPTER 32—
SOMETHING HAD BEEN BOTHERING ME

4:35 P.M., TUESDAY, JULY 4, 1972

This was my fourth July 4 in New York City. By now I was beginning to realize what most New Yorkers know: the city is all yours if you choose to stay on a holiday weekend. An overwhelming number of city dwellers flee to beaches, mountains, and lakes near and far. But along with the rest of a tiny minority, I generally liked it here when everyone else was gone. Less traffic, fewer people, emptier subways, the same number of theaters, restaurants, and stores, all available and nearly empty. The weekend was peaceful.

When the phone rang Tuesday morning, I was sitting alone in the kitchen. I'd gotten a good night's sleep the night before, first time in weeks. Ian and Jack were nowhere, and I assumed Liz was still up in her bedroom. The call was unexpected, considering who made it.

"Don't know what you've planned, if anythin', but Mother and I thought that if you've nothin' on, you should order up a car, come to town, and let's all go to this party we've been invited to. Jerry Rubin— you know 'im, don'tcha?—and some of his mates. Has a friend with a loft, top floor somewheres, where we can all go to the roof and maybe watch the rockets come nightfall."

By "rockets" he meant good old American fireworks.

No hesitation here. There had been no Farah, no Infinity, just a casual invite directly from John himself, which found me a few hours later stepping out of a town car in front of 105 Bank. Infinity was on duty, and possibly on something else. Her bright blue eyes danced behind the wire-rims, and her grin, always there, was broader than ever before. She actually bounced on tiptoe and seemed to glide around the apartment, fussing with dirty dishes, watering half-dead plants.

"And, well, I was, like, blown away when out of nowhere, and I didn't hint or anything, John asked if I'd like to tag along to like this great party and stuff, even said I could bring my new friend. His name is Dominick; I think you met him a couple times, 'cause we've been ordering pizza from this place where he works. His brother maybe owns it or something, and anyway he does deliveries, and that's, like, how we met."

Okay, I thought, *seemed like most people would be there in couples, and here I was hoping that an invite to a party would make me feel less lonely. Would Sam be there with Chris?*

Sitting at a chair in front of Farah's oak table desk, I realized that something had been bothering me for days.

Just where was it that Sam had gone to before he flew off? He seemed to disappear periodically, no explanation. I didn't see him as the type to hole up in a hotel, even a fleabag on the Upper West Side. I also couldn't imagine him crashing with friends for a night or two. Then it struck me.

"Infinity . . . "

"Yo! Whaddaya need?"

"You admitted a while back, few days ago, that you and Sam had been, well, close, you know. Intimate."

"Whoa!" she said with a start, turning to face me. "Like, so what? No big deal, and pretty please, don't bring that up any time tonight, like when Dominick is there. I mean, like, I'm not proud of it. It, well, just kinda happened."

Studying her carefully, I asked, "But where did this thing happen exactly?"

"Well, like, if you must know, it was in a bed, silly! I mean I wouldn't just, you know, do it out in the open like in a car, and anyway I don't think Sam even owns a car. Like I said, it was just the once, and it's only because he kinda has this magnetism thing going for him, like I was drawn to him."

Okay, okay," I interrupted. "But this bed, where was it located?"

"Oh, that!"

She was mostly relieved; I wasn't about to ask details.

"Like in this place he has, at least I think it's his, you know, on MacDougal, three flights up above this messenger place called Quicksilver, same as the Frisco band. I thought you knew."

I didn't know. And if *I* didn't, I was fairly sure Lt. Rosado had no idea either.

Infinity continued to rattle on, saying she couldn't remember the address, but the place had the messenger service on the ground floor, and it was a small studio, kitchenette along one wall, half fridge, and on and on. I leaned over the table, picked up Farah's phone, and put a call into the First Precinct.

—CHAPTER 33—
GOT A MOMENT, COWBOY?
8:10 P.M., TUESDAY, JULY 4, 1972

"We were told this shindig would be on a rooftop," John said to no one in particular, though he had the attention of everyone within twenty yards. "We were thinkin' tar paper and grit beneath our feet, maybe an old water tank, and on one side maybe a couple of clotheslines strung with laundry. Least that was in my mind's eye when Jerry invited us to join him and his mates."

It was a rooftop for sure. The space dominated fully one half of the top of a fifteen-story apartment building in the East Village. No tar paper though; the space was beautifully tiled with curiously shaped terra cotta pavers. A brick wall surrounded three of the four sides, with large stone pots scattered throughout, some of which contained nearly mature trees. A half dozen or so teak tables of various sizes completed the setting.

John, Yoko by his side, was casually holding court in the corner of the terrace, which our hosts had assured him would have the most advantageous view of the promised fireworks, slated for nine o'clock.

Gathered round were people John would call mates: Maria and her good friend May Pang, each with a male companion, neither of whom I knew. Farah stood off to one side with an older man, well past thirty and way overdressed. Bill Frost was on the fringe of the crowd with his live-in girlfriend and another almost-constant companion he called sister. Infinity leaned dreamily on the shoulder of her Dominick, a pleasant-looking kid with ink-black hair, every inch a Sicilian. Looking not too intimidated. Impressive.

There were at least two guests in our party I hadn't anticipated: Lt. Rosado and Sgt. Parker, whose date kept asking me with a strong

Georgia accent if I'd ever had a mint julep. The open bar on the opposite side of the deck could, apparently, provide almost anything but not, as it turned out, that signature Southern cocktail. Rosado was alone and apparently quite happy in that state.

Neither detective was there as a result of my call to the First Precinct a few hours earlier; rather, John had called them that morning. Neither was on duty this Fourth of July evening. Both had made it clear on arrival that they had nothing to do with drug enforcement, and so long as the consumption of grass did not lead to excessive antics, both were happy to remain completely off duty. Whatever pills, powder, and any other pharmaceuticals were traded or consumed in bathrooms or bedrooms downstairs would also be of little concern to either.

As it turned out, I was not alone. When two carfuls of us pulled up in front of the address John had written on a sheet of notebook paper, leaning against a planter containing a Scotch pine nearly twice her height was Liz.

"Slumming?" I asked and held out my hand. "Let's go upstairs. John says it'll be a blast, in every sense."

She joined in seamlessly as we moved toward the penthouse elevator.

She told me later, "When I answered the phone an hour after you left, well, at first I thought it was you running a goof on me. I mean, you do a more than adequate impression of John, and, well, I was blown away. Talkin' to your Beatle! He asked me if David's girl was there; I thought for a second he meant Katie. I think it was Infinity or Maria who told him you might have had a thing for her. Anyway, hope you don't mind, I just blurted out that it was me! Then he said he'd have another car sent to the house and bring me to this party, to surprise you. You're not pissed, are you?"

"No, not at all," I said, meaning every word. This confession came tumbling out after John, spotting Geraldo across the deck, broke away from the group to heartily embrace him and a couple of others I didn't recognize.

Liz looked somehow different. Was she wearing makeup?

I was on my second, maybe third beer when a solo rocket arced into the night sky, finishing in a loud boom. The entire show lasted less than forty minutes. Someone on the rooftop mentioned that it was synced to a soundtrack on one or another station. Indeed, snatches of marches by Sousa, a classical piece I didn't recognize, and "All You Need Is Love," which came drifting up from another terrace, were our night music. Actually, it was just perfect.

"Grand show," John proclaimed as a smattering of applause rose from an adjoining rooftop. A roar ascended from crowds gathered a few blocks to the east, at the water's edge. I heard them and looked at us, and for once I felt truly privileged. It wasn't just the rooftop setting, provided by some rich benefactor of Rubin's who was backing the antiwar movement, but even more so the actual gathering that was there: colleagues, decent people, two detectives, Liz, and John and Yoko.

John actually seemed to revel in the fact that the fireworks had been the main event, leaving him, like us, just one more observer.

There is a lull that occurs after a fireworks display. I mean, after you applaud, whistle, shout, or murmur, what do you do next? Up here, more than a hundred feet above street level, a buffet was laid out. Burgers, dogs, and barbecue appeared on silver trays, offered by uniformed waiters to this mostly denim and Frye Boots crowd, a bit of cognitive dissonance, but nobody seemed to care.

"Got a moment, Cowboy? Looks like there's plenty of food, no need to rush." Lt. Rosado lightly touched my right elbow, and only at that moment was I aware that my left arm had sought out Liz's shoulder. *I wonder how that happened*, I thought.

"Sure, Lieutenant, let's talk."

"No rank up here, Cowboy. Please try calling me Nancy for a while. If you call either me or Parker by our titles, you're liable to clear the rooftop."

"Lieutenant, I'd like to introduce . . . "

But Liz, realizing Rosado wanted me to herself, had gone to have a word with Maria.

"Oh, that was rude of me, grabbing you away from your date," Rosado apologized.

"She's quick on her feet and fine on her own for a while," I offered.

"Okay, I wanna meet her later. For now, let's grab a table in the corner."

Someone had set out citronella candles in different colors; the setting was almost intimate. Out of one of her back jeans pockets came the Moleskine notebook, likewise a pen.

"Again, you called, Cowboy? Spill!"

I did, filling her in, best I could about Infinity's revelation, Sam's pied à terre somewhere on MacDougal Street, and the fact that even though a studio, it apparently had something of a kitchen. My information didn't take long to impart; in fact, the silence that followed took almost as much time.

"Well, I'll be damned," exclaimed Rosado. "Okay, I knew she had slept with him, felt she'd told me pretty much all that was important; she did blush a bit, and dammit, I didn't even think to ask where it all took place."

She slapped her notebook closed with a flourish. However, she did not stand and make a move for the Penthouse door or, I thought whimsically, scramble down the fire escape to her car. The lieutenant sat there, looking at the East River and Brooklyn. Again, she said, "I'll be damned."

Then, quite unexpectedly, she gave me a broad smile, "And good for you, Cowboy. So while you're on a roll, don't you think it's strange Mr. Heintzelman and his wife are absent this evening?"

I nodded in agreement.

"Tomorrow we'll deal with this . . . tomorrow. Right now I'm going over to that fancy-ass wet bar, see if the man can build me a gin and tonic. That shouldn't be too hard. What'll you have?"

"Let me think about it, lieu . . . Nancy. It's well stocked, an open bar."

"Open? Well, in that case, I'm definitely buyin'!"

—CHAPTER 34—
I'LL GET BACK TO YOU
ON THAT

2:35 A.M., WEDNESDAY, JULY 5, 1972

"So, tell me true, don't hold back. Was that really awkward?"

The query came from Liz, curled up in the middle of the massive back seat of a stretch limo as we just began to cross the Verrazzano, headed for Staten Island. As the party had begun to break up less than an hour before, Farah had ordered what seemed to be a fleet of cars, lined up in front of the apartment tower. None was assigned; each of us just grabbed the next available car.

"Staten Island?" I said, startling the driver.

"Wherever," he replied. "How many of you are there?"

There was little if any traffic. And so it was that Liz and I had the back seat together.

"I mean," she continued, not really waiting for an answer, "John and Yoko were right beside us, really even with us in line, and we got the limo. Next car was just, like, something smaller, maybe a Lincoln. Do you think John minded?"

"Nope," I said. "If that's what you mean by awkward, you don't have to worry. Look, he knows who he is and where he is. Doesn't need, well, trappings, to reinforce his or anybody else's opinion of him."

"Really! I mean, that's nice."

"He told me a month or so back—I mean, we were just killin' time back in the kitchen at Joko, waiting for something to be cleared up in the edit room—anyway, he asked me what I thought my ultimate definition of 'comfortable' would be."

"'Comfortable?' Or 'comfort'?"

"Comfortable. John said he thought it was a word that had—how did he put it?—lost its way."

"Interesting. What do you think he meant by 'lost its way'?"

"We talked about that. Like he thinks this is a time when everything is on edge, everything is sharp, prickly. There's the war, the constant police hassles, pressures and issues with drugs, and then just the business of, well, his business. Do you know he told me that he actually had to borrow money from one of his lawyers in order to pay the rent, just to have money for him and Yoko to live on, one month when they first arrived in New York?"

"Really?" Liz cut in.

"Yeah, really. I mean, like, Apple is a mess, all tied up in lawsuits, back-and-forth arguments. It's just one of those edges I think John was talking about."

"So how did you answer him? What would be your definition of 'comfortable'?"

"I didn't. Fact is, I don't really know. I think I tried saying something clever, like 'I'll get back to you on that.'"

"Did it work?"

"No. You can't fool him, at least I don't think you can. I mean I've never tried, in a major way. He sat there on one of the stools and just smiled at me, nodding a bit."

"So? Did you ask him what he thought 'comfortable' was?"

"Of course. He said that 'comfortable' for him would be a bungalow, a small house someplace—three, four rooms, nothing fancy. A telly, a bunch of records, to be warm in the winter, airy in the summer, just a place where he and Yoko could, well, simply be."

Liz sat there a moment, taking it all in. "You know, I'm so glad I got asked tonight, that I came. I mean I almost didn't. When he called and asked, I was fucking intimidated."

"What decided it for you?"

"I was on the kitchen phone, looking out that window facing the driveway, and one of those black town cars showed up, and, well, it decided it for me. I thanked him, hung the phone up, ran upstairs, threw this on, and jumped in the car without thinking about it. Yeah, I like your Beatle. Sorry if I've seemed, well, derogatory."

"Not to worry," I said. "Everybody deals with his presence differently. It's been more than interesting to watch.

"So," I continued, "is that what you meant about 'awkward'?"

Liz took her time in answering. "I mean this, you and me. You know, when John called asking for your girl and I said I was that girl, I felt a little bit like a fraud, but I'm glad I did it. So again, do you find this—us—awkward?"

Now it was my turn to take my time in answering. "No, I was glad when I saw you standing there . . . near the door, I mean."

We both laughed at my accidental phrasing.

"And to start, I was morose thinking I'd be alone."

The overhead lights of Bay Street gave off their periodic glow that comes and goes through the back window of any car. When I glanced at Liz, we had just driven beneath a streetlight, and we locked eyes for more than a few seconds.

"Is this, are we, going to start up again, David?"

"I don't know." I answered more quickly than perhaps I'd intended. "What do you think?"

"Hmm . . . .. I'll get back to you on that."

—CHAPTER 35—
BLUEBERRY JAM UNUSED?
11:20 A.M., WEDNESDAY, JULY 5, 1972

For some strange reason, and after very little sleep, I awoke refreshed. I grabbed a quick breakfast and made the 8:45. Naturally, when I arrived there was no one in the office.

And Joko stayed quiet. No phone calls, even the end-of-the-world predictors seemed to have taken the week off. I wondered whimsically whether the guy with the guitar and amp had shown up on the Empire State Building Monday afternoon. This was the first I'd thought of it. Quick look . . . yup, sun was up, world not ablaze. Broome Street was well within the twenty-five-mile radius. All was good. I was just cleaning out the detritus from my top desk drawer when the front door swung open gently.

"Anybody home?" a small voice asked, though the speaker was still not visible.

For more than just a second, I thought I might be waking from a dream, that the voice belonged to Stephie, stepping in from the street.

"Like, hello! I mean I don't like coming here by myself much; it's still kinda creepy. So if anybody can hear me, like maybe say something. Somebody? Anybody, please?"

It was Infinity.

"Here, I am at my desk," I shouted, "but all alone."

She rolled in and somehow rose up on one skate, kicking the door shut behind her with the other.

"How do you do that?"

Ignoring my curiosity, she went on, "I mean, I didn't do anything wrong. I mean, like, golly. It really freaked Dom out, you know, this uniformed cop shows up at like eight o'clock, says he's been sent by Lt.

Rosado and that she'd like me to come over to the police station, you know, down near the ferry and talk to her and that cute Sgt. Parker, although don't get me wrong. I never would say anything in front of Dominick that I thought Parker was cute. I mean, like . . . "

The better I got to know Infinity, interrupting her became both easier and, definitely, more necessary. At first I looked for an opening, a space possibly in between thoughts. I sometimes just waited for her to take a breath. Now I jumped right in without compunction.

"What did she want to talk about, Infinity?"

She parked herself on the couch, removing her left skate and undoing the right. Her flow of conversation persisted.

"Oh wow, it was all about like me and Sam, where we had done it, you know, stuff like that. I mean, like, I'm sure I knew you had to say something to her, and, well, for a while I thought I was in real trouble. Then she explained to me she knew I wasn't holding back, like I hadn't lied or nothing and that she felt responsible that, like, she hadn't even asked."

She rambled on for a while; I let her. A long, quiet day stretched ahead. I could be patient. The conversation at the precinct had apparently been brief. Then Rosado and Parker had popped Infinity into the unmarked Plymouth, and the three of them headed uptown to MacDougal, where she'd pointed out the building that held Sam's other apartment. No one was home, or at least no one answered the bell. Rosado offered Infinity a ride back to the office, probably relieved when she said she could skate over, which meant Rosado was free to head wherever a detective heads to obtain a search warrant.

"And, like, of course I told her I would say nothing to nobody except for you, David. That was right, right?"

I agreed that it was, then asked if she'd go back to the kitchen area, poke around and tidy up, and especially see to the garbage, which was more than beginning to make its presence known. The phone rang for the first time that day.

"Joko Films."

"Cowboy, you'll never guess where I am at this moment. C'mon, take a shot!"

"Let's see, sergeant. You're either calling from a judge's chambers or you and your good lieutenant are threatening some magistrate in order to get a warrant. Or you're possibly already in Sam's alternate digs or . . . "

"Ding, ding, ding, ding, ding, bulls-eye, second try," replied Parker. "And my good lieutenant wanted me to make sure you're in the office and have some time for us early this afternoon."

"I am and I do, Sergeant."

"That's good, Cowboy. You'll never guess what we found here in what has to be New York's most underused refrigerator."

"Blueberry jam, partially used?"

"I must tell you," Parker replied, "even though your mother was a Yankee, sounds like Mrs. Johnson didn't raise any stupid boys. Stay put; we're going to drop this off at the lab; then we'll see you shortly."

As I hung up the phone, I felt both satisfied and disappointed. Despite Yoko's careful numerological calculations, it sounded as though Joko films had actually employed a murderer.

—CHAPTER 36—
'TIS A PUZZLEMENT
2:20 P.M., WEDNESDAY, JULY 5, 1972

My newfound friends the homicide detectives and I were sitting at a table in the Spring Street Bar. I couldn't seem to concentrate or pull my eyes away from an unused table at the other end of the place, the very two top where Stephie and I had sat for our lunch the afternoon of the day she died. For sure, I'd told myself, I'll stop coming here for a while. Maybe, just maybe, after all of this was over the creepiness of this restaurant would wear away somehow.

"Earth to Cowboy," Lt. Rosado quipped in a soft, determined voice. "Again, you had mentioned on a couple of occasions that Christine Heintzelman brought muffins, cookies, other home-baked goods as well as some jelly or jam to the office for the staff to enjoy, correct?"

Now Rosado glanced up from her notebook to stare me down.

"Uh, yeah . . . a couple of times."

"And tell me again, do you think she suspected her husband and Mrs. Bradley were involved? I do recall you telling me you thought she was more than curious."

I now remembered that morning three weeks ago when Chris had come in with Sam but stopped at my desk to chat. "That happen often?" Chris had asked, staring up toward the edit room where Stephie's bright laughter pealed.

"So, we now have two jam jars, both without labels, but each has two common sets of fingerprints," Parker inserted.

"Well," I mused, "let's see, I suppose Stephie's prints were on both and then, I guess, Sam's?"

"One right, one wrong," answered Parker.

"Indeed, Mrs. Bradley's prints were on both, David," Rosado

added. "It makes sense, as we feel that both jars were either given to or left for Mrs. Bradley at the office sometime, possibly only a day or two before she died."

"Okay. I see where we're going. Then I imagine Chris's prints were on each jar. From what the two of you are saying, it looks as though she actually made the jam, but can we, I mean you, prove that she put poison in either or both?"

"Back down a bit," Rosado said. "If indeed she cooked up the jam, it appears she or someone had wiped the jars clean of prints before leaving them at Joko. And Sam's prints were on one jar—the one we found earlier, in his studio apartment—but not on the jar we recovered from the Bradleys' apartment."

"Now I'm really confused," I confessed. "I don't imagine Jeffrey Bradley . . ."

"And, yes, the jar at the apartment obviously contained his prints as well as his wife's and, as we've just found out, a nice thumb and forefinger from one Socrates Ball."

"And the other jar? The one we picked up today? Same deal," said Parker. "Prints plain as day from what the lieutenant here calls the cat toy—big as life."

"You printed all of us, Maria, Bill, and me, the day we went downtown to the precinct following the discovery of Steph's body. But I don't recall you printing anyone else, like, you know, Sock, Danny, Infinity . . ."

"Well," broke in Rosado, "we are the NYPD, you know? Pretty lax if we hadn't? We happened to do that a week or two back, when we brought them into the First for a chat, Ball and Richter at least. It's more like a device we like to use. If someone is genuinely guilty, they tend to invoke their right not to give evidence until asking for an attorney or a court order. Dan Richter stuck out his hands without hesitation."

"And surprise, surprise," said Parker, "so did good old Sock. I don't think at that time he thought there'd be any way to connect him to any aspect of Mrs. Bradley's murder."

"This makes no sense," I said. "I can't see the likes of Sock Ball making jam, lacing it with poison, and then . . . what are you guys implying? Replacing some jars of Chris's jam with something he made? It's nuts."

Here, Rosado and Parker, almost as rehearsed, stared across the table at each other. The lieutenant folded her hands neatly on her open notebook while Sgt. Parker, with his ever-present slight smile, rolled his toothpick from the right side of his mouth to the left and back again. He broke the silence.

"To quote Yul Brynner in one of my favorite musicals, 'tis a puzzlement. Not our first, likely not our last, but confusin' nonetheless."

"You're quoting The King and I?"

"He's a musical theater nut," Rosado broke in. "Think he's seen Hair at least twice . . . "

"Three times," admitted Parker. "Twice with the original cast."

"Book, cover don't always match," mused the lieutenant, nodding toward the sergeant. "Now, David, can you remember a time when, for any reason, Mr. Ball would have been at Joko unseen by you and might have access to these two jars? Any time at all?"

I did stop to think for a moment; had Ball gone back to the kitchen on one of his two earlier visits to Joko? Maybe, just maybe he had had access to something in a paper bag left on the counter with Stephie's name scrawled on it.

"A man's gotta pick 'is own poison," Ball had said to me on one occasion I recalled, context forgotten. Just a metaphor? Then I spoke.

"Yeah, maybe, even probably." I lapsed into thought again. After a brief silence, I added, "So it's not as simple as one might think. I mean, like, it's not as cut-and-dried as either Sam or his wife. You guys think Ball might be involved?"

Not waiting for an answer, I went on, "So what are we all doing here? Why don't you pick all three of them up and question them? Grill them or whatever?"

"We would if we could, but we can't, Cowboy. Only one available for even light grilling is the cat toy, and currently he's sitting down at the precinct waiting for us to talk. There isn't a Heintzelman to be found anywhere in Manhattan, including the twin boys. Any ideas?"

"Nope, not a one," I responded. "But if I hear from anybody . . . "

"You will let us know for sure."

With that, both detectives rose, dropping some bills on their respective place mats, and exited the bar.

—CHAPTER 37—
THESE SHEETS SHOULD COVER THINGS

7:50 P.M., WEDNESDAY, JULY 5, 1972

The three of us, John, Yoko, and me, were in a stretch, something European, maybe a customized Mercedes or BMW. I hadn't checked when the sleek black limo glided up to Joko nearly an hour earlier to gather me up.

"They, and of course I mean Yoko and John," Farah had begun contemptuously on a phone call just after 5:00 p.m., "for some reason they want you to come to dinner with them uptown, The Quilted Giraffe. It's fancy, as you know . . . "

"Wait a minute, Franny," I interrupted, "I'm in jeans, my oldest boots . . . "

"Not to worry, David, I've notified the maître d' that at least one scruffy will be accompanying them this evening. Just don't make a scene of any kind and things should go fine. And David, for the very last time, don't ever fucking call me Franny."

John and Yoko were sprawled out comfortably on the leather bench seat in the back of the passenger cabin. I was on the jump seat, one of two padded leather fold-down contraptions that flanked the built-in wet bar. My mind, already cluttered with the conversation from earlier in the afternoon, wandered. *I'll just bet*, I thought, *the term "jump seat" dates back to the war, when paratroopers squatted on tiny foldouts, waiting for orders to free-fall over France.* I'd always wanted to ask John what memories he had of the war, but not tonight.

Yoko, seated at John's left, stared out the window while John fiddled with some papers in his lap. No one said anything for nearly five minutes after we left Bank Street. And then, almost too softly to be heard, Yoko spoke:

"You know, I hear, uh, John, that this place, the Giraffe, is very expensive. Did you remember to get the American Express card from the cigar box on the mantle?"

With that, John thrust the papers out toward me. "Hold these please, David," he said. Then, reaching into his left back pocket, he pulled out a thick wad of bills, all hundreds from what I could see, and peeled off five or six, which he then tucked into his shirtfront pocket. "Not to worry, Mother; I think these sheets should cover things. Agree, David?"

Our eyes met, and not for the first time I felt that this man who had already done so much at age thirty-two, was just a tiny bit proud of his financial, shall we say, independence.

I tried to answer John's question, "I guess. I don't really know. I've never been to . . . "

"Now," John continued, reaching for the papers I held. "what do we know, if anythin', about this crime of murder? New, anythin'?"

Before I could answer, Yoko cut in. "Farah, you know, could not find Sam, not to attend the fireworks party or to come to dinner tonight. He, you know, is not returning messages, and we even asked the last time we called, spoke, you know, to his answering service, to have either Sam or his wife please call. Nothing."

Then, turning ninety degrees to face me, she continued, "So, David, please bring us up to date."

I did. Well, as much as I could, telling both of them only of speculations the police and I had shared. I spoke of strange fingerprints and jars of poison jam, of murder and manslaughter and topics that just didn't seem right to discuss in the back of this elegant car on a clear summer night on the way to what would likely be a sumptuous meal.

John folded the papers he held longways and tucked them into an interior pocket of the fatigue jacket he wore. Looking up and to the left, as though through a nonexistent skylight, he spoke carefully:

"It doesn't look good. In fact, it does very well look, Mother, like there is a two-in-three chance someone associated with Joko or us may very well have been involved. I'm not likin' this at all, but we most likely need to prepare ourselves to face some facts."

"And you don't think, you know, that if it was Sam's wife who's responsible, she would not be seen as a member of our, well, family?" Yoko said. "This is simply awful, and I think I refuse to believe it."

We said little the rest of the trip, about twenty minutes. The Quilted Giraffe lived up to its reputation, with two interior dining rooms bustling with activity. The three of us were whisked down the central hallway through a pair of open French doors, into a softly lit garden where a dozen or so tables were scattered. Muted classical music drifted in from somewhere, though the dominant sound was that of splashing water, a fountain at the back wall of the garden where the face of a carved lion spat a continuous stream of water into a pond about ten feet wide. Standing in the middle of the pond, looking either perplexed or pleased, was a gaily painted stone giraffe whose skin did seem to be quilted. However, with Yoko graciously seated by the maître d' and John about to pull out a chair to her right, I would not get the chance to sit or eat—or continue the discussion. Over my shoulder I glimpsed Lt. Rosado, out of context but not entirely a surprise, heading into the garden and directly for our table. It seemed like I could not go anywhere without her showing up.

Greetings were exchanged, apologies made, and with little hesitation I agreed to accompany her back downtown. As I turned to follow, I felt a hand on my arm. It was Yoko.

"You know, David, I think that you and your lady detective will learn much tonight. If it's not too late, come by the apartment."

I assured her I would.

—CHAPTER 38—
FROM BEHIND A ONE-WAY MIRROR

2:35 A.M., THURSDAY, JULY 6, 1972

I don't care how long I live here or how many times I commute home on the ferry, I will never get tired of standing on the back deck watching Manhattan drift away on a warm summer night—or early summer morning.

Lt. Rosado and I left the First Precinct a little after 2:00 a.m. Turning down the offer of a ride home from Sgt. Parker and checking my watch, I decided to " . . . just stroll down to the ferry terminal. I've got plenty of time to catch the two thirty, and besides, a ride across the harbor will clear my head."

"Ya know, Cowboy," Parker said, "there are bushels of more than interestin' things about this city that I have grown to love, things my folks back in Salisbury wouldn't really appreciate."

"Such as?" I encouraged the North Carolina native.

"There's the obvious: skyscrapers, Broadway at night—by the by, have you seen *A Celebration of Richard Rodgers*? Just terrific!—Central Park by day, stuff like that there, and then there's the not so obvious, like, for example, tens of thousands of New Yorkers gliding by the Statue in the harbor every day before work. Mind-blowing, really."

"Interesting," was all I said, because it, and he, were.

I bade Parker farewell and tried to engage Lt. Rosado, but she was having none of it.

"Bitterly disappointed," had been her brief comment when, nearly a half hour earlier, she had more or less been forced to release Sock Ball, accompanied by a well-dressed attorney who'd appeared at his side as if by magic.

"Mr. Ball has been more than cooperative, officers," insisted the lawyer. He was in his early thirties with razor-cut hair, self-satisfied smile, and Brooks Brothers everything, no doubt down to his tailored BVDs.

"You are in a position to either charge Mr. Ball with a crime or allow him to go about his business, agree?"

Unfortunately, Rosado and Parker concurred, and more importantly, so did a young assistant district attorney who had observed the interrogation. Sock had been cooling his heels in this interview room for more than an hour by the time the lieutenant and I arrived. However, he became overwhelmingly cooperative after huddling with his attorney—less than a half hour into his unproductive interrogation.

Yes, Mr. Ball would very much like to see the Lennons return to England, where he and possibly Mr. Richter would resume their duties at the country household, agreed the attorney.

"And it is understood that Mr. Ball does have a temper and has in the past even expressed himself in a colorful manner. However, these two facts alone, you must agree, are both circumstantial and by themselves do not in any way rise to the level of evidence."

But when the attorney, the very definition of a mouthpiece, removed two signed affidavits indicating that Socrates Ball was accounted for from midday on the Thursday Stephie was murdered till early the following afternoon, much of the air seemed to leave the detectives' sails.

I had been situated in one of those little rooms adjacent to an interrogation area, behind a one-way mirror. And yes, thinking that dinner at The Quilted Giraffe would have been a treat. But here I was surrounded by the hospital green walls. It was creepy. On more than one occasion, Sock Ball stopped glaring at one or the other detective and raised his eyes toward the mirror side of the glass, appearing to look at or through me. I could swear he knew I was there. Then again, police procedures probably don't vary that much between New York and London. It seemed unlikely this was the first time Ball had been interrogated.

"Okay," I said after Ball and his attorney left, around one a.m. "He's accounted for himself for most of the time, but what about the poison? Couldn't he have fooled with the jam jars earlier in the week? Couldn't he still be responsible?"

Neither detective chose to respond immediately. Finally, Parker remarked, "We don't think so, Cowboy. There's this paraffin people sometimes use to seal home goods that are canned, another form of protection against mold and the like. Each jar had a lid, but that was either for show or just because they came with lids. At least on the one jar we recovered from the Bradleys' apartment, we found proof the paraffin had only recently been disturbed. The lab techs don't think there's any way anyone could have tampered with the contents after the paraffin had been poured on, cooled, and hardened. No needle marks, no nuthin'."

Speaking in muted tones, Rosado added, "Even if Ball was guilty of tampering with the jam jars, eyewitnesses can claim he could not have been at Joko that night to strike Mrs. Bradley. Personally, I never bought the theory there might have been two murderers."

"So," I said, "Am I to understand the two of you once thought maybe Steph was poisoned by someone, while somebody else, totally different, may have come in later that night and hit her?"

"Possibly, maybe, more than likely in my estimation," replied Parker.

"Whoa," I said. "So you guys don't really agree on this, right?"

"Happens sometimes, Cowboy," Rosado inserted. "We think that's the real reason there are two of us assigned on high-profile cases. It's good to bounce ideas off one another. Look at a situation from more than one angle."

With that, Lt. Rosado fell silent. Parker broke the silence.

"It's looking more and more like one of the Heintzelmans is deeply involved, and that is not made any less likely by the fact they've both disappeared."

I leaned against the railing on the starboard side of the *John F. Kennedy*, as it plowed across the harbor at a constant eighteen knots. Rosado had wanted me at the precinct "just to observe, to watch the cat toy while we talk to him, that is, if you don't mind, David," she said when we left The Quiltec Giraffe. Of course I hadn't minded. Again, the right kind of information kept falling in my lap.

However, I knew by one a.m. it was much too late to head uptown to the Bank Street apartment. As a drunk tourist leaned next to me and snapped a picture of Lady Liberty, using, as they so often do, a useless flash bulb, my stomach grumbled. I again wondered what delicacies I might have enjoyed in the garden of the giraffe.

—CHAPTER 39—
JUST CALL HER BACK
6:55 A.M., THURSDAY, JULY 6, 1972

"That's crazy. You always, I mean you *always*, cut through the kitchen and stop by the fridge, no matter what time you get in! It's nuts that last night you went right to bed. I can't believe you sometimes," said Liz at a ridiculously early hour. I turned over, plumped the pillow, and gazed at my indomitable housemate situated at the edge of the bed, clutching a piece of note paper.

Apparently she'd left me a note on the fridge urging me, no matter how late I got in, to talk to her; she had news, important news, the note indicated.

"What could be so all-fired important that it couldn't wait a little while till I got a smidge of sleep?"

"It's Katie. She called last night, three times in fact, and each time she sounded more upset, maybe even desperate."

"What did she want? I mean, like, no one's heard from her for days on end; then suddenly she demands attention? Personally, I'm glad she took off and . . ."

"Who cares, David? Look, get the fuzz off your brain and just call her back."

Liz thrust the note in my face; I was expecting a number with a 301 area code, from Maryland. Instead Liz had scrawled a number beginning 609, which I was pretty sure was southern New Jersey, not that far away. I held the paper in my hand, staring at the number, trying to clear my head.

"So?" Liz continued. "Pick up the damn phone and dial!"

"Should I bother to ask for privacy?"

"You can ask, but it won't do any good! Look, I know her probably better than you, and something's bugging her for some reason she wouldn't tell me, so dammit, call her!"

I did. The phone rang ten, twelve times. I hung up, feeling sure I must have misdialed. I dialed again and this time, after the fifteenth ring, there was an answer. A man's voice, scratchy and low and, like myself, recently awakened.

"Yeah, this is the Beach Comber, who's this?"

The Beach Comber? Oh, a place, not a nickname.

"Is there a girl, a woman, there, Katie? Pretty tall with . . . "

"Oh her, yeah, they was till about an hour ago. They woke me up early, had to check out quick. Hey, you a . . . David?"

"That's me. You said 'they.' How many of them were there?"

I was upset with myself. Who cared who Katie was keeping company with? Guess I did, at least a little.

"You still there, fella?" the Jersey voice asked, a bit more awake, and more insistent.

"Okay, so whoever left about an hour ago, did they leave a message or . . . "

"Gimme a minute."

"Yeah, but where is this I'm calling?'

"I'm in Asbury Park, and this is a beach hotel, with, obviously, just one phone, which ain't supposed to be used after ten p.m. I see here on the notepad that your redheaded lady friend made a batch o' calls last night. Left a wad of money, though. Let's hope she didn't call Paris or Hong Kong or nothin'."

"Okay," I said, "but you asked if I was David. Did she leave a message or anything for me?"

"Oh yeah, says here that if you called, your sister sez to be careful around someone called the Great Director.' That make any sense to you, bub?"

"Some," I said, and before I could thank him, he said, "Good to hear," and he hung up the phone.

"So," urged Liz, "give!"

"She's gone from wherever that was, in Asbury Park. Left some kind of cryptic message I should be careful around Sam, and that will be easy; he's been missing about a week."

Liz was leaning on the side of the bed, draped in an oversize U Cincy football jersey I'm pretty sure had once been mine. She pursed her lips in that nervous way I knew and said only, "Look, don't want to be dramatic, but either Katie's in some kind of trouble or she's trying to warn you about something. Or both. Does that make any sense?"

"No more than anything else that's happened in the last few days, Liz. Thanks anyway. Next time I come in late, I'll make damn sure I don't avoid the fridge."

Liz nodded and without further comment slid from the bed and out the door, down the hallway to her room.

Only three or so hours before, I had promised myself I'd sleep in. Now, turning over these new puzzle pieces in my head, I was more than awake, so I figured I'd head for Joko sooner rather than later.

—CHAPTER 40—
BLOODY HELL!
11: 35 A.M., THURSDAY, JULY 6, 1972

Taking my usual place at Joko, I had to ask myself what I was doing here. Maria had called, claiming she'd be in "pretty shortly or whenever." Infinity was nowhere to be found, same to be said for Bill. In the two-story building that usually shook with sound effects, music running forward and back, and the clatter of the editing flattop itself, there was no soundtrack to Joko Films this morning, just dead silence.

It was a Thursday. But no Thursday was ever going to be the same, at least not here. Three weeks ago this time, Steph was bailing me out of an uncomfortable situation with Richter and Ball, and we had yet to go to lunch. Uncontrollably, I glanced toward the ceiling, knowing full well on the floor above there remained a slight trace of a chalk outline. I glanced at the EOW calendar and saw that the world was scheduled to end three times this day: one prediction for fire, one for a cataclysmic ice storm coming from both poles simultaneously, and, most dramatically, one for a rogue comet, the kind that took the dinosaurs out, hitting somewhere in South America in less than half an hour.

The phone was silent, not a call since Maria. I had a thought: maybe I should emulate Bill and go into "conference," hold down a beanbag chair in the back room, and make up for some of the sleep I'd lost the night before.

I rose, stretched, and sauntered down the hallway that divided the first floor and into the dimly lit kitchen area; the only sound here was the gentle hum of the fridge and what I always thought were the distant protests of uneasy chickens just up the block.

Then, three things happened:

The phone on the wall unit behind the kitchen counter rang.

"G'morning, this is . . . "

"Oh, David, I'm so glad. Liz said you'd be at the office, but then I lost the number, and you know you guys are unlisted? And, well, I had to call Liz back, get the number, then more change and . . . "

"Katie."

"Uh, who else? Look, David, is, like, Sam around? I mean has he come in?"

Before I could answer, I felt, more than heard, the front door open—smoothly for a change. Footfalls across the front office, neither light nor heavy; too heavy for Maria. And Infinity would have stopped to take off her skates.

"Bill?" I called out.

"No, not Bill, I'm talking about Sam. Is Sam there?" Katie insisted.

"Dunno, somebody just came in but . . . "

"Look, David, just listen. I'm almost out of change for this phone again. Now, don't be pissed, but I spent a couple days with Sam, you know, hangin' out."

Indeed, I did listen, couldn't really say anything. I thought I should feel much more than I did. Instead, I felt a flush come over, not exactly jealousy. I just felt empty.

"You still there?"

"Yeah, so you were with Sam . . . "

"Well, it was just stupid, silly. I mean he is well, not bad looking, and he did say he'd make sure John heard my tape, and you weren't having much luck, so, well, fuck it. It is what it is; I'm not proud, but most important I need to warn you. I really think that Sam is . . . "

And then, the third thing happened. Sam Heintzelman filled the entire doorway leading to the front office, simply staring at me, not making a sound. I gave him a deadpan "Sorry, on a call here" look.

And was I ever.

"Anyway, he was talking crazy shit, really strange stuff the last two, three days, I mean, we shared a bottle of tequila or two. First claimed Stephie meant nothing to him, then that she was a real pain, you know, threatening to make trouble, and then he would go off on a tangent saying he hadn't meant to really hurt her but it just kind of happened, and look, David, I don't think he's stable, I know he's angry, and somehow, for some strange, fucked-up reason, he thinks it's all your fault. Says you turned Stephie against him, even thinks there might be something between you and his wife. I mean, how fucked up is that? And . . ."

Then Sam spoke: "David, hang up the phone."

Katie continued to chatter, though my attention was totally riveted on Sam's left hand, wrapped around a rather large revolver. Oddly, I didn't think of it as a gun but as a revolver—large cylinder, bullets in every chamber, and a long barrel pointed directly at me. Was the hammer cocked? I lost interest in the conversation.

"Katie, thanks, yeah, he's here and, well, I gotta go."

I hung up the phone. Then, for what felt like the longest time but was probably only thirty or forty seconds, the two of us just stood looking at each other.

Yep, I was scared, but I started to think somewhat strategically. The counter was between us; I could duck down, possibly before he fired, if he was going to, but then I considered the thin wooden construction that likely wouldn't stop a bullet. Where would I go then? I glanced toward the back windows, sealed shut since Marwood Press days. There was only one way out, and Sam stood between it and me.

"David, we should talk."

"About?"

"This has all gotten out of control. I never meant, not really, for any of this to be this way. As you know, I have a vision, not just within a single film, but for this enterprise. For film in general and, of course, for John and Yoko. You know, I was against them hiring you in the first place. Damn Frost, jumping in with both feet, introducing you, damn bad luck."

He wasn't raving. In fact, his measured tone and precise phrasing made him far more menacing.

Again, silence, so I broke it.

"Can I ask a question here, Sam?" Not waiting for an answer, I went on, "When you hit Stephanie, and I can assume you did hit her, did you give any thought to the consequences? What was going to unfold?"

Then doubt took control: what good was it to ask him these questions? Was I playing for time or could I try to make this discussion mean something?

"It wasn't s'posed to happen that way, David. Oh, I knew Stephie would have to go. You know she threatened not just to call Chris, but to go directly to John and Yoko and accuse me—me!—of making it terrible to work here. Me of all people! You would think I'd forced her into bed the first time at gunpoint."

With this statement, Sam glanced down toward his left hand, even grinned slightly. "Yeah, at gunpoint. That's rich!"

"So you couldn't just talk to her? Try to work it out so she and you and everybody could just go on? People have affairs all the time and nobody dies. How fucking important is it that any film, that anything be so . . ."

I stopped to search for a word. "Important" didn't seem right.

" . . . so consequential," I blurted. "Couldn't you just let it go? Let her leave or you leave, maybe even J&Y close up the entire crazy operation? I mean, dammit, Steph was a person, a good person, and she's dead."

"Yeah, that," he said.

He then raised the gun, the barrel going up at an angle, possibly a spot over my head or to the side. It was only then I realized I was gripping the countertop so tightly I'd begun to lose the feeling in both hands. Guess I was more scared than I thought.

"Yeah, well, it didn't and I didn't and it's over."

Looking directly at me, Sam went on, "Are Chris and the boys with you? That commune out in Staten Island? You know that redhead, the one who says she's your sister? Anyway, she thinks you're, well, still hung up on your college girlfriend. Bullshit. I see the way you look at Chris, how she confides in you. Well, fine. You can have her."

Chris? And me? I think I was finding it helpful to try to figure out what the hell he was thinking. Took my mind off the revolver. But not for long. Now Sam seemed to survey the entire back room, both couches, the scattered beanbags, the unplugged lava lamp, the kitchen counter, then back to me.

"Fuck it," he concluded. "It's too messed up to salvage."

Was he going to walk out, just walk away? Or did he intend to shoot me? And for what reason? To keep me from repeating what he just confessed, out of jealousy for what had not happened between me and his wife, or just to be ornery? I'll never know what Sam intended to do next.

Sam turned slightly to his right, just in time to see a blur come at him from the darkened hallway. I saw two men collide, and there was a grunt. As I started around the counter—still debating fight or flight—the large, ugly revolver gave a muffled report. As a result of the brief struggle, Sam had his back turned toward me. He rose to his full six and a half feet, then shuddered slightly. There was a thud, the gun slipping from his hand and hitting the floor. Sam crumpled more than fell. His knees seemed to yield to gravity, followed by his torso. I watched as he joined the gun on the floor, then glanced up to see his assailant, fists clenched, jaw tightened, an equally amazed Socrates

Ball, with fear and wonderment in his eyes.

"Bloody hell! Bleedin' door was open, I come in, saw through the hallway this bloke, this guy we've been tryin' to talk to for weeks standin' with pistol. Didn't know who he was tryin' to menace, but felt takin' it from him was best practice. Believe me, mate, I didn't make the contraption go off. It just happened. Meant to knock him over, take it from him . . . "

I looked down at Sam, a small pool of blood forming beneath where he lay. The bullet had done its work. His head was turned toward the door, one unresponsive eye on the hallway. I should call someone. 911? An ambulance? Lt. Rosado? All three?

"Bloody hell," said Ball again, "I think I'm gonna come sick."

With that, he turned and shuffled toward the bathroom. I headed for the phone, thinking this job was above any pay grade.

—CHAPTER 41—
FINE. I REALLY MEAN IT, I'M GOOD.

7:35 P.M., THURSDAY, JULY 6, 1972

"Just consider it. I mean, just stop to consider it."

The speaker was Sgt. Parker, more or less talking to Lt. Rosado but most assuredly addressing all of us gathered in the front office.

"I mean think of the *Post* headline: 'Cat Toy Saves Cowboy.'"

"Yeah, great, Quay, it rhymes and everything, but it would only be mildly humorous to those of us here, rather inconsequential to anyone else," Rosado replied, still writing in her notebook. She paused, considered something on the page, then snapped the book shut. "Again, you okay, David?"

This had to be the third or fourth time she'd asked, and each time my response was "Fine, I really mean it. I'm good."

And I was good. Hey, it's good to be alive. The Joko offices were packed. Maria was on the phone telling anyone and everyone she knew that another death had taken place at Joko. Lt. Rosado apparently didn't feel the need to put a lid on it. There were as well at least a half dozen crime techs, uniforms, and other NYPD personnel milling about, talking on handhelds. Socrates Ball, of all things, my savior, had been taken to St. Vincent's Hospital under police escort. "Me tum—Mom says an ulcer probably, don't think docs know—but at times—certain, sure times of stress—it hurts painful much. I needs a lie down."

That had been pretty much all Sock had had to say when Officer Sam Hatter, again first on the scene, strode in to survey this Thursday's mess.

"He's pretty pale, looks like he might've thrown up blood. You say he wasn't the shooter, Mr., uh, Cowboy? Let's see if he can hold those thoughts till homicide gets here."

Rosado and Parker had arrived together, less than five minutes behind Hatter and his sidekick, who once again was stationed out front to deal with what was, no doubt, a gathering crowd.

Parker had taken Sock into the corner of the front office, where they had spoken briefly. Then the sergeant slipped paper bags over both of Ball's hands, tied them off, and sent him on to the hospital with two other officers and one crime-scene technician for company.

"That boy is shook, real upset," Parker commented. "We'll have to follow up, get his statement later. I sent a tech along to try and see if there's any GSR on his hands, but if it happened the way you say, Cowboy, young Ball is probably fortunate the pistol discharged toward Heintzelman and not himself."

I had talked at length with Parker and Rosado, the sergeant explaining that if Ball had actually grabbed the gun and shot Sam, whether in self-defense or with malice, there would be gunshot residue on at least one of his hands. However, I played those few seconds back in my mind, imagining how the scene might be intercut within a film: long shot, established confrontation, ECU as Ball rushes from hallway, reverse angle, surprise on Sam's face as he turns, side angle to indicate collision, grappling for weapon, then back to establishing shot, as gun discharges. And it, and Sam, meet the floor. I knew there was no way, no time Ball could have grabbed the gun; it just went off. It was cocked and, for sure, it was loaded.

"So," mused Rosado, with both authority and whimsy, "we have two killings, one celebrity-owned film company, and no way that this isn't front-page and A-block news for the next forty-eight hours. Only good news I can see, Quay, is that this incident more or less wraps up both cases. Oh, and yeah, there is the fact that at least one of us, if not both, will wind up with serious overtime."

This time, none of us would have to go to the precinct to answer questions or make any statements.

"We'll get your official statement tomorrow, Cowboy, yours and Mr. Ball's. Just go home, try to put all this behind you. Get drunk maybe, watch a ballgame," Rosado advised.

"Love to, Lieutenant," I said, "but I gotta go over to Bank Street. J&Y need to hear this from me, unless there's already some sort of instant update on their bedroom TV."

"Nu-uh," sang out Maria, obviously monitoring the discussion while simultaneously talking on the phone. "They're at the Plant—all the Elephants, Spector, full session. I'll call a car. We can head there together, whaddaya think?"

Thinking was not high on my list. I glanced at the lieutenant, and before I could ask, she said, "Go to the studio, Cowboy, you and Miss Anastasia. It's a shame there's no backdoor out of this place, but we'll get you through the press."

Less than half an hour later, Maria and I were in the back of a town car heading up Sixth Avenue.

"Well, guess it's pretty much over, ya think?" said Maria, piercing nearly five minutes of silence.

"Maybe, hope so," I replied. "Stephanie's still dead."

"Oh yeah, that," Maria muttered. She fell into a melancholy mood. Neither of us spoke until the car pulled up to the Record Plant on West Forty-fourth. I guess it made sense to chalk it all up to the great director. But I couldn't.

I didn't think Sam poisoned anybody. And I didn't think Rosado thought so either.

—CHAPTER 42—
BREAKFAST AT HOME

1:20 A.M., FRIDAY, JULY 7, 1972

"Let's break early. Nothin' seems to be comin' together, and to be blunt, I'm out of sorts," John announced to a studio full of musicians and a crowded control room. "I'd say breakfast, but not whole group. Just a couple carfuls."

Oddly enough, this evening at Record Plant had been much like my first. I'd stayed on the couch, down and in front of the producer's dais, saying little while noticing far less than usual. Maria, however, had become reenergized somehow. She was up and down, in and out, running small errands and chattering to anyone who would listen. Her good friend May Pang was there as well, offering more or less a calming influence as word spread among the twenty or so gathered that John and Yoko had lost another member of their film company quite unexpectedly. John didn't mention who was and was not to go to Home, his and Yoko's favorite early-morning destination on the far East Side. The restaurant would often close early or reopen when word was received that J&Y and friends—from a handful to a bus full—were soon to arrive.

We had the place to ourselves. "Two carfuls" meant just John's immediate circle: Yoko of course as well as Farah, May, and Maria. The divine Miss Freedwoman felt the need to inform me that "Yoko and John would like you to come to breakfast as well if you're up for it, David." Phil Spector, John's current producer, opted out.

So there we were, just the six of us around a much larger table than we needed. Menus were passed out and ignored; each of us pretty much ordered what we wanted from an eager-to-please kitchen that would create anything for their most famous guests. As for me, I wanted a plain cheese omelet, a few strips of bacon, and an English muffin. For the first time in my life, I actually felt like I wanted a cup of coffee, though I didn't order it. It wasn't a day for starting anything new.

Clearing her throat softly, Yoko more or less called the group to order.

"You know," she began, "I am still finding it difficult, quite difficult, to accept the fact that Sam, someone in whom we'd put so much faith, so much trust, could, well, how exactly would you put it, John?" she concluded, quite out of character.

"Go off the rails, out of his skull, round the bend? Driven to do stupid things because of who knows what triviality? Don't know what he thought any of us would think, his dalliance—I mean shaggin' of poor Stephanie—would mean to any of us. It wasn't a really big deal; we coulda talked it out. Instead, all this pain and violence has come about."

With that proclamation, the table fell silent. Each of us surreptitiously scanned the other five at the table, looking for reactions. In my case, I fell into brooding.

Were the deaths of two people so important in this city of several million? Only because both Sam and Stephie worked for John and Yoko would the story make anything before the second section of the *Times* or page thirty of the *News* or *Post*. No one at any of the local stations, not even Geraldo, would take notice of a young, gifted, shy yet inconsequential film editor who had been murdered at her place of business. Likewise, no attention would be paid to a thirty-something film director who, during a confrontation, had accidentally shot himself; nobody at all would care if both hadn't worked for a former Beatle.

"So," said John, breaking nearly a minute of silence, "does this finish it? David, do your copper friends think this is the last?"

I took a deep breath and let it out slowly, and for perhaps the very first time, I was not pleased to be the one in any group singled out by John.

"Well," I began, "there is the matter of poison."

At this, I saw the blood drain from Maria's face. At the same time, Yoko reached out and put her right hand on top of Maria's left, a gesture that I could see was immediately appreciated. May, seated to Maria's right, put an arm around the girl's shoulder. I went on.

"Lt. Rosado did tell me that, and I think I mentioned this, Sock Ball's fingerprints were on both jars of the jam, you remember, the homemade blueberry laced with arsenic."

John inserted, "But yes, then wouldn't that indicate that Ball might well have been the poisoner, that maybe he . . ."

"No, no way," I said, interrupting John for the only time ever. "Ball told the sergeant before they sent him off to St. Vincent's that he vaguely remembered pawing around in a bag back in the kitchen, probably one of the first times he went to Joko. The jam was in the bag, sealed up tight, and Ball did confess lifting a muffin—pecan, as he recalled—but decided to leave the jars sealed. He just happened to touch the wrong jars at the right time."

"Well then, could it have been Sam, the one that slipped the poison into the jars?" wondered John.

"No way of telling," I replied, "and obviously no one can ask Sam; however, I did hear Rosado tell one of the crime scene techs, the one who bagged Sam's gun to take in for evidence, to make sure and test the entire piece. Apparently, she thought she saw some caked or dried blood on the side of the barrel."

"What meaning?" asked John.

"Meaning that Sam, self-confessed, struck Stephanie, perhaps with the gun, sometime that Thursday night three weeks back."

"Sheeez," said Farah, out of character and out of nowhere. "has it only been three weeks? It seems like this nightmare has been on top of us forever."

Before anyone could respond to anything else, a young man and a young woman, each carrying large overstacked trays, arrived with the food. Plates were passed around, mixed-up servings exchanged, and all of us went back to staring at each other. Nobody lifted a fork.

"Then it's not over, not at all," concluded John. "But without poor Sam to question, will there ever be a way of knowing who was responsible for the poison?"

"Maybe, maybe not," I replied, but in my heart I felt I knew. And if I felt I knew, I believed for sure that so did Lt. Rosado.

—CHAPTER 43—
WE'RE SUPPOSED TO BE A FILM COMPANY

4:45 P.M., WEDNESDAY, JULY 12, 1972

"D'ya mind the jump seat, David?" John asked as the Cadillac stretch pulled away from in front of the Bank Street apartment. "No, I'm fine, really," I insisted.

It had been like this for the last few days. Nearly everyone in my life seemed overly concerned about my well-being. Back at the house, Jack had gone out of his way to install a ceiling fan in my bedroom, something I'd bought last winter. He'd been promising to put it up for months. Twice this week, Ian had left the sports section of his morning *Times* open on the counter, where I would obviously find it. Finally, Liz had actually announced during our Sunday brunch, "Okay, like nobody make plans for tonight. I'm cooking." And she had, and all of us were blown away by her crab bisque, followed by grilled pork chops, sautéed snow peas, fresh garden salad, and a box of amazing treats she'd brought home from Jon Vie, the French baker on Sixth Avenue.

"This is for David," she said, lifting a half-empty champagne flute. "He's been through a lot, come out alive, and, well, after all he found this house we all live in."

Same had been true at the office, even though, in my estimation, Maria had every right to consider herself as traumatized by the last month's activities at Joko as I had. She had beaten me to work two out of three mornings so far this week. She even seemed cheerful about it. Infinity seemed almost diligent, going so far as to shorten the occasional rambling monologue. Finally, although he had been more than affected by what had happened to Sam, Bill had been in all three days, more or less straight and sober, sorting and doing some screening on his own, spending most of today up at Mag-Arts Sound refining the soundtrack to Imagine. John and Yoko saw fit to declare the film nearly finished. My contact at Fabergé had even called to ask for a contract for half the ad space on the film as soon as we got network clearance somewhere. But for one mostly solved murder and the untimely death of Joko's self-appointed creative head, it had been a pretty good week for all of us at Broome Street.

Lt. Rosado, Sgt. Parker, and I had spent quality time the previous Friday afternoon going over everything and anything to do with what the *New York Post* headlined in that morning's bulldog edition as "Another Outtake; Lennons' Director Dies at Joko. Linked to Murder, Sex Scandal."

"Seems clear to me, David," Rosado remarked as we headed out of the First onto Old Slip, "the great director's death was an accident. The only person to fault is Heintzelman himself, his loaded gun, his threatening intent, coupled with the timely intrusion of one Socrates Ball."

"Yeah, hard to think of him as the cat toy anymore," I mused, "since I owe him, but then there's Stephie."

"Like we said inside," stated Parker, "lab came back with positive matches, hair and blood type, to Mrs. Bradley, found on the barrel and cylinder of Heintzelman's gun. The gun was the blunt instrument."

We'd huddled on the sidewalk outside the precinct, moving aside while four uniforms approached hustling a frightened young Hispanic boy.

Rosado followed this bit of cop street theater with cold eyes, then answered, "Well, there is the issue of the poison, David. Only other person who could have possibly been involved in lacing that jam with arsenic is Heintzelman's missus, Christine. Yes, we found jam making and other canning supplies in the apartment when we searched it a while back, but none of her empty jars, not one, matched the make or size of the two we're now holding as evidence. Her fridge had fruit, strawberries, some aging raspberries, and a cantaloupe, but not a blueberry to be found, not to mention any arsenic. Whenever we get the chance to question her, I have every confidence she'll look back at us angelically and claim not to know anything about anything to do with poison whatsoever."

"Still no sign of her or her boys?" Funny, this was the first time I'd even thought about Sam and Chris's twins.

"The kids showed up in Cleveland late last night," interjected

Parker. "We had some locals covering the airport there to see if she showed up, since she seemed to be nowhere around here, in the city. Her sons got off the last United flight out of Philly."

"Clever girl. So much for our covering LaGuardia and Newark," Rosado interrupted briefly.

"Yeah, well, they were accompanied by a flight attendant and a note for her parents, who'd been told to meet the plane. All the note said was that her mom and dad should see to the boys for a while, an impromptu summer vacation, and she'd be in touch."

"Clever indeed. When do you think you'll catch up to her?" I said.

The two detectives stood more or less shoulder to shoulder, Parker, the taller of the two, seeming to stoop ever so slightly in deference to the Rosado. Two pairs of tired, very intelligent eyes didn't so much bore into me as gaze with concern and apprehension.

"Cowboy," replied the lieutenant. "I don't know how to break this to you, but in the month since your friend Stephanie was murdered, there have been several other major crimes in Mayor Lindsay's 'Fun City,' and there are only so many extremely intelligent homicide detectives to go around, but Quay and I will do our best. We're not gonna forget this one, trust me."

Five days later, I was on my way up to Record Plant with J&Y for no other reason than that John had asked me. He had been elated with the word that Fabergé was set to buy half of *Imagine*, jumping from the California king in their bedroom and nearly flattening me when I gave him and Yoko the news.

"Now we're off! Really going someplace! And David, I'm so confident that someone else, that you'll find another group to pick up the rest, and we'll get the film on the telly almost instant."

"David, are you in there?" It was John, leaning slightly forward from the back seat of the Cadillac, touching my left knee with his right hand to gain my attention.

"Yes, sorry, my mind was wandering a bit. What did you say?"

It was Yoko who picked up the thread of conversation, "We, you know, John and I, have been talking and, well, doing a great deal of thinking, and to be very clear . . ."

"What Yoko's trying to say, David, is what do you think the rest of the people at Joko think? Do you all want to press on? Course, *Imagine* will be fine, and we've been discussin' other projects . . ."

"And of course," Yoko added, "you know we have so much we must do, need to do, with the McGovern people, the election. Nixon cannot be allowed to win."

"Right, definitely. In fact, we haven't had a proper talk about your visit to the Democrats, when, last month? David, we need to catch up," John interjected.

"Yeah, I've been meaning to go over that. But what you're both asking right now is do I think those of us down at Joko want to keep the company together—do we want to keep on working?" I responded, looking first at John, then at Yoko, now holding hands. Yoko nodded, and a beat later, so did John.

"I know this might sound trite," I said, choosing my words carefully, "but I really think Stephanie would want things to continue. I mean, we're supposed to be a film company, so let's go back to making films."

About thirty seconds of silence followed, and I could swear all three of us, each in our own way, let out a sigh.

"Okay then," said John, sitting up a bit straighter and beginning to grin. "It's settled then. Mother, let's give the entire group, ya know, the staff, tomorrow and Friday off, and then Monday next we'll put our heads together, sort things out, and move on."

Yoko smiled almost shyly, and I could see her squeeze John's hand.

"That's fine," I said. "But I have one favor to ask. Y'know Sock Ball only spent a night or two at St. Vincent's, and he appears to be fine. Could we put to bed once and for all that neither he nor Danny needs to consider working at Joko as a possibility?"

"Well," said John smiling, "might you not need him as your personal bodyguard?"

"No, thank you, I'm good."

"Didn't think so," said John with conviction. "Fact is, we told Farah today to book them both out on a jumbo by the end of the week. I've given 'em quite a bit of instruction regardin' things we want sorted out at Tittenhurst. Fact is, Mother and I have been thinkin' of sellin' it. At one time, Ringo fancied the place. Anyway, that all should keep both of them occupied till September or thereabouts."

I smiled agreeably, and then Yoko said the most surprising thing just as the car turned right off Eighth Avenue onto West Forty-Fourth, less than a block from the Plant: "Wonderful, but please David, do stay with us throughout the entire session. Both of us, John and I, want to talk to you seriously about just one more thing."

—CHAPTER 44—
WHILE U WERE OUT
10:40 P.M., FRIDAY, JULY 14, 1972

St. George, my neighborhood near the ferry in Staten Island, is hilly to be sure, not quite San Francisco hilly but often daunting, a brisk uphill workout. I'd just made it up from the terminal in under fifteen minutes, not bad after a couple of beers and a burger I'd caught at the Dugout less than two hours before.

"Another red-hot Friday night, big guy?" Liz greeted me, standing behind the kitchen counter, pouring what I feared was my last Grolsch into a jelly-jar glass she favored. "In fact, where the hell you been the last few days?"

"Oh, around," I replied, hoping to sound cool. "You just get in yourself?"

"Uh-huh, I was on the nine thirty. Looks like you were on the ten, and before you ask or complain, there's another one of your fancy Dutch beers at the back of your shelf." She daintily wiped a smear of foam from her lip with the back of her hand.

I eased past her, opened the fridge, and was delighted to see a single chilled Grolsch alone on the shelf.

"So you here alone? The back door was left open again. We've gotta get better about that. I mean this is New York City, after all."

"I know. I think the biggest culprit is Jack. He blows in and out several times a day, and, well, his truck is parked out back, so I assume he's downstairs someplace. And oh yeah, before I forget, there's been some guy, I think his name is Paul Bloch. Anyway, he's called two, maybe three times over the last couple of days. Says he's called you at the office.

Anyway, I left one of those pink While U Were Out phone message thingies I swiped from your desk; it's up on your dresser, I think."

"I know. I owe him a call."

"He's persistent. What does he want?"

"Well, surprise, surprise, he wants John. Who doesn't"

"Whoa, you mean one of those end-of-the-world wackos has our home number?"

"Nope," I replied. "Sounds like he has a gig booking talent on this year's Jerry Lewis telethon. He'd love J&Y to perform. And I promised . . ."

"Well, that's not gonna happen," Liz stated. "Jerry Lewis? I can't see your Beatle hobnobbing with the likes of Jerry Vale, Joanie Somers, Steve and Eydie. I mean, like, ridiculous."

"Maybe—we'll see," I replied."

"So again, what've you been up to?"

I didn't bother with a glass but took a long pull at the ice-cold beer, then plopped onto a stool across from her.

"It's been busy, but also weird. I mean, like, I'm still sifting through a conversation I had with J&Y, well, really more with John, a couple of nights ago, late."

"And the topic was?"

"Oh, nothing really heavy, just about death," I said.

"Well if you think that's light fare, I shudder to imagine what you conceive as heavy. Care to elaborate?"

• • •

For the first time ever, I had gone back to John and Yoko's apartment after the Record Plant session broke, a little after three a.m. that Thursday morning.

"Not to Home tonight; let's just the three of us go back to our place," John had said as musicians, recording assistants, and a small group of others began to filter out. "Mother and me wanted to have a bit of a talk."

Less than a half an hour later, we were seated around Farah's circular desk in the kitchen area of the Bank Street apartment. Already I was a bit confused. This was the first time I could remember spending time with both not in their bedroom. Yoko wandered over to the cooktop, began to reach for a now-cold teapot then, instead, drew herself a glass of water. John leaned back in one of the cane chairs, took in a large breath, and let out a sigh.

"Glad we talked about what future there might be for Joko. We need to bring on some additional staff, and Mother has an idea or two about a new, well, creative type, someone she and Jonas are really high on. Met her only once myself, and she's top-notch."

"You know, I think, well, David, I do not imagine you'll mind working with, or maybe for, a woman, will you?" asked Yoko, standing with her glass of water at the table's edge, between John and me.

"No, not at all," I said.

"Super!" inserted John. "She's from the West Coast, LA, and will be here in less than a fortnight. You'll help her get settled in, meet everybody else, and then you can go about hirin' someone to replace . . . well you know, another editor."

"That's great. Bill has been really terrific this week especially, but ya know, he's best left to camerawork and especially mixing the soundtracks and . . ."

Abruptly, Yoko said, "Good night, John, and you too, David."

Yoko turned and disappeared through the shredded American flag on her way to the bedroom.

"And there's one more thing, somethin' else we need to delve into, at least I would like to," announced John, leaning forward on his elbows, looking up as he always did and just a little to his left.

Some time passed, maybe just a few seconds. I decided to say nothing. Still looking at the tin ceiling, John continued, "What has happened in all of our lives, especially yours and the rest of them at Joko, well, there's no other way to put it, death has happened."

I didn't know what to say, both glad and reluctant to discuss what had been haunting all of us for a bit more than a month.

"Well," I began, "I think it was Maria who said just yesterday that speaking for herself, she was surprised how easily all of us had come to get used to working in a crime scene. I mean, it is more than odd. We don't really use Edit One. The second edit room is more than fine, and I thought it was just me, but I saw both Bill and Infinity purposely or unconsciously walk around the spot where Sam fell in the kitchen. I think, well, I guess I hope time will help—you know, heal."

John took another few seconds, then replied, "Death is both final and an interruption, but sometimes a beginning. Well, I guess that's three things, but we don't just need to look upon it as only an ending. Things often begin from death. Do you know what I mean?"

I did not. But before I could admit it, John continued.

"I encountered death, an important loss, early, my mum, Julia, I'm sure you've heard the story—hit-and-run driver. And, well, after the usual mournin', some mewlin' and pukin' and many brave words about movin' on, I did. Move on, that is. And I was different, not just because I was motherless, but her passin' made me that way."

John now turned his eyes directly on me, looking for some sort of response, but I had none. He went on.

"Have you had a big loss yet, David, outside of Stephanie of course? Someone important? Maybe not even a family member, but someone you thought you wouldn't get over quick?"

"Whoa," I said, letting out a breath. "There was one summer, '66 or '7, when I was in college. Five guys, three from my own graduating class, all from my neighborhood, were killed in 'Nam, one right after the other. I think there were four straight weeks we went to funerals. The whole neighborhood was in shock. I think that's the first time I came face-to-face with real loss, when death became real, you know, not just some distant uncle or a cousin from out of town."

"Bloody fuckin' war. So much pain, so much useless pain."

"But then there was my grandma, Nana, we called her. She died pretty suddenly the first fall after I moved to New York, and that one I felt sure I would never get over. Don't think I have to this day."

"Indeed, and for me it was Brian, you know, Epstein. Wish you and lots of others could have met him. He was special in so many ways and fucked up in a few others, but again, when he passed, it made me different. It made me grow up more than a little bit. It made me say to myself, *John, this is your own life. This is your time and your life, and no one else can run it for you.*"

A long silence fell between us. Then John spoke again.

"See what I mean? Death is loss and then a beginning. And maybe Stephie and Sam, while one was a good soul and the other quite troubled, their passin' might well affect you in that same way. In other words," he continued, stretching and rising from the chair, "do try not to let it bring you down. Rise above it, learn from it." He yawned. "Now there's no one here to call you a car, but I'm sure you can see your own way home."

It was the only time in memory that while I wasn't quite dismissed, I realized I needed to leave the apartment, and I would be the last one out.

• • •

Now, recalling that conversation to Liz, I mused, "It was like he wanted to connect in a more intimate way, yet also stopped short." So I left. It was John who buzzed me out. I hailed a yellow cab and took it all the way home here, nearly thirty bucks including tolls."

"He's a complicated and fascinating man, your Beatle," remarked

Liz. "You know, I'm glad I've met him, got to know him a little through you, and of course he's right: death, especially somebody really important, does interrupt things and leaves us all more than a bit overturned.

"On that note," she added, glancing at the wall clock, "I'm on my way upstairs."

She grabbed her jelly glass with its dregs of beer, gave me a slight smile, and passed through the hallway and upstairs to the second floor. I took another sip of beer, then checked all the doors to be sure they were locked. It took a couple of good shoves for the back-door lock to engage. Why was it all the important doors in my life seemed to be troublesome?

Upstairs, I paused outside the door to my room, closed as I'd left it that morning. I polished off my beer, put the empty near the stairs, where I'd find it tomorrow, and glanced down the hallway, where there were three doors. On the right was the door to the third floor, where, most recently, Katie had stayed. Other side of the hallway was the door to Liz's room. I saw light coming from the crack at the bottom and heard the faint strains of what I thought might be Mozart. I stood there for a moment wondering for the thirtieth or fortieth time what my real motives might have been encouraging Liz into the household as one of my roommates. I started down the hallway, past both doors and through the third, the second-floor bathroom. Teeth brushed, I headed for my own room and opened the door. Home. I knew the space intimately, instinctively. There was a bright stripe of moonlight cutting across the bed over the rug and up onto my dresser, an eerie blue nightlight from the outside. Without turning on the light, I went to the dresser, emptied my pockets, and set my wallet on top of the note Liz had mentioned. I chucked off my boots and left my denim jacket draped on the nearby chair.

Only then, turning toward my bed, did I notice someone else already there, slumbering beneath the covers. I smiled inwardly. Had Liz turned on the radio and left the light on in her room as a decoy before she slipped into my bed? But then I saw a long pale leg protruding from beneath the sheets, much longer than Liz's. Katie?

I moved quietly across the room to the bedside and clicked the lamp on. I was prepared for a riot of red hair but instead found that at least two of my pillows were covered with black. The light momentarily blinded me, as well as my uninvited guest, who raised her hand as she opened her eyes, then yawned and made that comforting sound we all make when we stretch.

"Oh, David. Good. It's finally you. We need to talk," said Christine Heintzelman, sporting a wide smile. "Turn off the light and come to bed."

229

—EPILOGUE—

Joko did return more or less to normal—our version of normal—in the weeks that followed. After Sam managed to shoot himself, both Maria and Infinity became and stayed more diligent. In fact, either or both seemed to be first in at the office almost every morning. Bill Frost continued to take his job more seriously, adding layers of sound effects and other subtle audio extras to *Imagine*, rounding out the scenes not dominated by the album's ten cuts.

A contract was sent up to Fabergé. Signing it, however, was predicated on getting network clearance for the late fall or early winter. Meetings were scheduled at both NBC and CBS to discuss just that issue, and more intimate screenings of the film were scheduled in search of an additional sponsor.

Farah continued to reign over the Bank Street apartment. The Elephant's Memory Band remained fluid in its membership, though always ready to support John at Record Plant with little or no notice.

Sock and Danny flew back to England, or so we heard. One way or another we saw no more of them that summer.

Paul Bloch stepped it up. He continued to call about the Jerry Lewis telethon every third or fourth day. Somewhere, I don't think I made it up, I heard John thought Jerry Lewis was really very funny. Maybe? If I ever had the time to ask him. He and Yoko might agree.

And somewhere in that flood of phone calls, I heard from Katie's former assistant manager in Washington that she and the band had taken a cruise ship job and would be entertaining in a second-class lounge for the foreseeable future.

The Cincinnati Reds continued through the summer at or near

the top of the National League Western Division, although I was not following the season and their exploits so closely.

And of course, the world didn't end that summer, but late in July, Geraldo Rivera did a puff piece about Joko's overcrowded "End of the World" calendar, which, the newsman claimed, he had discovered John Lennon kept personally on a daily basis. John loved the report and forbade me to complain about it or deny its authenticity.

In early August, Sam's replacement arrived. Mahalia Joanne Washington ("Call me 'Hey Joe,'" she said when we first met), a tall woman of about thirty with a lush Afro, had little trouble fitting in with any of the staff with the possible exception of Bill, who dealt with the "inconvenience" of working for a woman by upping his drinking just a bit.

I did have one more lengthy session with Lt. Rosado and Sgt. Parker that early morning, after talking Christine Heintzelman out of my bed and into their custody. It was a process that was actually oddly placid.

"She's bonkers, Cowboy," Rosado stated that morning as the sun rose over Manhattan. "The DA, I'm pretty sure, will charge her with a count of either murder one or murder two, not to mention manslaughter for Stephie's husband, but I gotta tell ya, we never thought she'd come out and admit the entire deal."

After that meeting, I headed back to Staten Island. More walking, more head clearing. I wondered if I would ever see either detective again. I thought for a bit that I would miss them. Then I thought, *No, I won't.*

—AFTERWORD:
A DOSE OF REALITY—

Nobody was ever murdered at Joko Films. But the author did work there. Here are some details.

Joko Films was in business until mid-1973. John and Yoko did live on Bank Street. Toward the end of December 1972. They began to move their household from the sublet there to the first of several co-op apartments in what would become their home at The Dakota on the Upper West Side.

Geraldo Rivera was always on the periphery.

An actual "End of the World" calendar did occupy wall space in the front office of the tiny film company at Broome Street, packed with real paranoids' actual predictions of the world's demise.

Joko Films (Joko Productions) remains hard to trace online with the exception of credits at the bottom of a movie poster and a piece in *The New Yorker*, December 2, 1972, by Henrik Hertzberg, "Poetic Larks Bid Bald Eagle Welcome Swan of Liverpool," which, among other things, describes the film company at its inception:

"The Lennons bought a narrow two-story loft building in SoHo and installed in it six people who work for a movie company they own, Joko Productions. In Wall Street and on the Staten Island Ferry, they shot scenes for a feature film, 'Imagine,' planned as a companion piece to the record album of the same name. Joko Productions set to work editing the film . . ."

Imagine remains available in many video forms, after many edits, to this day.

The author worked in film and television for many years, always living on Staten Island and thinking of writing a memoir or murder mystery, until Victoria Hallerman suggested he do both.

–ACKNOWLEDGEMENTS–

I'd like to thank my publisher David Bushman, who is patient and extraordinarily wise. I'd like to thank Tom Hill, an important early reader, as well as the entire team at FMP. A loyal band of supporters and additional readers includes: Eleanor Schaffner-Mosh, Sarah Moon, Chris Cato, Jody Borie, and Elizabeth Nott. Thanks to Thom Moon and Victoria Hallerman, my partners in crime. Many thanks to Robin Locke-Monda for cover design and general consultation. Of course, thanks to Yoko Ono and May Pang. Finally, here's to an old college friend, Bob Fries, who bumped into me in Times Square one December afternoon in 1971 and changed my life by inviting me to a screening of the original rough cut of *Imagine*.

THE
FIRST CYLINDER
A NOVEL
BY
JOSEPH DOUGHERTY

NO WRITE
WAY TO DIE
—A NOVEL—
NEAL
LIPSCHUTZ

CONFESSIONS OF
A
ROCK
'N' ROLL
NAME-DROPPER
My Life Leading Up to John Lennon's Last Interview
LAURIE KAYE

PUBLIC COMMENT
A DEBRA WOLFSON MYSTERY
S. L. JACOBS

Forget It, Jake,
It's Schenectady
A Police Department Under Siege,
and the Man Who Led It
David Bushman

"WHAT
DO YOU
MEAN,
MURDER?"
CLUE AND THE MAKING
OF A CULT CLASSIC
JOHN HATCH

9 781959 748236